THE
BABY
SWAP

BOOKS BY DANIEL HURST

The Holiday Home
The Couple's Revenge
The Family Trip
The Husband

THE PERFECT NURSE SERIES
The Perfect Nurse
The Nurse's Lie
The Nurse's Mistake

THE DOCTOR'S WIFE SERIES
The Doctor's Wife
The Doctor's Widow
The Doctor's Mistress
The Doctor's Child

THE BABY SWAP

DANIEL HURST

bookouture

Published by Bookouture in 2025

An imprint of Storyfire Ltd.
Carmelite House
50 Victoria Embankment
London EC4Y 0DZ

www.bookouture.com

The authorised representative in the EEA is Hachette Ireland
8 Castlecourt Centre
Dublin 15 D15 XTP3
Ireland
(email: info@hbgi.ie)

ISBN: 978-1-83618-566-6
eBook ISBN: 978-1-83618-565-9

PROLOGUE

The maternity ward is quiet. Quieter than it has been since I arrived here. When I entered the hospital full of nerves and angst, my baby was still inside me, but now he is out in the world. Now he is a proper little person, I can look at him and hold him instead of only feeling him wriggling around my womb. I am cradling him in my arms as I stand beside my bed with the curtains drawn around it. It's nighttime, so the ward is still as everybody tries to get some sleep, from the new parents to the newborn babies, though it won't be long until somebody wakes up. The peace will soon be shattered when a baby cries for a feed or a nappy change or simply for the need to be held by its mother – because this new world that they have been born into is big and bright and scary.

There are four beds in total in this section of the maternity ward, though only three of them are currently occupied. The woman who was in the bed opposite mine went home with her baby daughter and her husband a few hours ago, and they looked blissfully happy as they went. I haven't seen much of the woman in the other bed across the room because, like me, she's had the curtains drawn for most of the time she's been here.

From what I have seen of her and her partner in brief glimpses, they've seemed happy too.

But I don't care about them.

I care about the woman in the bed directly next to mine.

I recognised her as soon as I saw her arrive on this ward, though she didn't seem to remember me. Maybe she was just too busy taking deep breaths as a nurse showed her to her bed. I was trying to focus on taking deep breaths at the time as well, more than ready for my baby to come out.

I keep listening out for any sounds, the footsteps of an approaching midwife perhaps, anything that might make me stop and reconsider what I am about to try and do. But it's still so quiet, eerily so, as if time has stopped in this part of the hospital.

Maybe that's a sign. If one of the babies here were crying, everyone would be awake and I would know what I've planned to do wasn't meant to be. But they are all quiet and it's as if I have been presented with a golden window of opportunity.

So it's now or never.

Approaching the curtain that separates my bed from the woman next to me, I carefully pull it back with my spare hand, whilst cradling my tiny son in the other. As I create a gap, I'm able to peep through it and I see the other woman is asleep in her bed, lying on her back with her eyes closed and her mouth wide open. No surprise there. She must be totally exhausted from her dramatic and draining childbirth, not to mention full of all sorts of drugs that would make anybody sleepy.

As my eyes move away from the woman, they land on the sleeping baby boy in the plastic hospital crib. He looks so small, his face all wrinkled and his little fingers barely visible poking out of his oversized Babygro.

He looks like almost any other newborn baby on day one of life.

He certainly looks like the baby in my arms.

Which is why I have a shot at pulling this off.

I step towards the crib and, after one more check to make sure no one is watching me, I place my son down beside this woman's child – both newborns looking tiny in the big crib. To save time, my boy is already naked, and now all I need to do is remove the clothes and nappy from this other baby boy and put them on my child.

My heart is thumping as I make the switch, and it feels like it's beating even faster than it was when I was in labour earlier. It only increases when I realise the clothes aren't the only thing I need to swap, but the little tag that is looped around the ankle, the tag that bears the name of the baby. These tags are added soon after birth to allow for easy identification and also prevent any mix-ups in the earliest stages.

That's exactly why it needs to be swapped.

I'm perspiring as I cautiously slide off the first tag before making the switch with the other one, having to work quickly, but it's difficult due to how small and delicate the tags and the babies' ankles are.

The beads of sweat on my forehead are forming quicker now and that's because I know what is at stake here if I am caught. I will be arrested, and I'll be known in the news as the woman who did something unthinkable.

The woman who swapped her baby with someone else's.

But as everyone continues to sleep on the ward except me and the nurses who aren't currently around to witness this, that is exactly what I am doing.

I put the other woman's Babygro on my own son, so now he looks like he is hers. I panic for a second when he screws up his face, but he doesn't cry or open his eyes. He is disturbed but not awake.

With the babies still asleep, all I have to deal with now is the pang of guilt and sadness that emanates from deep within.

Then I pick up the other woman's baby and carry him back to my bed.

I look down at the little face in my arms as I close the curtain again and, as I do, I hear my own baby start crying on the other side of it. There's a tug on my heartstrings, a realisation that I cannot even try to comfort my child now even if I wanted to, because I'd only get caught. But I'm also aware what I've just done was years in the making and, while I might be to blame for what has happened now, I wasn't to blame for what happened back then.

I hear the other mother stirring from her sleep before she picks up my child and starts comforting him, performing the role that should be mine.

I did it just in time and it's too late to go back.

The swap has been done.

She has my baby.

And I have hers.

BEFORE

ONE

AVRIL

Oh God. I think this is it.

It's really happening.

My baby is coming.

'Bobby! Quick! Grab the hospital bag! My waters have broken!'

It's not often I raise my voice to my husband, shouting at him through the house to get his attention, as both of us prefer a quiet, peaceful home. But we might as well say goodbye to that concept because soon there will be a child living here with us. It is the beginning of a very new life for us both.

'Are you joking?' is my husband's response before he comes rushing into our en-suite bathroom and sees that I am not.

'No! Get the bags and get the car started! We have to go now!'

Bobby doesn't need me to tell him what to do because we've already gone through this routine dozens of times over the past few weeks as my due date neared and my bump grew bigger. But it's one thing to talk about our plan of going to hospital to give birth whilst sitting on the sofa having a cup of tea and eating a piece of toast. It's quite another to put the plan into action when it's the moment of truth. The fact is, if we aren't quick enough, it'll be us delivering this baby rather than a team of skilled midwives, and that makes me feel panicky, hence my raised voice.

As my husband moves quickly, I try to do the same, although it's not quite as easy for me to get around as it is for him, on account of what feels like a bowling ball strapped to my lower torso. And, whilst it's a nice problem to have, I'm also not helped by the fact that our home is a big one. It takes me a while just to make it out of the bathroom and through the master bedroom before going on to the top of the spiral staircase that descends down the centre of the hallway. I love this house, not only because it's huge and cost a lot of money, but because of how it looks now that Bobby and I have finished putting our stamp on it since we moved in here three years ago.

I also love it because it's a daily reminder of how all my hard work has paid off.

I've always been a career-driven woman, which is how I made it all the way to being the Marketing Director for one of the biggest luxury cosmetics brands in the UK. As a child who would spend hours going through my mother's make-up collection, trying all the different lipsticks, eye shadows and enhancers, it was a dream come true when I got a job working in a competitive but glamorous industry every day. Over two decades, from graduating university at twenty-one up to a couple of months after my forty-first birthday, it felt like I spent every waking hour either doing my job or thinking about my job. I'll admit I was a workaholic, but only because I loved what I did and felt I had little choice if I wanted to keep climbing the ladder. Some of my previous boyfriends didn't appreciate my drive and fell by the wayside very quickly, but Bobby embraced me for who I was, which is how I fell for him so easily in the end. From there, he persuaded me to walk down the aisle towards him in a flowing white dress, and while I initially thought that might be the most dramatic thing we would do as a couple, things have gone up a notch since that day. Now my darling husband is scurrying around downstairs by the front door as he prepares to drive me to the hospital, and my heart squeezes because I know he'd do anything for me. I love him as much now as I did on our wedding day in Santorini, which took place shortly before we got the keys to this gorgeous house, and I know I'll love him even more when we're holding hands and staring into the eyes of our baby.

As I reach the top of the stairs with both hands on my swollen stomach, I catch a glimpse of myself in the mirror and have to accept that I look very different to how I did when I got married. The slim figure that often turned heads has gone, possibly never to return, depending on how postpartum life goes for me. I also look tired, no longer able to pump my body full of caffeine like I did when I used copious amounts of coffee to get through my long days in the office. Most of all, I move slowly now, not like the woman of purpose and energetic vigour I once was, although I guess that will change when I'm chasing a little boy around this place in the coming years.

So how do I feel about all these changes? As I uncomfortably make my way down the stairs to see Bobby has already taken our bags out to the car, I could be forgiven for fearing that motherhood is changing me rapidly and I'll never be the woman I once was.

But that's okay because I no longer wish to be that woman.

I want to be different.

I want a new start.

And my son is going to give me the opportunity to be someone else.

'Here, let me give you a hand,' my gentlemanly husband says as he takes one of my arms and helps me navigate the last few steps. It's help that I appreciate because with my bump so far out in front of me, I can no longer see where I am placing my feet beneath it. Once I'm downstairs, it's just the short walk to the car before I'm seated again, and Bobby opens our mahogany front door before returning to my side to help me again.

As we leave behind the marble flooring in our hallway and step out onto our pebbled driveway, I see my SUV parked to the left. But we're heading for the smaller vehicle beside it, which is my husband's. We're taking that car because he always moans mine is way too big for him. It's funny because you'd think a man who works as a taxi driver for a living would be comfortable driving anything, but apparently not. Bobby said I didn't need such a big car, and perhaps he had a point when it was just me sitting in it as I drove myself to the office. But soon, my car will have a baby seat in it and will be full of changing bags, toys and maybe even a bicycle in a few years' time, so he'll surely be glad of the extra space then. He might even decide to drive it himself every once in a while. For now, we are taking his car, which is a registered taxi and has the official licence plate on the front and rear ends to prove it.

'I should be charging you a fare for this,' he jests as he unlocks the car, but this is not exactly the time for jokes, though I do roll my eyes because it is classic Bobby behaviour. He often likes to try and ease any tension with humour, whereas I prefer to go into practical mode when things get tough.

'Easy does it,' Bobby says as he helps me get into the front passenger seat before rushing around the vehicle and getting in behind the wheel. It's impossible not to notice that his movements are a lot more effortless than mine, thanks in part to his athletic build, but also to the fact that, unlike me, he was able to maintain his normal exercise regime over these past nine months.

'Have you definitely got the bags?' I double-check anxiously.

'Yeah, they're on the backseat,' he says as he starts the engine.

I glance back to make sure, not that he would lie. Sure enough, there they are, the three bags we need for our hospital stay – one for him, one for me and one for the baby boy we are going to meet very soon. The bags are sitting beside the baby seat that Bobby has installed, and as he reverses us off the driveway, I guess we are as ready as we'll ever be, which makes me relieved and nervous at the same time.

'That was the last time in our house as just the two of us,' I say as I look back at our beautiful property before we turn onto the main road. 'When we come back again, we'll be a trio.'

I glance at Bobby and see that he is smiling widely, clearly ready for our life-changing day ahead and the transition from being a couple to being a growing family.

'I love you,' he says, still beaming, and as he drives us towards the hospital, he momentarily takes one hand from the wheel to take hold of one of mine.

I grip his hand and give it a squeeze, which is something I expect to be doing a lot more of once I'm fully in the throes of labour when we reach our destination.

'I love you too,' I say back, meaning it even more than I did when I said it at the altar shortly after we had been declared husband and wife.

Life has been full of ups and downs, with both personal and professional challenges often making me doubt if I was ever destined to be a wife and a mother, and instead, considering whether I'd have been better off staying solo. But as we get closer and closer to the hospital and the baby inside of me gets closer and closer to being in my arms, I realise this is everything I ever wanted and needed.

I'm very lucky because not every woman gets to have such a devoted partner by their side on such a momentous day.

But if I'm so lucky, why do I have a sinking feeling in my stomach that tells me I don't deserve it?

I almost have it all, and when this baby is born, I really will have everything I've ever wanted. But rather than make me happy, it makes me feel like I have even more to lose than other people do...

TWO

JADE

This is it. The moment I have been dreading. The moment my miserable life becomes even more of a challenge.

I think I'm going into labour.

I think my baby is finally ready to join me in this messed-up world.

I grimace as I hold my stomach and feel discomfort, though it's exactly what all the books and online articles have told me it will feel like, so I know there's nothing wrong. This is just how painful it is when a child prepares to leave its mother's body, and this is just the beginning.

It's going to get a lot worse before it gets better.

Not wasting another second, because I don't know how long I have, I pick up my phone and call a number I am very familiar with. It's the number for a local taxi company, and I'm familiar with it because they are far more reliable than the bus I used to catch that was always late. That damn bus made me miss many important things like work shifts, new job interviews and, most recently, hospital appointments to check on the baby boy growing inside me. I'd prefer to take the bus over a taxi because that's the cheaper option and saving money is everything to a woman in my position, but I can't risk public transport letting me down today. I'm hoping I can make it to the hospital in time, but if not, giving birth on the backseat of a taxi seems preferable to giving birth at a bus stop.

'Hello. Yes, I need a taxi, please, as quickly as you can. Going to Green Meadows Hospital. Twenty minutes? Is there anything quicker? It's urgent and there's nobody else who can take me. Can you send a driver right away? Okay, just please be as quick as you can. I'll be waiting outside.'

I end the call, frustrated that a driver won't be outside for me in the next few minutes, but I'm totally at the mercy of the taxi company. For them, I'm just another passenger making a simple journey. But to me, this is potentially the biggest journey of my life. I hesitated to tell them I was going into labour, though, for fear of them refusing the fare and telling me to call an ambulance instead. That would have meant more waiting, and even if a paramedic came, I'd have just been told to go to hospital, which is what I'm already trying to do.

With the taxi booked, I put my phone in my tatty rucksack along with the other items I have packed in preparation. They include pyjamas and a change of clothes for me, as well as a few nappies, a dummy and a Babygro. It's not much, and I know a baby will need a lot more than that but, for now, it's all I can afford.

Putting the straps of the rucksack over my shoulders, I wince again as I feel more discomfort inside my aching body. I also notice it is starting to rain outside, which means I'm going to get wet if I go and wait for that taxi by the kerb. I don't have an umbrella, though, so I'll stay in here because it's still nineteen minutes until that taxi arrives.

Trying to keep calm, I take a seat on the armchair that was in this flat when I moved in. It's not the most comfortable and some of the old stains on it are questionable, but it's either this or the solitary wooden chair by my small kitchen table, so I choose this one.

Taking several deep breaths, I look around at my more than modest home as, not for the first time, I wonder how I am ever going to fit a baby in here with me. I know they are small, but all the things they need are not. A crib and clothing. Nappies, creams and wipes. Toys, eventually, too. They all take up space and they all cost money, but I need to try and not worry about this now in case the stress of it only speeds up my labour.

I'll figure it out. I'll get through this. I'll survive.

Somehow.

Those are the things I tell myself as I wait for the taxi to arrive, and they are the same things I have been telling myself ever since I discovered I was pregnant, a shocking moment which, for me, came much later in pregnancy than I guess it does for most. I had no morning sickness, no unusual cravings or any other sign from my body that there was a child growing inside me. As far as I knew, I hadn't even been missing my periods because they have always been incredibly light, so it felt like everything was normal. That was until I noticed my stomach seemed swollen, and after a few days of it not going down, I sought medical advice by visiting my local doctor. After a long bus journey on a very stormy day, I made it to my appointment, expecting the doc to have some simple explanation for my apparent bloating. Maybe it was something I ate that hadn't agreed with me, and maybe there was a pill to make things go back to normal. I was just hoping it was nothing serious because, as bad as my life was, I didn't need a deadly diagnosis to make it even worse.

'There's nothing in your notes here,' the doctor had said, frowning at his computer screen upon which he presumably had my medical history. 'Sorry, but how many weeks are you now?'

'Excuse me?' I had replied with absolutely no idea what he was talking about.

'Your pregnancy,' he had said simply, as if that was a word I should have been expecting to hear. But it was not, and within minutes, I was in a blind panic, tears running down my face as I realised the doctor was suggesting the reason for my growing midsection was a growing baby.

The test that told me I was pregnant came quickly. The tests and the scan to determine the duration of that pregnancy took a little longer but were just as conclusive. I was eighteen weeks pregnant. Almost halfway through the term. I was told that getting so far in and not knowing was rare, but not unheard of. But that didn't make me feel any better, nor did the sight of my baby on the monitor. That's because it looked so big and formed already and I knew I didn't want to terminate then. Things only got harder when one of the nurses at the hospital slipped up and accidentally told me I was having a boy, even though I hadn't asked to know the gender. That's because I didn't want to get attached to the baby, but the more I was told about him, the more difficult it became to feel like I could do anything to prevent it. I considered putting the baby up for adoption, but there was a whole arduous process to get under-way, and it felt daunting on top of the exhaustion I was battling throughout my pregnancy. Before I realised how much my time, and options, were slipping away, the weeks passed by and now here I am, preparing to meet this child that was not planned for and who I may not be able to provide for.

I want this baby to have a good life, certainly a better one than I can give him. But I haven't as of yet figured out how to do that, and it's not as if I have much time to consider it now.

I'm overwhelmed.

And I'm all alone.

So who is the father and, more importantly, where is he right now? He's a guy called Gavin. It has to be him because he's the only person I have slept with in the past year, and that's because he's the one guy who had shown me any attention in that time span.

We met in a pub that I used to drink in once a month if I had any spare money left over from my last paycheque, which I didn't always have. He bought me some tequila shots, which tasted sickly, and then we came back here and we did the deed, which also left me with a slightly bitter aftertaste when I woke up hungover and feeling like it was a bad idea. But I never saw him again after that night, at least not in person anyway. I did see his face online, though, in the local news article I read on my phone, the one about him being sentenced to two years in prison for possession of drugs with intent to supply. Apparently, he was out on bail when he slept with me, though he obviously failed to mention that as we got drunk together and fell into bed.

I wasn't stupid. I could tell he wasn't exactly a model citizen, not many people who live in this area are, but I didn't know he was facing jail time. However, he's behind bars now, none the wiser that he has fathered a child, a child who will be a toddler by the time Daddy is a free man again. I haven't told him, nor do I plan to. I doubt he would care anyway. I doubt he even remembers me. Our night in bed would have been utterly forgettable for me too if it hadn't resulted in such a life-changing outcome.

The rain is falling harder on the other side of the window, but fifteen minutes have passed, so I better head outside because my taxi will be here soon. I head for the door, pausing once when I feel a contraction that takes my breath away, but there are no more as I leave my flat on the ground floor of this eyesore of a tower in London's East End. The building rose up in one of the most impoverished areas of the city, but it's been my home for a couple of years now and, as bad as it is, it's better than the last place I lived. I'm thirty-eight, estranged from all my family and friends up north where I originally hail from, thanks to a lack of effort on my part to keep in touch and the burning of a few bridges after arguments with my closest relatives about my life's direction. The only things more depressing than my current situation are all the dead-end, minimum wage jobs I've had to do just to maintain my 'lifestyle', a word I always use lightly because there is nothing stylish about it.

Everybody has hopes and dreams when they're younger and I was no different. I moved to London when I was in my twenties, alone but with stars in my eyes and my head full of grand visions of making it big in the biggest city in the country.

Nobody expects their life to turn out bad. That's not the dream. But mine has, mostly because of one big moment that was out of my control, sending me careering off into years of more misfortune and poor circumstance. Now I'm about to bring some poor little boy into it too, and I don't want him to suffer alongside me.

I step outside and feel the rain hitting my head as I walk to the spot where I'm hoping the taxi will arrive any minute now. As I go, I give some thought to something I've considered a lot ever since I decided to go through with my pregnancy.

I could give the baby away when he's born. Admit I can't do it and let someone adopt him. Someone who can give him more than me. I know it could be a lengthy process, but not as lengthy as living the rest of my life struggling to care for another human being. It seems so sad to consider, especially whenever I feel my baby kick. I could bond with this little life if I took the time to, but if I give him up, I would be totally by myself again. That is most likely for the best, though, because, as I spot the taxi coming towards me, I know the baby would have a better life and more opportunities with someone else. The thought of ruining someone else's life alongside my own is terrifying.

But can I really give my baby away?

It's either that, or both of us struggle, right?

What other option do I have?

THREE

AVRIL

As I ride the painful wave of another contraction, the sound I make causes Bobby to increase his speed. He's probably desperate to get out of this car now, but believe me, I am desperate to get this baby out.

The hospital is getting closer by the second, but so is the impending birth.

I cannot wait to be in the safe arms of the doctors and the midwives.

I considered going private for the birth and paying money to have my own room in a fancy hospital rather than taking the free option via the NHS healthcare system. I knew we could afford it, and it promised to provide me with a more comfortable environment to begin motherhood, but Bobby eventually talked me out of it.

'There's nothing wrong with our healthcare system,' he had said over dinner one night as we discussed the topic for the umpteenth but final time. 'Our parents were born at Green Meadows, I was born at Green Meadows, you were born at Green Meadows and our son is going to be born at Green Meadows.'

Some people might find it slightly depressing to have one hospital play such a big part in a family's life, wondering if they should have gone out further into the world, but not Bobby. He liked the fact that both he and I, and our parents well before us, had been born at the hospital that was a twenty-five-minute drive from our home. The fact we grew up in the same part of London was a factor in how we got along so easily when we met, so I can hardly use it against him now, I suppose.

As I see the sign for that hospital come into view through the windscreen of my husband's car, I tell myself that he was right. Everyone in our families, including ourselves, was born right here, at this hospital, and there's something wholesome about that. It's a good hospital; sure, a little rougher around the edges than a private one, but the staff here are just as caring and capable, and that's all that matters. Perhaps what swung it for me was when Bobby suggested we use the money we save on having a private birth to splurge on a holiday, which would be our first family vacation as a trio. He mooted the Maldives or Dubai, two places we have been to before and places we wish to go back to again, although it would be a slightly different experience with a baby in tow. The flight would certainly be more gruelling with an infant than it was back when all I had to do was pick which movie I wanted to watch on the in-flight entertainment. But I agreed, though maybe it was something other than the prospect of a sun-kissed holiday that made me reconsider spending thousands of pounds on a birth that I could have for free on the NHS. Like the fact I was preparing to leave my high-paying job and never go back to it again.

As Bobby brings the car to a stop and rushes out to the meter machine to pay for a parking ticket, I'm aware that my life isn't only about to change dramatically when this baby is born as I navigate parenting. It's also changing because I am leaving my job, just as soon as the maternity pay ends. Of course, my employer has no idea about my plans to quit yet and I doubt they'll be too happy about it when they find out, given the senior role I hold with them and the difficulty there will be in replacing me.

As I watch Bobby hurriedly putting a few coins into the parking meter, I get why he is nervous about the thought of me walking away from a six-figure salary. That's a huge drop in household income, and while he'll still be driving his taxi, the money is nowhere near comparable. But it's not as if I'll never work again, just in a different, less demanding industry than cosmetics, and we have plenty of savings, so we won't have any immediate worries for a while. It's more that I don't want to be at the office all the time and missing out on my son growing up, and rather than pay for a nanny to raise him for me, I want to do it myself. At least, they are the reasons I have given to Bobby to be a stay-at-home mum. But there is another reason, one that I have kept quiet because I don't want anybody to know it's something that has been playing on my mind.

I want to be the best person I can be for my baby.

I cannot be that if I keep working in the job that was turning me into a monster.

As Bobby rushes back to the car with a ticket in hand, I am relieved that whatever happens over the next few years as I tackle motherhood head-on, my child won't ever get a glimpse of the woman I had to be to achieve such success in my career. I had to do things I didn't necessarily want to do, things I am not proud of, and things that would shock anybody who knew me outside of work – my husband in particular. I don't want to be that person anymore, not when I am going to have to be a role model, so this is what I have decided. I'm quitting my day job, and my only job now is to be the best mum I can be.

I hear it's the most demanding job in the world. But I like a challenge.

Bring it on.

Bobby throws the parking ticket on the dashboard so it's

visible should an inspector come by to check while we're inside. Then he helps me out of the car before grabbing the bags and now we're making our way to the entrance and this is getting more real by the second. It's not unfamiliar because we have done a couple of practice runs before, ensuring we know exactly which way to go once we get inside the hospital. I'm glad we did because it's an absolute maze inside.

The electronic doors slide open and we step in, me and my big bump attracting a couple of lengthy glances from a few other members of the public already in here. That's okay, I know it's hard not to stare at a heavily pregnant lady because it's not every day a person sees someone who looks like they are about to burst.

'This way,' Bobby says, taking charge as I need him to because I'm too busy focusing on my breathing and trying to figure out how far apart my contractions are so I can pass that information on to the first midwife who comes to consult with me.

As we reach the locked door of the maternity ward and Bobby presses the buzzer that will alert the reception staff to let us inside, I see a man approaching the same door behind us. He is holding a balloon and a box of chocolates, and if I had to guess, I'd say they are presents for his partner who has already had their baby. That means the stress is over for them, but as the door unlocks and we go into the ward, it's only beginning for us.

As we approach reception, I see another heavily pregnant woman waddling to a bathroom before I glance through a door and see a young couple cooing over their newborn. It's just another day here where babies are born and go home before new ones take their place. I allow that fact to reassure me rather than worrying too much about what could go wrong.

'Hi. This is my wife, Avril,' Bobby says to the nurse behind the desk. 'We called ahead as I think she's going into labour.'

'Oh, okay,' the midwife says before glancing at me and

checking something on her computer. But she's not being as receptive as I would have hoped and now I'm worrying again that we should have gone private. I'd probably already be in a bed by now with multiple doctors fussing over me. But then the nurse smiles casually as if this is just another day at work for her and beckons one of her colleagues over, who quickly offers to show me to where we will be based until I'm taken to the birthing suite.

We're led into a large room with four beds in it and I see two of them are taken by other couples who, like us, are anxiously awaiting their new arrival. The third has a solitary woman in it and the chair beside her is vacant, making me assume her partner is at work or has gone out to get her snacks. We are led to the empty bed and Bobby puts down our bags as I feel another sharp pain and prepare for the next contraction, which I make sure the nurse who is still with us is aware of so she can judge the severity of it.

Once that passes, I lie down on the bed and try to make myself comfortable, which is impossible, while Bobby takes a seat in the bedside chair, and we are aware it could be many hours yet until we actually meet our baby. I've heard all the horror stories of three-day-long labours and while I hope this doesn't last for that length of time, it's hardly likely to be quick either with a first baby.

After a nurse has told me that a doctor will be with me shortly to ask me a few questions, I think about closing my eyes and trying to get some rest because I'll need all the energy I can get for what is to come. Just before I do, I look over again at the woman on her own and there is still no sign of anyone else joining her, no boyfriend or husband or parent or sibling or even just a friend. This woman, who looks even more ready to give birth than I am, seems to be preparing to go through it all by herself, and as she lies down on her bed I hear her ask the nurse to draw the curtains.

The nurse goes to do just that but as she is pulling the curtains around the neighbouring bed, I get a few more seconds to look at the solo woman and as I do, I get the strange sense that she is familiar. I can't place her, though I can see that she looks very sad. Perhaps she is nervous. Maybe her partner is away on business, and she is worried he might not be able to make it here in time. Or perhaps she really is alone, and the impending arrival of a baby is making her feel worse rather than better about things.

But just before the curtains close, I see one more thing.

The woman is looking right at me.

She's caught me staring at her and, at first, I assume that is why she looks so strangely at me. But as the curtains close and I lose sight of her, I'm not sure that is it.

I get an uneasy feeling that there was another reason why she was glaring at me. But I don't know what it is, only that I'm actually glad those curtains have been closed so she isn't making me uncomfortable anymore.

FOUR

JADE

I was barely in the bed on the ward when my contractions sped up and I was suddenly whizzed down to the birthing suite because my baby was coming a lot quicker than anticipated. That's why I've not had much time to process the shocking thing I saw when I was waiting on the ward.

I can't believe who was in the bed next to me. I knew it was her the second I saw her. I recognised her instantly.

It's that bitch I've hated for a long time.

The person who crushed my dreams and shattered my confidence.

It's Avril.

But there are more pressing matters at hand than thinking about her and I am reminded of that by the amount of pain I am in, as well as the very loud voice in my ear.

'Okay, Jade. One more big push! You can do it. Three, two, one, push!'

The midwife giving me the orders is only doing her job but it's far easier to tell me what to do than it is for me to actually do it. This hurts so much. Every cell in my body is in agony.

'I can't,' I scream breathlessly, my face drenched in sweat and my hands gripping the bedsheets beneath me.

'Yes, you can, Jade. Come on. You can do it!' the midwife cries, but if she says anything more, I might take my hands off the sheets and use them to shut her up.

'I need more drugs!' I cry, frustrated that the pain relief I have already been given seems to have worn off or not worked at all.

'You're nearly there. You can do it,' the repetitive midwife tells me again, and despite not feeling like I can, somehow, my body finds its last vestige of strength and I push with all my might, if only to get this damn thing over with.

The sound of crying a second later is shocking but it's not me who is upset, nor is it any of the midwives around me. The sound is coming from the baby I have just given birth to. As they hold him up to me to give me the first look at my child, I have tears in my eyes. But they're not tears of joy, or even exhaustion.

They are tears of fear because this little life is totally dependent on me, yet I don't believe I am capable of doing this.

'He's gorgeous,' a gushing midwife says to me. 'Look at him, not a single hair on his head. They're so cute when they look like that. Mine was bald too when he was born. Don't worry, you'll be paying for haircuts before you know it.'

As the bald and bawling baby is taken away to be cleaned and have the remainder of the umbilical cord cut, I close my eyes and pray that my heart rate will come down soon. I feel shaky and cold, uncertain and afraid, and I have to wonder if this is what every new mother goes through or if it's just me. I open my eyes to check the midwives around me to see if they seem concerned about my appearance or any of my readings on the machines I am hooked up to, but they seem fine, so maybe this is normal. Everyone seems calm in here, everyone except my baby, that is, who is still crying his little eyes out, or at least he is until a midwife places him down on my chest.

I read about this online. It's done as quickly as possible after birth so that mother and baby can bond instantly. But as I feel my son's skin on my own, I am not sure it is working. I feel cold, though not just in temperature, even though I am shivering. I feel cold in general, numb almost, and while it might be the drugs, I fear it might just be me and how I feel about being a new mum.

'Congratulations. He's very handsome,' another delighted midwife says to me as she beams at me and my baby, who is still crying. She is looking far happier than I feel. I'm jealous of her and the fact that she gets to leave this room and take a break now while, for me, the work is just beginning. What do I do now? Try and feed this child? Dress him? Cuddle him? Where's the guidebook? What are the rules? I really hope somebody is about to share them with me because if not, how can I possibly know how to navigate this new life?

'Why is he crying?' I ask, my desperate question a torrid cocktail of anxiety, frustration and sheer naivety.

'It's perfectly normal,' the midwife tells me, as if that is supposed to make being deafened any easier. 'Here, put your hand on him like this.'

She repositions my hand, which was resting limply on my baby's back a moment ago, proving I'm utterly useless at this, though it doesn't make the crying cease. I guess she did it because I look like I don't know what I'm doing, which is true, but at least I'm surrounded by people who have a clue. The problem is, I'm not going to be in this hospital forever and I'm already dreading the time when I'm told I can go home because then I really will be all alone. Or at least as alone as a person can be when they have a little person who depends on them for absolutely everything.

'Do you have a name yet?' another midwife asks me over the sound of the incessant crying. Maybe it's not so fun to be surrounded by all these fawning faces after all.

'No,' I reply quietly as my upset baby wriggles on my chest, and I wonder if he is uncomfortable, still adjusting to this strange new world he has entered or simply sensing that I'm not going to be a good mother and already making his unhappiness clear.

'Not to worry. Plenty of time for that,' the midwife says. 'It took me three weeks to name my eldest. Hubby and I just couldn't agree on anything.'

I watch her as she saunters away, this woman who seems to have parenting all figured out. *Hubby and I*. It must have been so much easier having a partner in the room with her at a time like this. I wonder how old her kids are now and how much it has taken out of her to raise them. Maybe not that much if she has the energy to come here and do this job every day. She also has somebody to split the duties with. Or maybe she really loves babies and wants to be around them all the time, both at home and at work. There are so many people out there like that – people who seem to live to care for others – and despite how noble that is, I know I am not one of them. But because of how many people there are out there, people desperate to be in my position here, I know adoption is still a possibility. Some women would kill to have my baby, so is giving him away really that bad if it fulfils someone else's dream?

'Let's wrap this little one up so he doesn't get too cold,' yet another midwife says to me, and as she picks up my baby it's a relief to have a temporary reprieve from holding him. It feels like a lot of pressure to have to handle, and I've never been good with pressure. I need things to be ordered and balanced, which is why I have struggled so much for so many years as my life has got steadily worse and more chaotic.

I'm taken into another room for a while where me and my baby are monitored before being told that I can be wheeled back onto the ward now. As soon as I am told that I will be returning to that bed where I was taken first, I realise that means I am also going to see the woman who was in the one next to me.

The thought of being close to Avril again is even more daunting than what I have just been through, though I try and relax by assuring myself that she did not recognise me when our eyes met just before the curtains were drawn around my bed. Why would she know who I was? I've changed a lot since we met, definitely as a person, but certainly physically too. I have a new hair colour, going back to my natural brunette rather than the blonde I used to have. I also keep my hair very short these days, a big change from how it used to hang halfway down my back, and I have several ear piercings, a desperate stab at some identity after so long not expressing that side of myself either because my family disapproved or because I thought it might not help me get a serious job back when I tried to be career driven. I've put on weight too, not necessarily because I eat a lot – I can't afford to – but because I've got older and having not kept up with exercise, the pounds gradually accumulated around my midriff and face, even before I got pregnant. While I can't be proud of my added weight, and I only changed my hair-style because I wanted to disassociate with the younger me, at least the differences have prevented Avril from recognising me. Although she might get a sense that she knows me from some-where if she gets to look any longer, which is why I will keep the curtains closed around my bed as much as possible.

I'm planning on telling the nurse who takes me and the baby back to the ward to close the curtains promptly until I see that Avril is not in her bed at all. There is no sign of the man she was with either, just their bags sitting on the chair. I recognised him too, and as much of a shock as it was to see her, it was even more shocking to see him. But like Avril, I don't think he recog-nised me. Now, they are elsewhere in this hospital, their minds are on far more important things than me.

I guess she has gone to give birth too. I wonder how it is

going for her. I'm sure she's in control of the situation like she always used to be.

I should care less, but as I get into my bed whilst the nurses place my constantly crying baby down into the crib beside it, I cannot stop thinking about Avril and how she will be coming back here very soon. I've been unable to clear thoughts of her from my mind ever since I saw her, that blast from my past, that unforgettable time of torture and pain. When she comes back, will she recognise me and, if so, what will she do? Just as unknown is what will I do if she does?

When Avril returns, she'll have her own baby with her; perhaps she'll only have eyes for her newborn and won't notice me.

But I told myself that if I ever saw her again then I would take revenge. Now's my chance. Will I go through with it?

FIVE

AVRIL

When I open my eyes, everything is blurry. I can't see anything yet, but I can hear something. It's the sound of a crying baby and it's very close.

It takes me several seconds and plenty of blinking before a few things finally come into focus. The first thing I see is a pale blue curtain. It seems to totally surround me. The next thing I see is the smiling face of my husband, though I'm not quite sure why he is so happy. At least, that is until I see what he is holding in his arms. It's a little bald baby, dressed in a baggy blue 'gro, and he is currently asleep, so that crying must be coming from the baby on the other side of the curtain.

'Wahhh hurggh,' is the first noise that comes out of my mouth, though that's not what I intended to say. What I was trying to say is 'What happened?' but my throat is incredibly dry, whilst my brain feels scrambled. If it wasn't for the fact that Bobby seems so happy, or that the baby he is holding seems very content, I'd think I have some kind of a hangover. That feels like the only thing that could explain my grogginess. But I haven't been drinking. So what is going on?

As Bobby passes me a cup of water and I take a refreshing

sip, I try to figure this out. The last thing I remember is being in a lot of pain as a doctor and several midwives rushed around me, while Bobby looked very worried, asking all the medical staff what was wrong. I don't remember anything after that, until this moment here.

Did I pass out? Was I drugged?

I'm not sure. All I know is when I went to sleep, I did not have a baby.

But as I wake up, I do.

'Meet our little boy,' Bobby says, still smiling widely. 'And he's absolutely fine. The nurses want to take him for a few tests shortly, but they said it's nothing to worry about. Just a precaution.'

So much information to process and it would be a lot even if I didn't have brain fog.

I take another glug of water, more to ensure my throat is lubricated enough to allow me to speak properly this time, before trying again.

'What happened?' I ask, relieved that my words come out sounding normal.

Bobby doesn't answer me straight away and instead takes the time to gently place the baby down in the plastic crib. He doesn't stir, still sound asleep, looking peaceful and perfect, and I keep staring at him as Bobby takes hold of my hand.

'There were a couple of complications during the birth,' he says gently. 'They had to do an emergency caesarean.'

I look away from our son and at my husband's concerned face. Is he worried that I'm traumatised? If so, he needn't be because I can't remember much of anything.

'The doctors were a little concerned about your heart rate, so they gave you something to settle you,' he goes on. 'But you're okay now and our baby is okay and that's all that matters.'

He has tears in his eyes, but he's not upset in the typical way. He looks overjoyed, like he's proud of me and what I've been through to give us this child. That's when the emotion hits me too. I find myself blubbing like that baby in the next bed, the one that hasn't stopped crying since I woke up. But unlike that baby that I can't see behind the curtain, I am not unhappy. I am overjoyed, albeit exhausted and still a little unsure, because it seems as if my dream, our dream, has finally come true.

Bobby and I are parents.

We have a baby boy.

And he is perfect.

'I want to hold him,' I say as I quickly wipe away a few of my tears, putting my hands out to let Bobby know he is to pass me our child immediately. I don't know exactly how long it has been since he was born, but it already feels way too long a time for me not to have held him.

'Are you sure you're feeling okay?' Bobby asks me, but I assure him I am and lean forward in my bed to show how eager I am to hold our baby. As I do that, I feel pain in my midsection and regret the sudden movement, grimacing and gritting my teeth, which only makes Bobby look even more worried.

'Okay, just stay still. You need to rest,' he tells me. 'Lie back. I'll pass him over to you. Just get comfortable.'

I do as my husband says, not used to him telling me what to do when it's usually me bossing him around, but he seems far more in control of this situation than I am. I get an even stronger sense of that when he picks up our baby again and just watching him carefully cradle the small child puts me in awe of my partner and how naturally he seems to be taking to this new responsibility. He looks like he knows exactly what to do, how to hold the baby just right, where to place his hands so the little head is supported and how to not do anything that will wake him up with a start.

As Bobby passes him to me, I fear that I will not be anywhere near as competent as he clearly is, but I have to learn fast. Although, as I take hold of my baby for the first time, I realise all the pre-birth classes I took have been for nothing. It's very different holding a doll to holding an actual living, breathing baby. As I try to get both myself and the baby comfortable, I see him stir. I feel bad that I seem to have woken him up, but as he opens his eyes and looks up at me, I can't feel regret when I'm so overwhelmed with love.

'What shall we call him?' Bobby asks me as tears fill my eyes and my baby's face goes all blurry.

'What about Luca?' I say, naming one of the top two suggestions we had whittled it down to if we had a boy.

I'm prepared for a bit of a discussion with my husband over this because he has just as much of a say in the name as I do, and he might have a different opinion. But then—

'I think he looks like a Luca too,' Bobby says, and I guess that decides it.

I want to hold onto my baby boy forever, never let him go and cherish every single second I am in his presence. But the reality of the situation is that I'm in a lot of pain, my thoughts are still foggy and I'm aware that I'm not in the best physical condition to be holding on to him for too long.

'Here, let's put him back down and he'll probably go back to sleep,' Bobby says as he takes Luca from me and places him gently back in the crib. Within seconds, our son has closed his eyes again and already seems to be drifting back into a slumber, which is impressive considering the loud crying that is still going on nearby.

'You need to get your rest too,' Bobby tells me, and while I feel too wired to sleep, it is nice just to lie back and not have to move much because I'm definitely not feeling myself yet. The problem is, I'm not finding it as easy to relax as my son is with the incessant crying going on in the next bed over and I wonder why it is taking so long for somebody to help settle the child down. Judging by where the crying is coming from, I figure it is the baby belonging to the woman who came in here all by herself and I wonder if that explains it. If she's alone, she might be unsure what to do and she doesn't have the help of a considerate partner like I do. I get proof of that a moment later when I hear that woman call out.

'He just won't stop crying! Can somebody help me?'

I look at Bobby then, wondering if he should dart through the divide in the curtain and try to assist, though it's not really his job to. Then I hear footsteps and realise some nurses are arriving to help, which is good, particularly a moment later when the crying ceases.

The ward is temporarily at peace, and I can relax for a moment.

'I'll go and tell a nurse that you're awake,' Bobby tells me before he goes to step through the sliver of a gap in the curtains. Just before he does, I have something to tell him.

'I love you,' I say, smiling at him from my pillow, and while I probably look awful considering what my body has just been through, he smiles back at me as if I am the most beautiful woman in the world.

'I love you too,' he says before he leaves me momentarily.

As soon as he leaves, I hear the baby in the next bed start crying again.

SIX

JADE

'Why won't he stop crying?'

My tired, exasperated question is directed at the latest nurse who has come to try and get the baby in the crib next to me to be quiet for more than two seconds. Just like all the others before her, this nurse picks up the baby and starts shushing it and just like the others, she quickly gets him to settle. But as soon as she puts him down, he starts crying again.

'He wants to be held,' the nurse tells me, smiling, as if having to deal with constant crying is not enough to drive any woman mad. I also get the rather large hint that she is dropping, which is that I should be making more of an effort to pick up my son and hold him myself. The fact is, I have barely touched him since we got back to this ward, not only because he's been crying so much and the noise has quickly left me feeling frazzled, but also I am struggling to feel a strong bond or attachment with him. Maybe it's because I have no real, time-tested bond with his father, which is usually the way after a one-night stand, or maybe I'm really not cut out to do this. I'm aware that I'm unlikely to feel any closer to him if I don't hold him, but I can't bring myself to do it. Maybe if he was quieter and less agitated then I'd be willing to try but I feel so out of my depth with a crying baby. Maybe if he was as quiet as the other babies on this ward, who have barely made a sound whilst mine has done nothing but bawl.

My inner turmoil is only compounded by the fact that I know Avril is in the bed next to me, on the other side of this curtain, and her baby seems to be perfectly at ease. I haven't heard any crying coming from there, just a couple of small sneezes and some soft snores. *Typical.* That woman always lands on her feet. While I'm struggling here with an unhappy child, she has been blessed with a serene one. I know she's had a boy like me, as I heard her partner tell her so, as well as hearing the name they gave for him. Luca. They're even ahead of me there. I haven't thought of any names for the little boy in the crib next to me. I didn't ever dwell on the subject of names during my pregnancy. It made the pregnancy feel even more real and I did not want that: it felt far too scary.

However, as seemingly perfect and peaceful as it is on the other side of the curtain, I have heard a few clues that suggest the birth didn't quite go to plan. It's been difficult to hear everything that has been said between Avril and any nurse who has come by to speak to her, what with the baby by my bed being so loud. But I have heard snippets of conversations, and by the sounds of it, Avril had a tough experience. I heard the term 'emergency caesarean' as well as someone saying, 'we administered drugs', 'doctors want to make a few checks' and a few more things that hint that it wasn't plain sailing for them in the birthing suite. But since then? It seems as if everything is going swimmingly, and if Avril's baby is content, and the mother herself is okay, I imagine they will be going home together very soon to begin their new life as a family of three.

It makes me furious to think of Avril getting to bask in the warm afterglow of having a new baby, relaxing at home as, presumably, many friends and family flock to visit her and the welcome addition. I bet she'll get so many visitors and so many gifts – baby clothes, toys, maybe even some offers to babysit so the two tired parents can get out for a little break. I bet Avril will have a really wide and supportive network around her as she navigates the first few months and years of motherhood, and that will undoubtedly make things easier for her. It's in stark contrast to my situation. I'll go back to an empty flat and the only visitor I'll get in the coming weeks will be a health visitor, duty-bound to check in on me a couple of times to make sure everything is okay with my mental health and the physical health of the baby. I'll be left totally alone after that. No gushing family and friends visiting me with armfuls of gifts, no offers of giving me a brief break to get out for some fresh air and clear my head away from the sight, smell and slog of dirty nappies, dirty clothes and a dirty home.

It won't be as hard for Avril as it is going to be for me and not only because her baby isn't crying every goddamn minute.

Her life is better than mine in every way and it really isn't fair.

If I'm honest, I'm surprised, and possibly even shocked, that she would even want a baby, given what she was like when I first met her. She was the most selfish, ruthless woman I'd ever met. What could possess someone like her to make the ultimate sacrifice, to put somebody else before herself, to dedicate the next several years to being totally at the beck and call of another human being? It doesn't seem to fit with the person I knew Avril to be, and although I did only meet her briefly on a couple of occasions, I saw the darkness of her character come out. The few instances we crossed paths were enough for her to ruin my life and that's why I've always hoped I'd never have to meet her again. Yet here she is, going through exactly the same life-changing thing as I am at exactly the same time.

What are the odds? Probably about as astronomical as any

of us being born when we were. Or maybe it's all fate. Maybe we were both meant to be here at this precise moment.

After all, I have dreamt about getting revenge on Avril for a long time.

Now I've seen her and the life she is living, it only makes me want it even more.

As I watch the nurse try in vain to soothe my crying child in her arms, I think back over all the ways I have fantasised about getting my own back on Avril after what she did to me. The fact I barely made a blip on her radar of life whilst she completely altered the course of mine has meant that I have spent plenty of time wishing there was some way I could get back at her. Hurt her. Make her feel inferior. Cause her to cry. Ruin her life. Wish she'd never met me. *Make her feel like she made me feel.* After all, she's the reason my life is such a mess now.

As all the old feelings of hatred are stirred up again, my disturbed mind is only fuelled further by the unabating cries of the child I am supposed to go home with.

I'm completely out of my depth.

That's when I have a thought.

It's one that is almost too frightening to entertain for longer than the second it takes for it to flash through my head, and such is the horror of it that it must have been dredged up from the deepest and darkest recesses of my imagination. But I can't change the fact that I had the thought and, rather than ignore it, I allow it to marinate, working through all the possible ways I could do it and what would happen if I did.

The baby keeps crying, the nurse keeps looking at me like I'm useless, I feel no connection to the child in her arms and, all the while, Avril is sleeping in the bed next to me alongside her perfect child and partner.

I can't think straight. I can barely hear my own thoughts over the crying.

How do people do this? How do people not go crazy?

That's when I suddenly contemplate the unspeakable.

That's why I'm considering doing as drastic a thing as any mother could do, and it's in the name of revenge, envy and sheer desperation.

That's why I consider swapping my baby with Avril's.

SEVEN

AVRIL

I feel so alone. My husband and my son are not with me, and I miss them both terribly, feeling like I could cry the longer I sit here in this bed by myself and wait for them to return. It makes me realise how grateful I should be for having them both.

It makes me feel grateful to not be the woman in the bed next to me.

I still can't see her because her curtain is closed, but I can hear her baby crying and I know she is having to cope with that without the help of a partner. I have no idea how she has the strength to persist all by herself, and I'm glad I don't have to find out. The only thing I want to find out now is if everything is okay with my loved ones.

A couple of nurses took Luca away for tests about an hour ago, and while Bobby went with them to make sure our son was okay, I have been advised to stay here and rest. It might have been sensible advice considering what my body has just been through and how my thoughts still feel clouded and confused, but it doesn't mean I'm happy to simply lie here and wait for my loved ones to reappear.

'It's just a precaution,' one of the nurses said to me as they prepared to take Luca away. While that is true, it doesn't stop me worrying.

As I lie in this bed, hearing all the sounds of a busy maternity ward around me, I think about what an exhausting, stressful start this has been to parenthood. But I still wouldn't change it for the world. That's because of the journey I have had to go on just to get here.

'I think I want to try for a baby.'

That was the short, simple sentence I said to Bobby one night after I got home from another very long day in the office. The idea of saying it had been on my mind for a few months before, but it took a lot of courage for me to blurt it out to my husband because I knew he'd be surprised by it. What I didn't know was if he would be receptive to the idea too. Neither of us had really discussed having kids and whenever anyone we knew had a baby, not even that was a catalyst for a discussion. I assumed I was happy focusing on my career and I figured Bobby knew that too, so he never broached the subject either. That was why, when I said that simple sentence to my husband, he dropped the knife and fork he had been using to eat his dinner and stared at me with his mouth wide open for several seconds before answering.

'A baby?' was his eventual reply, and I nodded to make sure he knew he hadn't just dreamt it.

'What's prompted this?' was his next question, but I didn't really have a great answer for it, only that the thought of being a mother had started to play on my mind more and more as I got older.

'I think we should try,' I had said. 'Who knows, we might not be able to have kids. But we might always wonder "what if?" So what do you say? Shall we give it a go?'

In hindsight, I'm glad I was already aware that wanting a baby and actually having a baby are two very different things because that mindset made me slightly more prepared for what was to come. Only slightly, but it helped. That's because, as Bobby and I laughed and hugged that night after deciding that we were going to try and make a baby, we had no real idea of the struggle that was to follow.

The crying baby in the next bed suddenly goes quiet and it's a brief moment of respite that I, as well as surely everyone else on this ward, appreciate. The temporary peace allows me to think about how there were many times I thought that I'd never end up in this position, in a hospital, with a baby, being fussed over by nurses, contemplating going home and being a mother just as soon as we get the clearance to leave. After over a year of trying and failing to conceive, even after using every single app in the world that told me when I was at my most fertile, we made an appointment to see a specialist. It was there I was told I had a medical issue that was making it difficult for me to conceive.

The crying starts up again behind the curtain, which is apt because I could almost cry when I think back to the time when I was told it was not guaranteed that I would ever be able to bear a child. It wasn't just upsetting though; it was frustrating too. It was frustrating because if I hadn't tried then I wouldn't have known there was an issue and I could have gone my whole life blissfully unaware. But the thing was, I was trying, we both were, and as any couple will know, once you warm to the idea of having a baby, it quickly becomes the only thing you ever think about. That's why it was devastating to be told that barring paying for an expensive round of IVF and hoping we got lucky, there wasn't much else we could do.

'Shut up!'

The loud and desperate cry from the woman in the next bed startles me and everyone else on the ward. She's obviously reached breaking point with her unhappy baby and needs some help. I'm sure a nurse will be on hand soon. Although I don't see one arriving yet and, as the crying continues, I wonder if I should try and offer assistance myself. It's not as if I really know what I'm doing with a baby yet either, but I could try and offer support to this poor woman who obviously needs it, so I peel back my sheet and go to ease myself up. But no sooner have I done that than I remember why all the nurses have been telling me to rest. The lower half of my body is in pain while my head still feels like it belongs to someone else. I've barely begun my recovery from the birth and the seriously strong drugs I was given, so what help could I be to this woman in my current condition? Thankfully, I don't have to find out, as a nurse appears a second later and goes behind the curtain to assist.

As the crying quietens again, I wonder what that baby's mother went through to get her child. For me, it was making the decision to pay for IVF treatment, an expensive decision, but one we were financially fortunate enough to be able to explore. Even then, the doctors warned us the odds weren't necessarily in our favour, my age being a factor, but we had to try. Try we did, three times, in fact, and it was third time lucky, not just for us but for our bank balance. Of course, that didn't mean the party could start. I still had nine months of pregnancy to endure, and I use that word to describe it because I felt nauseous almost every day throughout it. All that just to get to this point right here where I am lying in bed after an exhausting and unpredictable birth and having to wait for somebody to come and tell me if my baby is okay.

So, the question is, was it all worth it?

I get the answer to that question when I see my husband walking towards my bed with our little son in his arms. My heart swells with love as I watch them approaching, the two people whom my life now revolves around.

Luca looks asleep whilst Bobby looks happy and, as he reaches me, I find out why.

'Everything is absolutely fine,' he tells me. 'He passed all the tests, so there's nothing to worry about.'

'Really?' I cry, feeling immensely proud of my little boy for acing a load of tests on what is only his first day in the world.

Bobby goes to put him down in his crib, but I want a hold, so I gesture for him to pass me our baby. As he does, Luca stirs and begins to whimper, but he's not unhappy to be going to me. I think it's because he's hungry.

I knew from an early stage of pregnancy that I wanted to breastfeed if I could and I haven't changed my mind, so I have a go at doing just that. I was visited earlier by a lactation consultant who gave me some tips and showed me how to position Luca for optimal chances of success. While I'm still finding my feet and it feels really awkward, not to mention painful, I am able to get him to latch on and I presume he is feeding now. He's stopped crying anyway, which is always a good sign. I wish the same could be said for the baby in the next bed. But I can't worry about anyone else other than the little life I am now tasked with nourishing and, as Luca feeds while Bobby stands by my bed and watches me with pride, I know I made the right decision.

I don't need my career anymore. I have everything I ever need right here. Now all I hope is that the three of us get a good night's sleep so that we can go home in the morning.

It'll be great to be back in our house and feeding Luca in my own home. I hate to say it, but it will also be great to get away from that crying baby behind the curtain.

Just one more night. Then hopefully we'll be out of here to get on with the rest of our lives.

I cannot wait.

EIGHT

JADE

The maternity ward is as quiet as it has been since I arrived here. It's nighttime, so the ward is calmer as everybody tries to get some sleep, from the new parents to the newborn babies, though it won't be long until somebody wakes up. The peace will soon be shattered when a baby cries for a feed or a nappy change or simply for the need to be held by its mother – because this new world that they have just been born into is big and bright and scary.

The thought of noise, of more crying, more stress, makes me extremely anxious, to the point where I wouldn't be able to relax and get some sleep even if I wanted to. But I don't because, while everyone else rests, I am preparing to take action.

There are four beds in total in this section of the maternity ward, but I only care about the woman in the bed next to me. With her in mind, I stand over my baby's crib and look at the sleeping boy inside it. As I do, a tear rolls down my cheek as I say my goodbyes.

'I'm so sorry,' I whisper, my voice barely audible to me never mind my baby, as I cannot risk anybody overhearing me. But it's still important that I say this. 'I don't know what will happen next, but I just want you to know that I'm sorry.'

Then, whilst telling myself that my baby is better off without me, I pick him up and hold him tightly for a moment.

As I do, I keep listening out for any sounds on this ward, the footsteps of an approaching midwife perhaps, anything that might make me stop and reconsider what I am about to try and do. But it's still so quiet, eerily so, as if time has stopped in this part of the hospital.

Maybe that's a sign. If one of the babies here were crying, everyone would be awake and I would know it wasn't meant to be. But they are all quiet and it's as if I have been presented with a golden window of opportunity.

So it's now or never.

Approaching the curtain that separates my bed from the woman next to me, I carefully pull it back with my spare hand, whilst cradling my son in the other. As I create a gap, I'm able to peep through it, and when I do, I see that Avril is asleep in her bed, lying on her back with her eyes closed and her mouth wide open. No surprise there. She must be totally exhausted from her dramatic and draining childbirth, not to mention full of all sorts of drugs that would make anybody sleepy. Her husband is asleep too, though he looks a lot less comfortable, propped up in a chair with a very thin-looking pillow at the side of his head. But he can't complain as he's not the one who has put his body through such a physical ordeal and I'm sure he knows better than to try.

As my eyes move away from the couple, they land on the sleeping baby boy in the plastic hospital crib. He looks so small, his face all wrinkled and his little fingers barely visible poking out of his oversized Babygro.

He looks like almost any other newborn baby on day one of life.

He certainly looks like the baby in my arms.

Which is why I have a shot at pulling this off.

I step towards the crib and after one more check to make sure no one is watching me, I place my son down beside this couple's child. To save time, my boy is already naked, and now all I need to do is remove the clothes and nappy from this other baby boy and put them on my child.

My heart is thumping as I make the switch, and it feels like it's beating even faster than it was when I was in labour earlier. But that's because I know what is at stake here if I am caught. I will be arrested, and I'll be known in the news as the woman who did something unthinkable.

The woman who swapped her baby with someone else's.

But as everyone continues to sleep on this ward except me and the nurses who aren't currently around to witness this, that is exactly what I am doing.

I make the necessary changes between our babies so now he looks like he is theirs and theirs is mine. The Babygro, the nappy, the ankle tags – all are swapped as quickly as can be.

Then I pick up their baby and carry him back to my bed.

I look down at the little face in my arms as I close the curtain again and, as I do, I hear my own baby start crying on the other side of it. Then I hear Avril stirring from her sleep before picking the child up and shushing him.

I did it just in time and it's too late to go back now.

The swap has been done.

She has my baby and I have hers.

But will I get away with it?

NINE

JADE

The first light of dawn is easily infiltrating the thin blinds that hang over the large windows at one end of this maternity ward. That's why I'm able to see the baby sleeping in the crib next to me. He looks so peaceful and he hasn't made a noise since I took him. The same can't be said for the baby I swapped him with. I can hear that baby now, crying his eyes out, screaming at the top of his little lungs. My baby. I should be with him. It hurts that I'm not and being parted has made me realise I did care about him after all. But it's too late for that now. He's on the other side of the curtain, and I can hear the two people who are with him trying to calm him down, though it's not working.

They seem to be confused as to what the problem is. But I know something they don't.

They have my baby now.

And I have theirs.

As crazy as what I did during the night was, such is my hatred of Avril that I did it anyway.

I gave up my baby, but I still have one.

I still can't believe I actually did it, though. I could have been caught. All it would have taken was somebody waking up and seeing me, or one of the babies waking up and crying out. Or a nurse wandering by and making a check behind the curtains, or perhaps one of the other parents on this ward coming back from the toilet in the dark and mistakenly going to the wrong bed before spotting me leaning over the crib. There were so many ways I could have been caught, and surely only one place I would have ended up if I had been. It's a place I still might end up: it's not that I haven't been caught.

Not really.

It's that I haven't been caught *yet*.

The thought of prison is terrifying, but then, in the early hours of the morning, staring into the abyss of a miserable home life with a constantly crying child, I decided that the risk was worth it. It's worth it when I think about what Avril did to me, the things she said to me, and the downturn she caused my life to take. I know I wouldn't even be here now if it hadn't been for her, so if she's screwed me over, it's only fair I do the same to her. Except she doesn't know she has been screwed over yet and if I'm lucky, she never will. But is that possible? Can I really get away with what I have done? What if I don't? I know I'll be in serious trouble with the police, but getting caught would also mean that one day, my son would know what his mother did.

We could potentially be reunited.

Or most likely, *he would hate me until the day I died*.

I believe there is a chance because our two babies are barely a day old, of the same gender and same size, and now they are wearing each other's clothes and wristbands, could anyone really tell them apart? I mean, even away from the accessories, newborn babies look so similar, don't they? Sure, there might be the occasional one with very distinguishing features, perhaps a freckle or a mole on their face, or larger ears, or more hair than usual on their head. But most newborns look the same – totally bald with squished faces and black pupils that haven't developed their pigment and shown their true colour yet. And they sleep a lot, so it's not as if their personality comes out quickly. So it could work. I could leave here with Avril's baby and she could have mine and it may go unnoticed. I know our babies were a similar weight and even if they weigh them again before we leave, I read somewhere that it's common for a baby's weight to fluctuate greatly early on, depending on how much milk they are taking in. They gain or lose weight quickly, so any discrepancies there can easily be explained away and masked.

This can work, but I think the longer either one of us stays here, the less likely this plan is to succeed, so I need to get home as quickly as possible and, ideally, without Avril getting a look at the baby I leave with.

I decide I'll ask the next nurse who comes by if it's okay for me to go home, and while I wait, I listen to Avril telling her partner in exasperated tones that she has no idea why their baby is crying so much.

'He won't latch on,' she says, presumably trying and failing to breastfeed him, and maybe it's because the baby senses something is wrong. As if that feeling is spreading, the baby I stole starts crying then. I instantly panic, fearing Avril might recognise the cries and realise a switch had been made in the night. I also panic because despite potentially having an easier baby now, I still don't really know what to do. How can I calm this baby quickly so no more attention is drawn to us?

I get out of bed and look down at his unhappy face, wondering if he is hungry. If so, he is probably expecting to be offered breast milk, but I'm not Avril and I can't and don't want to do that. That's why I reach for the tiny bottle of formula milk by my bed, but before I can offer it, a nurse appears through the curtain.

'Good morning. How was your night?' she says, all smiles which tells me she has just started her shift and hasn't yet accumulated the fatigue that comes from a full day on this ward.

'It was okay,' I say, instantly fearing that my guilty

conscience is going to give me away and she will guess that I did something criminal. But she is still smiling and as she looks at the baby, *Avril's baby*, she doesn't seem concerned about anything. In fact, she seems pleased.

'Well, he looks a lot happier than yesterday,' the nurse says. I guess she is comparing this situation to when she saw me trying to deal with my crying child to no avail during her last shift. She is right too because the baby has stopped crying now, which might mean he wasn't hungry at all. But while it might appear that I am managing, someone else on this ward is not. I hear Avril call out for help, and the nurse I'm with quickly scurries away to check on her. I guess she came to see me first because, based on yesterday's evidence, I was deemed the one who needed assistance the most. Not anymore, not now Avril has all the crying to deal with while I have her placid baby.

As I stand there, listening to the commotion on the other side of the curtain, I constantly remind myself of the person Avril is and that makes it much easier to feel less guilt. Although I'm still very much on edge, fearing that I'm on the verge of being caught. When another nurse appears, my stomach drops.

'Good morning. Shall I open these curtains and let some more light in here?' she suggests, reaching to pull back the curtains that have been closed around my bed ever since I was put here.

'No. Leave them!' I cry out, lunging forward to stop her.

'Oh. Okay. I'm sorry,' the nurse replies, visibly startled at how desperate I am for her to stop what she was about to do, though she thankfully has no idea why I require so much privacy. She probably thinks I'm feeling unconfident with my child and don't wish to be judged by the other mums on this ward, or that I'm self-conscious about people looking at my post-partum appearance, which is bedraggled to say the least. As long as she doesn't know that it's because I am harbouring someone else's child, and I want to ensure that the real parents don't see him before I leave here.

'So how are you feeling today?' the nurse asks me with the curtains still very much closed around us.

'Me? Why?' I ask nervously, paranoia seeping out of my every pore.

'Well, you did have a baby yesterday,' the nurse replies with a chuckle, and I force myself to relax.

'Oh, right. Yeah. I feel fine. Good, actually.'

'Excellent. And your little one looks well too, so how about we see if we can get you guys home in the next few hours?'

'That would be great,' I reply, because it would be. Anywhere other than here.

'What am I doing wrong?' comes the cry from the next bed. I recognise Avril's voice, now sounding even more distressed than the last time I heard it. The baby, *my baby*, is still crying, and she is obviously getting upset about it, which is why the nurse leaves me and goes to help her colleague with the trickier patient. I need to get out of here, away from the sound of those cries that cut me to my core. But to make myself feel less guilty, I tell myself that my baby is better off being cared for by a couple rather than one person. Then I think about getting back into my bed and trying to rest. Just before I do that, I notice a small gap in the curtains and, despite the risk, I can't resist taking a peek at the next bed. When I do, I see the two nurses working to try and calm the crying baby, while behind her, Avril's husband is doing his best to console his worried wife. It could be a scary moment for me to see her like this because it could really bring everything into sharp focus and cause me to crumble. But it has the opposite effect. Seeing her so upset gives me pleasure, which is why I end up staring for too long and getting caught.

Every muscle in my body tenses when I see Avril look up and notice me peeking through the gap in the curtain and, as our eyes meet, I fear she is going to know what I have done and start screaming at me. Thankfully, that doesn't happen. She just holds my gaze for a few seconds before looking back to the baby she is worried about and, with that, I am free to move away from the curtain and return to privacy.

I think this is going to be okay, both for me and for my own baby, the one who will now grow up with access to so many things that I could never offer. That is the silver lining: my boy will have the lifestyle I dreamt of.

Who would have thought it? Me, getting the upper hand over her. But I needed a break.

That bitch had to pay at some point.

The past always comes back to bite those who deserve it the most.

TEN

JADE

'How do I look?'

I'm not nervously asking my question to my boyfriend, or a family member, or even anybody remotely close to me at all. That's because I don't know anybody in this city that I moved to in pursuit of my dream. I'm all alone, except no one is ever really alone in London. There is always someone nearby. I've actually just asked this question to the woman who I have been sitting beside on the bus for the past twenty minutes.

The bus has just reached my stop and, after spending the journey telling this stranger about where I am going and why it is so important to me, I need a confidence boost before I depart this busy vehicle. Hence why I am now standing in the aisle and letting my fellow passenger get a full look at the outfit I have chosen for today.

'You look like a woman who is about to get the job of her dreams,' comes the very kind reply.

I smile and say thank you before heading for the exit so as

not to hold up the people on the bus who wish for it to continue on to the next stop.

'Good luck! You'll be great!' my passenger friend calls out to me as I disembark. As my heels hit concrete, I turn back and smile before giving her a wave as the bus departs.

I'm alone by the roadside, but only a short walk away from somewhere I definitely won't be by myself. I begin walking before the nerves in my stomach can debilitate my legs and prevent me from moving at all. As I told that friendly older woman on the bus, today is a big deal for me, although I only actually mentioned it to her when she commented on how incredibly stressed I was looking. Thankfully, she has calmed me down a lot, but as I see my destination come into view down the street, my breathing becomes shallower again and I am afraid all her pep talks and positivity were for nothing.

If I'm this nervous out here, how am I going to be when I get inside there? That's where it counts, not out here, where nobody knows me, but inside that very tall and very impressive building that I am almost at the front door of now.

As I enter the offices of this cosmetics company, I am comforted by how familiar the place looks, even though I've never actually been here before. I've never physically stood in this grand and expansive reception area, though I have looked at photos of it online countless times and visualised myself being here. You can find almost anything on the internet if you look hard enough and I certainly looked hard to find photos of this place, the place I have dreamt about working since I was a little girl. I've analysed every image, from the ones posted on social media by employees here or famous models who are passing through, to the pictures that the company themselves have published. All of them have done the job of making this place look alluring, ambitious and, most of all, an amazing place to ever set foot in.

Not just any person can have the privilege of being here.

There are basically only three ways you can get inside and stay inside for the more than five seconds it would take for a security guard to escort you back out. One, you need to work here, and getting a job in a place like this is as difficult as winning the lottery three weeks in a row, or at least that's how it feels for the countless people who try and fail. Two, you are a fashion icon, a superstar model who travels the world walking catwalks in the latest fashionable threads and most glamorous make-up and you are here to visit and discuss what look is going to take the world by storm next. Thirdly, and last but not least as far as I'm concerned, you get to be here because you have an interview to become part of this world.

That's exactly why I am here. I have an interview for my dream job. That explains why I feel like I could puke all over this gleaming marble lobby area any second now.

'Jade White. I have an interview with—'

'We have your name down here. Please, take this security pass and go up to the fifteenth floor. The other candidates are waiting there.'

The receptionist is incredibly efficient, not even wasting a second to allow me to finish my sentence. She was obviously expecting me, so I take my pass and head to the elevators. As I push the button, I think about what she just said.

The other candidates are waiting there.

As I ascend, I wonder how many people are standing between me and what I want.

It's only as the elevator doors open that I get my answer.

At least ten, if not more, other women are here.

I try my best not to look inferior as I take a seat amongst the other candidates, although it's difficult when I notice that all of them are wearing far better clothes than me, as well as shoes. This being one of the top cosmetics brands in the world, it shouldn't bother me what everyone else is wearing because I'm not here about fashion, but I instantly feel inferior. I thought I had done a good job with my appearance today. I'm wearing a suit dress and a pair of shoes that I could scarcely afford but decided to spend what little I had in my bank account to at least make it look like I could belong in a place like this. I also made sure to buy some very expensive make-up because I presumed I'd be judged on that. However, the other women look far better than me, or are at least wearing more expensive clothing than me, as I'm glancing around spotting five hundred pound shoes, five-figure handbags and the kind of cosmetics on their faces that don't come cheap either.

I'm hoping it's not a big deal. We'll ultimately be hired based on our personality and fit for the job and I believe that's where I can shine. I've put together what I think is a very thorough and impressive portfolio of work experience, all unpaid, but I have to start somewhere. I have also volunteered with make-up artists on weekends for the last few years whilst studying at night college for qualifications in beauty, skincare and cosmetics. I might not have been born anywhere near where the prettiest models showcase cosmetic products, be that the catwalks of Milan and Paris or the huge events in amazing places like Dubai or Monaco, but I have worked hard to inch my way closer to them. I must have done something right because I have been selected for an interview here.

I have been selected for an interview with...

There's a collective intake of breath around the room as a door opens and standing right before us is a woman we all admire. A woman we all want to gain the respect of. A woman we have to impress today.

A woman we all want to be one day.

Avril Anderson stands before us looking as beautiful and powerful as she does in every piece of online content I have seen her in. I've watched her be interviewed, post social media updates, get pictured beside famous models and designers, and stand with her arms crossed beside her desk as a magazine features her as one of the most influential women in cosmetics. Her hair and make-up are impeccable, her stylish outfit just as perfect, and the aura around her almost visible.

'Come in,' she says calmly. She is the only person here who doesn't appear to be on the verge of having a nervous break-down. Without hesitation, I and all the other candidates rise up out of our seats and follow her into the room. Once inside, I see a row of chairs and take a seat in one of them, as does everybody else except the last candidate to come in. There are no chairs left.

I watch as the candidate awkwardly looks around for some-where to sit, but there is definitely no chair out for her to take, and while it initially seems like a mistake, I realise it is not when Avril leans back in her seat.

'You can leave now,' she says to the only person standing in the room, and the candidate looks puzzled.

'I'm sorry?' she replies, not getting it.

'I said you can leave. There is no chair here for you because I did not put one out for the last person to enter the room. I didn't bother because whoever came in here last obviously doesn't want to be here as much as everybody else.'

All of us stare at Avril as we process her explanation, none more so than the unlucky candidate who seems to have blown her interview simply by not walking into the room fast enough. But surely somebody had to be last?

'You're joking,' the candidate says with a nervous laugh, but Avril's expression remains stoic, and if I didn't know from stalking her online, I know it now. This is not a woman who makes jokes.

'Please, don't make this any more embarrassing for yourself than it already is,' Avril says, looking down at the pieces of paper in front of her, and I wonder if they are our résumés. 'Good luck with the rest of your career.'

The candidate stares at Avril before looking helplessly at

the rest of us, but there is nothing we can do, even though I wish there was because I feel terrible for her. She was a rival, but this doesn't seem fair, although I dare not say anything in case it hinders my own chances. Eventually, after a few more awkward seconds, the crestfallen candidate leaves the room and those of us remaining wait to see what Avril does next.

She gets up from her seat then and walks over to our row of chairs and slowly moves along the line, looking each of us up and down but not saying anything, her eyes doing all the talking. She appears to be checking for something, but what?

'What's your name?'

My heart skips a beat when I realise she is talking to me.

'Erm, I'm—'

'It doesn't matter. Names are meaningless. A person doesn't need to know a name to form an opinion of someone else. They can get everything they need just by looking at them.'

I'm not sure what to say to that so I stay quiet and hope that Avril's opinion of me based on my appearance is a positive one.

'You can leave,' she says then, shattering that hope.

'I'm sorry?'

'So you should be. But thank you for coming.'

Avril turns away from me then and retakes her seat and, as she does, I feel the eyes of the other candidates on me. Just like the poor woman who left this room because there was no chair for her, now it's my turn to let out a nervous laugh.

'I don't understand,' I say. 'You want me to leave?'

'That's right,' Avril replies breezily.

'But why? You haven't interviewed me yet.'

'Did you not listen to what I just said? I can get everything I need just by looking at someone and I've done that with you now, so you can go.'

She's actually serious. She's dismissing me from this process based on nothing but my looks? This is even worse than turning away the last person to enter the room.

'What's wrong with me?' I have to ask. 'Is it what I'm wearing? My shoes? The way I've done my hair? My make-up? I've tried my best. What could give you the right to dismiss me based on looks?'

'Stop being so needy and leave before you embarrass yourself any more than you have done already,' Avril replies harshly, not even looking at me as she speaks. Her eyes are on the papers in front of her.

I stand up then, incensed, and in shock, but I can't leave as quietly as the last person. Not when this is so unfair.

'I've dreamt of working here my whole life,' I admit openly. 'I made it through to this final interview out of thousands who applied. And you're just going to throw all that away because you don't like the look of me?'

'Why are you still here?' Avril asks bluntly as the other candidates sit entirely still, too afraid to move a muscle in case they attract the wrath of the interviewer next.

'You're judging a book by its cover?' I go on, stubbornly refusing to accept this injustice. 'What is it that's so bad about me? My clothes and shoes aren't as expensive as yours or anyone else's here? None of that means I would not be able to do this job. I don't need to be rich to work here, I just need to be creative and energetic and passionate and—'

'For goodness' sake, Jade. Just leave before I have to call security,' Avril says, finally looking up at me. At least she used my name then, although it was hardly polite.

I can't believe this. My dream of working here is over, and not because I failed to answer some questions about the industry or didn't dazzle with all the ideas I have for future cosmetics. Instead, my dream has died because the woman running the interview process is a complete and utter bitch. Worst of all, she doesn't even seem to care that she has just crushed my dreams.

'This isn't over,' I say as I reluctantly leave the room. 'I'm going to make a complaint. You can't get away with treating people like this.'

I look back to Avril just before I leave, wondering if anything of what I just said has made her reconsider her behaviour towards me. But she's already looking back down at the paper and, presumably, preparing to get rid of somebody else in here who doesn't fit the lofty and unrealistic standards she sets.

I should have just left it there.

But I didn't.

Because of that, it was so much worse the next time I saw that woman.

ELEVEN

AVRIL

Present Day

I thought we'd be out of here by now. I thought we'd be home, all three of us, our little family ready to start life in our natural surroundings. So why am I still here, in this noisy hospital, feeling like everything is going wrong?

It's because my baby seems to hate me.

He's gone from breastfeeding easily and sleeping peacefully to refusing to latch on and crying all the time, and in a very short lifetime, it's as if his personality has totally changed. A nurse has told me babies are unpredictable and every day brings with it a new set of challenges, which I guess she told me because she wants me to know that this is normal. But I don't want this to be my normal. I want that peaceful, happy, breast-feeding baby back, not the one he is now, the whinging, upset baby who only takes my milk from a syringe.

Luca is crying again now. I can hear him, though I can't see him because he's on the other side of the curtain with Bobby. My husband is holding our child and trying to settle him, which is feeling more like an impossible task with every hour that goes by. I know my mind is frazzled and fatigued from the birth and all the meds I've been on, not to mention the waves of sleep deprivation that already feel soul crushing. Bobby is struggling too, worried about both me and the baby, and also desperate to get out of here.

'Let's just go home and figure this out there,' he said to me a few hours ago, but I dismissed the idea because I don't want to leave until Luca is breastfeeding again. He did it before and I want him to do it again. Bobby doesn't seem to get why that is important to me. He just thinks it's fine that Luca is taking in any milk as he is getting what he needs, regardless of how he gets it. Except I envisioned feeding naturally, so why is this not going to plan?

I also know Bobby wants to go home because everyone else who was in the beds around us has already gone and we're starting to see new people arriving. That is making my husband frustrated, or perhaps even embarrassed that we're still here, needing the nurses' help, while the other new parents have braved going home and figuring it out themselves. Even the single mum in the bed next to me has gone, taking her baby and walking out of here this morning. I saw her glance at me through the gap in my curtain. She looked tired and pensive about the journey ahead, but she still had the guts to get up and go. Maybe I need to do the same. Things aren't getting any better here. Luca's cries are proof of that.

'I think we're going to go home and try things there,' I tell the first nurse who comes by to check on me an hour later, much to Bobby's delight.

'Are you sure?' the nurse asks, having already made it clear that we don't have to feel rushed and should only leave when we feel ready.

I'm not sure at all, but this environment is so suffocating and maybe Luca is picking up on the chaos of it. He might be better in our quiet house, and maybe I will be too.

'Yes, we're ready,' I say, unconvincingly, and with that, our departure from the hospital is set in motion.

I try to hold Luca as Bobby packs our belongings, but his cries become too exhausting, and a nurse has to take over while I get myself out of bed and try to get dressed. It takes me ages; I'm a little unsteady on my feet after so long lying down, and my stitches hurt, as does my head. I'm still taking meds, but I want to get off them as quickly as possible because I can't think straight on them. I want to feel like myself again. And I want my eyelids to stop feeling so damn heavy.

Once we're packed, Bobby straps Luca into his car seat and heads for the exit while I wearily follow behind, the three of us leaving with the best wishes of the nurses who cared for us during our time here. As Bobby walks ahead, he reminds me to take a photo, wishing to capture that very overused but sentimental image that always appears on social media these days. It's the one where the dad is carrying the newborn out in the car seat along a hospital corridor and while neither of us has been the type to follow the crowds, it felt like a fun thing to do. I was excited to take this photo, but the reality of it here is far different from the dream. Luca is screaming his head off again, my body aches all over, and in my drug-addled haze, I forget how to complete the simple task of navigating my way to the camera app on my phone. It strikes me then that I haven't actually taken any photos of Luca yet, another thing to blame the difficult birth and high volume of drugs for. But such is my feeling of being overwhelmed, I forget about trying to get the photo and just focus on putting one foot in front of the other.

'Did you get it?' Bobby asks optimistically as he reaches the secure doors that we came through, back when we were still child-free.

'Yeah,' I mumble, not in the mood to tell him that I failed. When he finds out later, I'll just blame it on the phone not working properly.

It's an arduous journey through the hospital's maze of corridors to make it out to where our car is parked, and it's just as arduous watching Bobby try to fit the car seat inside the vehicle. He practised lots beforehand but it's a different story when there's a real baby in the seat and that baby is crying incessantly.

I feel like my head is going to explode and that feeling does not diminish during the drive home as Bobby crawls along well below the speed limit, obviously nervous about the precious cargo he is transporting but not getting us where we need to be as quickly as he could. All the while, I have to try and soothe Luca while my own aching body makes me want to cry just as much as him.

Our house eventually comes into view and as we get out of the car, there is the chance to experience another moment that Bobby and I dreamt about before becoming parents. It's the moment we enter our home for the first time with our baby. But once again, it's not as we fantasised, because Luca is screaming. I feel like I could faint, and Bobby lets out a loud expletive when he bangs his elbow on the doorframe as he's carrying our son in his car seat inside.

'Do you think he needs a feed?' Bobby asks in frustration, as if I'm already some oracle who can instantly translate whatever sound my child makes.

'Just give him the milk from the syringe. I don't have the energy to try and feed him myself,' I mumble. To sort the milk out, Bobby needs two hands, so I take over.

I hold Luca, who stops crying for three seconds, giving us both hope that he might be calming, before he gets agitated again. I take the syringe from Bobby and feed our son with my last reserves of energy and, mercifully, Luca falls asleep, his little stomach easily filled.

'Go and have a lie down. I'll watch him,' Bobby says, taking Luca and sitting back on the sofa with our son asleep on his chest. It's a wonderful sight, the two males in my life looking so peaceful together. But all I want is sleep so I stagger upstairs and head for the bedroom, only pausing as I pass the nursery on the way.

This room, with the animal prints on the walls and the cuddly toys on the shelves, is a room we have spent many week-nights and weekends decorating. It's for our baby, a place where he can feel safe when he is old enough to sleep by himself. It looks perfect, but as I trudge on to my bedroom and collapse onto the bed, I fear that is where the perfection ends.

Is any baby perfect? He is crying a hell of a lot.

And what about me? Am I going to be the perfect mother?

I have no idea. It's too early to say. Although I do have a very unsettling feeling inside me that makes me think I already know the answer to that one.

There's another unsettling feeling too. It's the memory that I have not been perfect in my past and, as I lie here trying to rest, I worry that karma has come for me.

Good people get good karma.

Bad people get the opposite.

I'm trying to be better now, I really am.

But is it too late to alter my fate based on what I've done before?

TWELVE

JADE

Everything is quiet. Too quiet? Maybe, which is why I get off the sofa and check inside the crib in the bedroom. When I do, I see that the baby inside is still asleep.

He's slept a lot since I brought him home, and he's barely cried.

He's been the total opposite to me.

Running a hand over my tear-stained, sleep-deprived face, I stare down at the little boy and think about how I haven't named him yet. But then he already has a name. Avril gave him one. Luca. That's what she called him. I presume Avril and her husband shortlisted that along with a few other potential ones. Luca was the winner. That should be his name. Now he's mine, he could have another name. The problem is a name makes him more real and it would be easier if I didn't personalise him.

I decide to make myself a drink so wander into my kitchen, a pathetic room if ever there was one. It's tiny, with one sideboard made of peeling plaster and with a rusting sink and a leaky tap. I don't prepare many meals in here, not just because I don't have the money to buy lots of ingredients and cook but because it would surely pose a serious health hazard. I've cleaned this place countless times as best I can, but there's only so much I can do. This entire flat is a dump and nowhere is that more obvious than in this part of it.

I boil the kettle and take out one of the two cups I own, before feeling relieved when I see that there is one teabag in the box. I'm glad I've not run out because I really need my favourite drink, but I'll have to go to the shops to get more teabags if I want another soon. That should be a simple enough task but, with a baby to look after, it feels like a huge obstacle to overcome. I can't just leave the baby by himself, so I'll have to take him with me, which will surely turn an easy five-minute walk into something more challenging. I was able to get a basic, second-hand pram at a knockdown price from a local charity shop a few weeks ago after realising I had nothing to transport the baby in, but do I want to use it? Going outside with some-body else's baby makes me anxious, as if every member of the public I pass on the street will know my secret. Instead of leaning over the pram and cooing at the sweet little child inside, they will point at me in horror, call me a baby snatcher and then call the police. At least that's what I'm imagining anyway. In reality, nobody should know what I've done. How could they?

As the boiling kettle gets louder, so do the worries in my mind, but they're interrupted by a knocking at the door. The sudden sound causes me to spin around and stare at my door, terrified as to who could be on the other side of it. A health visi-tor? The police? Avril? I consider not answering it, but then I hear a voice.

'Jade? Are you okay? Sorry if you're sleeping. I just wanted to check on you.'

I recognise who it is, which means I don't have to panic about being in handcuffs in the next few minutes. Although I'd still prefer to be by myself than have company, so I need to think of an excuse quickly or else...

'I saw you come back with your baby! I'm so excited! Can I see? I won't stay long, I promise!'

I realise that I can't hide in here forever. My excitable next-door neighbour is desperate to meet the baby I have been carrying for the last nine months and will keep coming back until she has got her wish. That's why I decide to just try and get this over with as quickly as possible.

I unlock the door. As it opens, I see Linda, my dowdy fifty-something neighbour, in dreary clothing, staring back at me. But what she lacks in sparkle on the outside, she makes up for on the inside because she is an incredibly warm-hearted and kind-spirited woman and that is why she has become a friend to me since I have lived here. When I first saw her, this older woman who seemed as down on her luck as I was, I felt pity for her, figuring I'd sort my life out where she had failed to fix hers. As time has gone by, I think it is more Linda who pities me, because even though I am younger than her, she possesses the ability to be positive in this environment. That is something I have never been able to do since I have been living here.

'Are you okay? Congratulations! I did see you come in here with a baby, didn't I?' Linda asks, looking past me, eager to see a child but nervous in case she was mistaken, even though she surely knows she was not. I was hoping I'd snuck in here without anyone seeing me, but it's difficult to get past a curtain-twitcher as proficient at snooping as Linda is.

'Yes, but please be quiet, he's sleeping,' I say.

'So it's a boy! Oh, my goodness, that's so exciting!' Linda shrieks, ignoring my request.

I hear a noise from the crib then and I guess the baby is stirring, which is no surprise with a loudmouth like Linda in the vicinity.

'Can I see?' she asks, already entering my flat before I've had a chance to reply, and now she's rushing towards the crib, so I close the door and hurry after her.

As she reaches the crib, I'm on edge, afraid that she's going to take one look at the little boy inside it and decide that he looks nothing like me and therefore cannot possibly be my child.

'Oh my, he's just beautiful!' Linda cries then, and I relax slightly because she hasn't instantly figured out that he is not my real son.

I see her marvelling over the child, his little eyes wide open now and staring up at the stranger's face above him, but he's not getting scared or upset. He's incredibly calm, as he has been since he was born, and it must be notable because even Linda comments on it.

'He's so peaceful,' she says, her face showing such happiness that it could almost be her child she is looking at. 'You're so blessed. Most babies cry, but I haven't heard him once since you brought him back and you know how thin the walls around here are.'

I certainly do, though I'd prefer not to think about all the questionable things I have heard coming from neighbouring flats over the years.

'So what is he called?' Linda asks me now, finally looking away from the baby and back to me, though I wish she wasn't because that is a very awkward question.

'Oh, erm...' I say, stalling, searching for an answer, trying to say anything but Luca.

'You haven't decided on a name yet,' Linda assumes then, which gives me an easy out.

'No, not yet.'

'That's okay. These things can take time, and you want to make sure you get it right. Do you have any ideas at all?'

'Erm...' I stall again, which basically answers the question once more.

'Well, just keep thinking about it. Something will come to you. You'll get a sense of what name would suit him. Some babies look like a certain name, if you know what I mean.'

I do know what she means. This baby right here looks like a Luca.

'Can I hold him?' Linda asks, and before I can answer, she has scooped him up and is carefully supporting his head with her arms. 'Just beautiful,' she gushes as she stares into the little boy's eyes, while I stare at the door and wish my neighbour would use it so I could be left alone again. But before that happens, she looks around at my humble home and asks another question.

'Have you got enough nappies? And bibs and clothes?'

'Erm,' I reply, the answer to that being no, but it seems silly to just say it and admit how unprepared I am for this.

'I don't mean to make you feel bad,' Linda goes on, 'but babies need a lot of things.'

I don't need telling that, just like Linda shouldn't need telling that all those things cost money, which I don't have much of. Then there's the fact that even while I was pregnant, I was preparing to give my baby away at some point.

I definitely won't mention that, technically, I've already given him away.

'I'll go to the shops and get you and baby a few things, just to tide you both over,' Linda offers, very generously.

'No, you don't need to do that!' I try, as if I'm capable of knowing what to buy myself, which I'm not. But I'm also aware that she can't have much more money than I do, but she insists and I'm in no position to turn down free help if it keeps being offered. But I wish that was all Linda was here for, as it seems there's something else she wants to ask me.

'I'm sorry to ask, but it needs to be done,' Linda says as she looks back to me. 'The father. Does he know about this new arrival yet?'

That's an even more awkward question than asking me what this baby's name is, but I know I won't be able to get out of it by saying 'erm' several times until she drops it.

'Jade?'

'I told you, he's bad news and I don't want him to have anything to do with me or the baby,' I snap back. 'I told you this before. He's in prison and I don't want him seeing him when he gets out.'

'I know you told me that, but now the baby is here, have you reconsidered?'

'Absolutely not,' I say before I gesture for Linda to pass me the baby back. She reluctantly does so, and once she has, I head for the door.

'Please, I'm really tired and he needs a feed, so if you don't mind leaving now,' I say. Linda gets the message, following me to the door and opening it while my hands are full.

'I'll be back soon with the shopping,' she tells me, still feeling generous enough to give me that help despite my sudden desire for her to leave. 'And if you need any help, anything at all, you know where I am.'

I have to thank her for that, but only because it speeds up the process of her leaving. Then, finally, she is gone, and as the door closes, I let out a sigh of relief.

That was not fun, nor do I imagine any future visits from her will be either when I have so much to hide. And bringing up the father? I told Linda the truth at the time, which is that I got pregnant during a relationship with a man who turned out to be trouble, so I'm better off staying away from him. He didn't know I was pregnant, and he never needs to. He certainly doesn't need me to tell him about this baby because it's not his. Not really.

It's not mine either.

This baby in my arms belongs to the woman who never deserved him.

THIRTEEN

JADE

Seven Years Earlier

She might have won the battle, but I am determined to win the war. I will see to it that Avril does not treat anybody else the way she treated me and those other candidates during that job interview, and I have already made a start on that. As soon as I had left the room where she had embarrassed me by dismissing me from the process based on nothing but my appearance alone, I had gone to reception and demanded to speak to somebody about her behaviour.

'I wish to make a complaint about Avril Anderson,' I said, before looking around to see if the poor candidate who had been dismissed before me was here to do the same thing. But there was no sign of her, so I figured it was just me.

'A complaint?' the receptionist had replied, looking and sounding shocked, as if she had never known any reason why somebody could possibly have a problem with the great Avril Anderson.

'Yes, that's right. A complaint. That woman was incredibly rude to me and another candidate too, and she's probably doing the same thing to another person right this minute. She's probably been doing it for years. So I want her to be stopped.'

The receptionist looked tense before handing me a form.

'Why don't you write down your grievance here and I will pass it on,' she had said, as if it was that simple. But could I trust her to do that? Or would it end up in the wastepaper bin as soon as I left?

'Can't I speak to somebody?' I had asked then, preferring to make this more formal.

'I'm afraid everybody is busy, but I will see to it that this gets given to the person who needs to see it.'

'And who is that?'

'Please, just write down what the issue is and I will pass it on.'

I'd seen little choice then but to do what I was being told, conscious that I could have made more of a scene, but it might have gone against me when I tried to find another job in this industry. People talk, especially in this world, so I didn't like the idea of being known as the woman who had a meltdown in the lobby. That's why I kept calm and wrote down my problem with Avril's behaviour before submitting it and asking when I would hear back.

'I'll get somebody to call you when they have investigated this,' was all the receptionist told me, and with that, I had little choice but to leave.

That was four days ago, and I haven't heard a damn thing from anybody at the cosmetics company since, despite calling every day to see what action was going to be taken. It's frustrating, not only am I desperate to see Avril disciplined and hopefully apologise to me, but also I could have used this time to apply for other jobs.

After the disaster that was my interview, I'm still very much unemployed and as far away as ever from achieving my dream of working in the cosmetics industry. I should be hustling now, trying to get another opportunity, yet I'm still too scared and shaken by the way my biggest chance ended up going for me. I've also been hustling ever since I came to this city, and I thought my hard work was about to pay off. But Avril really has knocked my confidence, which is particularly galling because she seems to possess so much confidence herself. It's not fair for her to hoard it all just because she's already made it. I haven't. How else is anybody supposed to climb the ladder and scale the heights that she has if she is going to keep knocking down any person who dares to dream of one day having a job like hers?

I look around at my feeble flat, the one I was aspiring to move out of if I had been successful in getting my dream job, but now it feels like I'm trapped here for a while yet. No such problem for Avril, I imagine, in her fancy house on the posh side of the city. A fraction of the items in her pantry probably cost more than everything in my entire place.

I'm trying not to freak out about how I'm going to pay my rent or the possibility of a lifetime of dead-end, unfulfilling jobs when I hear a knock at my door. It's weird to me because I don't get many visitors here, not since I left home in the north and moved to London all by myself to follow my dreams. So who could it be? Then I open the door and see the last person in the world I expected to see standing there.

'Nice place,' Avril says, a satisfied sneer on her face as she regards my humble surroundings.

'What are you doing here?' is the obvious question I blurt out. 'How do you know where I live?'

'Your address was on your application,' Avril replies before stepping in without any invitation from me. 'We need to talk.'

'Hey!' I cry out, but Avril doesn't slow down and once she's firmly in my flat, she waits for me to close the door before speaking again.

'You really thought making a complaint would help you,'

she says with a shake of her head. 'I knew I was right to get rid of you when I did, but you just went and confirmed it.'

'I wasn't trying to help myself, I was trying to stop you,' I say in my defence.

'Stop me?'

'Yes! You're rude and unfair and it's not right for you to treat people the way you treated us in that interview.'

'How can you know how I treated everybody? You left before the interview even got going.'

'Because you threw me out based on how I looked! How do you think that made me feel?'

'Worthless. Small. Like you being there was a total waste of time. Am I right?' Avril says, not at all looking embarrassed by what she has just said.

'Yes!' I cry. 'That's exactly how I felt. Why would you want to make me feel like that?'

'Look, whoever you are and whatever you think you were doing coming into that office, it's not the right fit for you. Don't take it personally. I've been doing this job a long time and I know what it takes to succeed. You don't have it, and you have proven my point by moaning to other people about me.'

'I'm not moaning! I have a right to a fair interview!'

'Now you listen here, you stupid bitch,' Avril snarls, a dark look coming across her pretty face. 'You don't have a right to anything in this world. Not a damn thing. You have to make your own rules and look out for yourself, that's it. The fact I'm having to tell you this proves that you don't belong here. Pack up and go back to wherever you came from and leave the grown-ups to get on with what they need to do to be a success.'

Avril turns to leave, clearly having said all she intended on coming here to say, but she can't be serious? Rather than come to apologise, she came to insult me even more?

'Hey!' I call out as she goes to leave, grabbing her arm to let her know that it's not going to be that easy for her to just walk away, but she instinctively pulls her arm back, freeing herself before she raises her fist and slaps me hard enough to send me stumbling backwards.

I'm stunned that she would strike me. I've never been hit before. Until now. The scariest thing is, Avril doesn't even look flustered by what she's just done.

'You don't even need to drop the complaint. It won't go anywhere, anyway. I'm too important. But you do need to stay away from me, and you'll be staying away from this industry now too because I'll see to it that nobody hires you, no matter where you apply. Not when I've given them my personal opinion of you. Give up on your dreams and go home, you silly little girl.'

With that, Avril walks out of my flat, leaving me cowering on the floor with a hand on my sore cheek and a ringing in my ears from what she just told me.

I'm to stay away. Forget about my dream career. Forget about all of this and just leave.

But how can I do that?

She's mad if she thinks she will get away with this.

She might be right about nobody at her workplace taking my complaint seriously.

But I think the police are going to be very interested in it.

FOURTEEN

AVRIL

Present Day

Sleepless nights. They're part and parcel of being a new parent, aren't they? But what about an entirely sleepless night? I would have thought there would have been at least an hour somewhere in the time between the sun setting and rising that a new parent might get some sleep. But nothing at all? That's exactly the kind of night Bobby and I have just had and it's thanks to Luca, who did not stop crying despite the pair of us trying absolutely everything to settle him down.

I felt like I'd lost the will to live many times during the long, dark hours whilst it seemed like everyone in the world was asleep except those of us in this house, but never more so than at dawn. It was then, as the sunlight was filtering into the bedroom and hitting my bleary eyes, that I told Bobby we needed some help. A health visitor is due at our home in a couple of days, a standard procedure for new parents to ensure they and their baby are settling into their new routine. But two days seems a long time away, especially without sleep, so I told Bobby to call and demand that a health visitor come and see us today.

As I see the car parking outside our house, I am guessing she is here.

I'm lying on the sofa, trying to rest, although that word is laughable because Luca is crying again. He's in his crib while Bobby is on his way to open the front door for our guest. I try to ignore the pain from another splitting headache for a few seconds longer until the health visitor walks in.

'Good morning. How are we all doing today?' she says, clearly already in character as the perma-positive patron saint of all things babies. I am the opposite, drowning in a swirl of doom and gloom, and I make that clear when I burst into tears no sooner than she has finished asking her question.

'Oh dear. Come here, it's okay,' the health visitor says, rushing towards the sofa and taking me in a hug while Bobby picks up Luca and tries to settle him.

My poor husband now has two criers to deal with, and as such, he looks like he's on the verge of tears himself, but he's holding it together because one of us has to. But he has reinforcements in the form of the kindly health visitor who holds me until I have got all of my emotion out, and only when I have wiped my eyes and composed myself does she speak again.

'Why don't you tell me what's been happening?' she says, asking me directly, so she must be eager to hear my thoughts on it rather than my husband's, who presumably gave her his version of events over the phone when he called earlier.

'I don't know what's gone wrong,' I say as honestly as I can. 'He was fine when he was first born. I was able to breastfeed. He slept well. He was happy. Something changed and now I can't feed him, and he won't stop crying and it's just like...'

My voice trails off.

'Like what?' the health visitor prompts me to finish my sentence.

'Like he's a different baby,' I say, instantly wishing I hadn't because it sounds foolish.

'I've told her every day is going to be different,' Bobby chimes in. 'Some days he'll be more upset than others, some days he'll be happier.'

'It's not different anymore,' I remind him, though I shouldn't have to. 'Day one was great but since then, it's been hell. Utter hell.'

'I'm sure it's not been that bad,' the health visitor says. 'You have a beautiful baby boy, and you are very lucky.'

'He just doesn't stop crying,' I lament, which leads to the health visitor getting up and offering to take Luca from Bobby. He is still crying, which proves my point, although he does settle somewhat when the health visitor has him.

Great, so now it's me who is the problem.

'I'll make a few checks on him if that's okay, just to rule out if there's anything in particular that might be bothering him,' the health visitor tells me.

I watch as Bobby strips Luca down before laying him naked on his mat on the floor while the health visitor makes her checks. Having read about this online before birth, I know that when the health visitor does this, it's as much to make sure the parents aren't physically harming the child as it is about making sure the child is okay. But, of course, we haven't hurt our baby, and the health visitor is quickly satisfied that he is okay, at least on the outside anyway.

'Okay, so you say you've not been able to breastfeed. How about formula milk? Is he taking that?'

'Yes,' Bobby replies as he re-dresses Luca, who cries again until the health visitor takes him once more. 'I've been tracking it on an app. I can show you. And I've been writing it down too on a piece of paper on the fridge, just so we can both see it.'

'Good, so he shouldn't be hungry,' she summarises, looking impressed that Bobby seems on top of the feed schedules.

'So what is it then?' I ask because nothing has been solved yet. 'Why does he cry so much? And why won't he sleep?'

'It could just be because this world is very new and very scary to him. He spent nine months inside you, where it was safe, and now he's suddenly out here where it's bright and loud and he doesn't have the constant ability to feed or feel protected like he had before.'

Hearing that makes me feel sad, not just for little Luca but for the fact that I have been thinking there is something wrong with him when what the health visitor just said makes perfect sense. How would I like it if I was dragged out of a warm, safe place and thrust into a chaotic world like my baby has been? I can't imagine I'd like it very much.

'There's also the fact that the birth was difficult,' the health visitor goes on. 'It didn't go to plan, which would have caused a lot of stress for you and, indeed, Luca here. He could be carrying some tension, not to mention babies pick up on when their parents are anxious, so that all plays a part as well.'

'So basically, you're saying this is quite normal and things will get better with time,' Bobby intervenes, sounding pleased about it, and the health visitor agrees.

'Yes. I know it's not easy, especially when you don't get enough sleep, but it will get better. And if for some reason it doesn't, we can come and help you. Okay?'

I feel teary again and I think a big part of it is that I feel so helpless and in need of assistance from others. I'm aware I can't do this on my own, which makes it very different to how I used to operate in my professional life. I was the boss there and was always in control. But motherhood? I feel utterly useless, like I'm constantly on the first day of a job where I don't know what to do or even if I'm capable of doing it.

'Go and have a lie down upstairs,' the health visitor tells me. 'I can stay here for a little while and look after Luca. And Bobby, why don't you have a break too, or do a little tidying up? Whatever will make you feel better.'

My husband and I are incredibly grateful for this help, and

well aware that it is help that will vanish as soon as the health visitor leaves us at the end of this appointment, so I don't waste any time taking her up on the offer of a rest.

Heading upstairs, I know I will fall asleep as soon as my weary skull hits the pillow, but just before I get to the bedroom, I hear the low voice of my husband talking to the health visitor below me. He must assume that I'm out of earshot up here, but I can just about make out what he is saying. I listen as he voices his concerns to this woman who has come to help us.

'I know it might be too early to say for sure, but my wife is struggling, and I was wondering could it be postnatal depression?' Bobby says, shocking me because I had no idea he was thinking such a thing about me. 'I mean, she's crying all the time, and she admitted to feeling like she isn't bonding well with Luca earlier, so those are classic symptoms, right?'

I grip the door handle to my bedroom, the room I should already be in, as I keep listening for the health visitor's verdict.

'It's possible, but we'll have to give it time and see how she is in a week or so,' she tells my husband. 'She needs some rest, and hopefully, Luca will settle better soon. Then we can assess things.'

It feels awful to be standing up here listening to the pair of them discuss my mental state as if they know me better than I know myself. I am a lot of things, but I am not depressed, I know that for sure. I'm just tired and upset and scared. I'm also confused. I'm confused as to why my baby seems different to how he was when we first had him.

Something is not quite right with him. I just can't pin down what it is.

I only know that while I'm far from the perfect mum, there's something else going on.

Something with the baby.

But what is it?

FIFTEEN

JADE

My kindly, albeit nosey, neighbour did as she promised and went to the shops for me to get some baby supplies. I thanked her as she unloaded the shopping bags in my kitchen. I now have enough of the basics to get through a few more days with a newborn child, as well as more teabags, a basic need for myself. Although one thing Linda didn't pick up, probably because I totally neglected to realise I needed it, was nappy rash cream. Luca's bum looks a little red and sore and I think it must be bothering him because he cries now, which is something he never did.

I've considered going next door and asking Linda if she could go back to the shops, but I don't want to become dependent on her, nor invite the opportunity for her to ask me more questions about the baby. That means I'll have to go to the shops myself, with Luca in tow, of course, which then means I'll have a very nervous time until we're both back here in the privacy and safety of my home.

Maybe it'll be fine. Nobody will pay me any attention. I'll just be one of many mums pushing a pram on the street. And maybe it will do me good to get out and have some fresh air. I have been holed up in here ever since I got back from the hospital, which was three days ago now.

I decide to go for it, figuring the worst that can happen is that Luca cries somewhere along the way.

Before I put him in the pram I give him a feed because I'm sure it will make him drowsy, and sure enough, he is asleep by the time we get out the door. The peace allows me to walk away from the flats without any noise attracting Linda's attention. As I head for the shops, I'm pleased to see that there aren't too many other people out walking at this time, presumably because it's mid-morning on a weekday and most people are at work.

There's a pang of regret then as I briefly contemplate a world that I never really felt a part of. The working world, where people have professional responsibilities, where they grow and develop and progress in all aspects of their lives. It turned out that I was never destined to experience that properly, barring the few meagre jobs I've had, and it will always be something that makes me sad, not that I'm the only one to blame for it.

I reach the supermarket quickly enough, but it takes me much longer to find what I need inside. Having barely spent a second on the baby aisle before, I'm now forced to have to try and navigate the numerous shelves piled high with all sorts of confusing things. All I need is a tube of nappy rash cream.

But it's like looking for a needle in a haystack.

Or the right baby in a maternity ward full of newborns.

'Awww, she's gorgeous,' a female voice says, and I look to my left to see an elderly woman with a basket leaning over the pram.

'He,' I say, correcting her gently.

'Oh, I'm so sorry!' she replies, embarrassed at her faux pas, not that she is to blame because Luca is wearing all white, so the neutral colours must make it a little harder to discern his gender. 'He is gorgeous. What's his name?'

'Luca,' I reply without thinking, but my heart skips a beat when I realise what I've just done.

'What a nice name,' the woman says, smiling. But what if she figures out what I've done one day soon? What if, when Avril realises she has the wrong baby, she goes on the news and says that she has a missing son called Luca? Will this woman remember meeting me in this supermarket and, if so, would she tell the police that she thinks I am the woman who stole the baby?

How many Lucas are there in London? Ones that were born around the same time? The more the better, but I can't just use odds and statistics to lessen the worry. I need to get out of here quickly, before I can become even more memorable to this woman, so I ditch the nappy rash cream and head for the exit, pushing the pram as fast as I can.

I make it outside without anybody calling after me but freeze when I see what is parked at the front of the supermarket.

A police car.

I see two officers getting out of the vehicle, but while they are moving and getting closer towards me, I am frozen to the spot, physically unable to operate my legs and get away from here before they notice me staring at them.

Now they have seen me, and the pram, and if they get any closer, they will see the little boy inside it.

'Good morning,' one of the officers says to me, nodding out of respect as he passes, and his colleague smiles too before they walk right on by and enter the supermarket.

I hold my breath as they pass me and only allow myself some oxygen once I am sure they aren't going to stop smiling and start arresting me. Now they're gone, it's time for me to do the same, so I push the pram away, headed for home, grateful that my legs seem to be working properly again.

It was an awful feeling to be so close to the police with the knowledge of what I have done, and the feeling doesn't leave me even when I'm safely back in my flat with the door locked. Luca, the baby with the name I stupidly blurted out in the supermarket, is still asleep, totally oblivious to the panic I just went through while ferrying him around, but while he rests, my mind races.

If that's what it's going to be like every time I leave home, how can I possibly do this? Maybe I need to leave Luca somewhere now, somewhere safe where he can be found by a person who can look after him, whilst I run away and hope never to get caught. Or perhaps I should try to contact an adoption agency, although they are bound to ask so many questions that I'll eventually be unable to answer them.

As I think back to the sight of those police officers in their uniforms, I'm reminded of the last time I was nervous in the presence of the police. It was the day I went to report Avril for coming to my home, assaulting me and threatening me with further force if I didn't drop my complaint about her.

Little did I know, after filing a report with the police, that things were about to get a whole lot worse for me.

SIXTEEN

JADE

Seven Years Earlier

I hate police stations. Then again, does anybody love them? They're like hospitals. Nobody ever visits one unless something bad has happened. And nobody ever goes back twice in quick succession because they want to. But here I am, at a police station for the second time in a week. The first time was to report Avril and urge the police to investigate her and, hopefully, punish her for her actions. Now I've been summoned back here, and I assume it is for an update on the progress of the investigation.

As I enter the station and wait to be seen by an officer, I am guessing that Avril denied the charges against her and is doing everything she possibly can to wriggle out of this one. I would expect nothing less from a woman like her. She's hardly likely to admit to trespassing in my home, striking me and threatening me. To do so would result in a prosecution that would affect her carefully curated life. No, she surely denied everything and is hastily assembling a team of expensive lawyers to try and prolong this as best she can in the hopes that I'll just drop it. But if she thinks that way, she is wrong. There's no way I'm letting this go. So what if she threatened me with the thought that I'll never work in my dream industry if I try to bring her down? That doesn't have to be true. I can still forge my own career there one day if I want to. But more and more, that world feels like one I don't wish to be a part of. But right now, my focus is on her, not my career or lack of it.

'What's the latest? What did she say? Did she admit it?' I ask hopefully as I enter the small room with the officer I spoke to last time I was here. His name is PC Lever, and he waits for me to sit down before he speaks.

'Not exactly.'

'I knew it. Well, what did she say?'

'Ms Anderson has made some allegations against you.'

'Against me?'

'That's right. She's accused you of stalking her.'

'Stalking?'

'She says you have been obsessed with both her and getting a job with her, which is why you were at the interview. But when you didn't get the job, you had a vendetta against her, leading to all these false accusations.'

'They're not false! She came to my home! She attacked me!' I cry, simply telling the truth.

'Ms Anderson says she has never been to your home, nor has she ever laid a finger on you.'

'She's lying!'

'She says the same thing about you.'

I don't know what to say to this. I was expecting Avril to fight back, but only to deny things, not to make up all sorts of things about me.

'I'm telling the truth. Avril is the one in the wrong here, not me,' I try again.

'It's difficult because it's your word against hers and...' PC Lever's voice trails off.

'What?'

'Well, she is the director at a very successful company, a very respected and high-achieving woman. She has no criminal record, no history at all of anything you are accusing her of, whereas you, on the other hand...'

I cannot believe this.

'You are unemployed, which suggests you would have a lot less to lose than Ms Anderson. It would also lead some people to think that you could become enamoured by Ms Anderson and the lifestyle she has as opposed to your own.'

'That's not what's happened here at all!' I cry, but PC Lever doesn't lose his train of thought.

'Then there's the fact that, unlike Ms Anderson, you do have a history of what you are being accused of.'

'Wait, I can explain!' I try, but PC Lever seems to have the facts laid out on a piece of paper in front of him.

'Two years ago, a complaint was filed against you in Manchester by a Mr Adam Harris. He accused you of stalking him, both physically and via social media. It says here you sent him over fifty messages after he ended your relationship, and you went to his workplace on six separate occasions before you accepted that relationship was over.'

Nothing the police officer has said is false. I'm just shocked that this is being brought up as a reason to believe Avril more than me.

'That is a totally different case. I was younger then. Stupid. I was very unhappy. I moved here to London to better myself. My ex-boyfriend didn't even press charges in the end. I didn't realise that complaint was still on record.'

'Yes, it is,' PC Lever says calmly. 'And now someone has made another complaint for a similar thing. So, tell me, Jade, how do you wish for this to go?'

'How do I wish for it to go? I want Avril to be arrested and punished, of course! I want her to pay for what she did. I want her to pay for these lies she has said about me too! I have not been stalking her, at least not in a sinister way. Sure, I did my research on her before I went to the interview, but that's it! Everything that happened since then is her fault, not mine!'

PC Lever lets out a deep sigh, the kind that a person makes when they feel like they're not getting anywhere with the conversation they have been having.

'If you pursue this, based on it being your word against hers and no actual evidence at this point, with your history, and your two characters being examined, I can't expect it to go the way you want it to.'

That's a very blunt way of him telling me to drop this and move on with my life. Basically, it's the same thing Avril said to me when she left my flat. But if I do this, she wins and what do I have?

'Be careful,' PC Lever tells me then. 'You're young. You have potential. Don't throw it all away over whatever this is. Seriously, if I was you, I'd just move on. Focus on the future. Okay?'

The future. It was hard to see in that room in the police station how the future could get much worse for me. But it did.

That's even after I decided to take the police officer's advice and leave Avril alone.

The problem for me was that Avril did not do the same thing.

She did not leave me alone.

In fact, she was just getting started with me.

SEVENTEEN

AVRIL

Present Day

I stare at my reflection in the bathroom mirror, analysing every detail of the haggard face that looks back. As I do, I am asking myself one thing:

Have I brought all of this on myself?

Knowing that I was not perfect in the past, I have often feared that anything bad that has happened to me since then is the universe trying to get back at me. As if a higher power has been trying to right the wrongs that I was guilty of committing by giving me some difficulties to deal with myself.

There were times when something would go against me at work, maybe a new product I had overseen would fail to dazzle when it hit the supermarket shelves, or something that I was sure would be a hit on social media didn't reach the numbers it should have. As many of my colleagues at the time said, not everything is a winner, and we have to take the rough with the smooth. But I always worried that there was more to it than that. That, in some way, my past indiscretions were making me fail at things that I would have been successful at if only I hadn't behaved so badly.

Then there was my personal life, like the problems we had with this house when we moved into it. It all seemed perfect at the time, and it is now, but there was a period when we discovered we had mould growing and the previous owner had done well to conceal it during the sale. It cost a lot of money to fix, and while Bobby just shrugged and said it happens, I wondered if it was another bad thing sent my way on purpose. Or when my car broke down on the morning of one of the most important meetings of my career, as if it couldn't have been any other morning when the stakes were lower. As I stood by the roadside, I felt as if a higher power was looking down and chuckling. Then, of course, there was the big one, which was mine and Bobby's struggles to conceive. Was it down to a simple medical issue? Plain bad luck? Or was it cosmic karma rearing its ugly head again? I know it was always bound to be a physical issue rather than something written in the stars because that's not how the human body works, but in my worried state, I managed to convince myself that our issues were down to something far beyond biology, which is nonsense.

I've spent a long time, and possibly wasted all that time, worrying that my past bad behaviour is cancelling out all the good I have been trying to do since. And that's exactly what I am worrying about now as I stare at my reflection after yet another sleepless night.

I thought that having a baby was one of the best things that would happen to me. How can bringing a new life into the world not be a blessing? How can it not be a positive thing? And how can it not make up for the sins of the past? Am I proud of who I was before? No way. Should I be punished for it forever? I hope the answer is no to that one too.

But as I hear my baby's cries from downstairs, whilst

thinking about how my husband discussed my mental state with the health visitor, I feel like I'm drowning in a sea of despair.

Worst of all, I feel like I have to accept that I deserve it.

'I'm going to take him to my mother's for the day,' Bobby says as he walks into the bathroom with our upset son in his arms. 'She's offered to help, and we certainly need it. It'll give you space to get some rest after everything you've been through.'

My husband might be dressing this idea up as a way of him helping me, but I see it for what it really is. He thinks I've been totally useless with our baby in the month since we got home from hospital, so he is enlisting a woman who might be of more help, in this case, my mother-in-law. To be fair, she will be great because she's very maternal, so it's a good idea in that sense. But I don't feel good knowing that. I don't feel good knowing that she'll probably handle this baby better than me.

'Have you taken the painkillers today?' Bobby asks me as he packs a few things.

'No. I told you they were making me feel worse. I couldn't think straight on them, so I've stopped.'

'And I told you that you need to finish the dose just like the nurses said. That's why you're feeling so bad now.'

'Are you sure it's not depression?' I snap back, instantly regretting it because it might give away the fact that I overheard his private conversation with the health visitor back when she visited us.

'What?'

'Never mind,' I snap. 'I'll try and get some sleep. Have fun at your mother's.'

I get into bed then and Bobby quickly gets the things he needs before scurrying away with our son. It is a huge relief when I hear the front door close downstairs, and the house is silent for the first time in an age. But just because it is quiet, it doesn't mean I can sleep. I'm staring at the ceiling, still worrying about this thing called karma, and how it might be haunting me now.

If it is, it's all down to her.

Jade.

That's a name that I have done well to keep from my mind for a long time, mainly for my own mental health. That's because thinking of her, or more specifically, what I did to her, is not something that leaves me feeling warm and fuzzy inside.

Jade White. There. I've just allowed her full name to run through my mind and, right on cue, here come all the sickly feelings in my stomach as the memories come flooding back.

The first time I saw her, she was sitting with several other candidates for a job that had become vacant in my workplace. I was the person who would make the final decision on who got that job, so the candidates had been whittled down to a final ten, and then I, in my own unique way, was going to decide who the successful candidate should be. The problem was my unique way was flawed and led to an issue.

Jade complained about me. Whilst at the time, I thought she was a silly, naive young woman who didn't have a single clue what it took to succeed in my world, I have since come to realise how badly I treated her. The problem is, I can't turn back the clock.

Jade was not the only woman who I removed from the interview process in a way that could be described as harsh. Stupidly, I thought getting rid of one candidate by purposely putting out one less chair than was required was a brilliant idea. At least that candidate just took it on the chin and left without a word. However, Jade did not take her rejection quite so well and, in hindsight, who could blame her? I belittled her in front of the others, telling her that she did not look like someone who could work with me simply based on the clothes she was wearing, the heels she had on her feet and the average make-up she had on her face.

What a terrible thing to do.

I'd never done anything like that before and I haven't done since, but I did it that day and, perhaps unsurprisingly, Jade made a complaint about me. In my defence, I was having a particularly bad day when that final interview stage was underway. I'd just found out that two of my best friends were each having a baby with their long-term partners and it had made me suddenly question if all the sacrifices I was making in my career were worth it. They were happily married and about to start a family and there I was, miserable and alone, keeping myself busy with work to fill the empty void inside myself. While that was positive for my bank account, it was not so good as I was getting to a point in my life when I knew that if I ever did want what my friends had, I'd better act sooner rather than later.

My reluctance to settle down and do what my friends were doing was driven by two things: one, my mother's experience. She had been a very successful businesswoman, just like me, until she had fallen in love with a man, fallen pregnant shortly after, and then given up her career to be a stay-at-home mum. That drastic life change led to a personality alteration in her, or so she told me, and that was why her partner – my father – had an affair and ultimately left her to raise me alone. While my mother loved me every day until she passed away a couple of years ago, I could also sense the unhappiness that accompanied that love. The 'what if' question that lingered over her life. What if she hadn't had me? What if she had focused on her career instead? Would she have been happier? She certainly would have avoided a lot of the days when, as a young child, I caught her crying in the bedroom.

Her experience made me want to be different. I didn't want to take the risk she had. I was going to play it safe, be career orientated and, as such, I would avoid putting my heart at risk of being hurt by another man and potentially being left to raise a child on my own.

But the problem was, as the years went by, I started to worry I was taking the wrong route. Not falling in love and having a family simply out of fear that it might go wrong was a terrible reason to stay alone and be a workaholic. This particular crisis of confidence was at its peak when Jade walked into my office that day for her interview, which is why I was a terrible person to her on that occasion.

It was also why I didn't stop there with her either.

When I heard about the complaint she had made against me, I knew I was powerful enough at work to make it go away. But I also wanted to ensure Jade went away, which is why I visited her home and made it clear that she was to drop it. I never meant to hurt her physically; she just grabbed me and I lost my temper. I did feel bad about it immediately afterwards. But I couldn't show any signs of weakness. I had to keep trying to make Jade feel like I had the upper hand. I thought I'd done that, right up until the point when a police officer came to my workplace and told me what Jade had said about me.

I had no choice but to go on the attack and make up lies about Jade being the one in the wrong. I created a stalker story, said that she was the one who had been bothering me and was obsessed with working with me and being just like me. I knew it was mainly going to be Jade's word against mine, so if I was more convincing, I had a chance to get the police to ease off. They did that, no doubt helped by the fact that I was seen to be a respected businesswoman with everything to lose. It was easy to paint Jade as the desperate wannabe who had it all to gain.

I kept myself busy with work after that, which was always my answer to everything, but every now and again I felt bad about what I did to Jade. But I can't have felt that bad because it didn't end there. Something else happened between us, something that didn't just occur in a spontaneous moment but took planning.

The thing is it didn't need to.

After the police dropped the investigation, Jade did as she was told and stayed away from me.

But I did not stay away from her.

EIGHTEEN
AVRIL

Seven Years Earlier

I don't need to be here. I could be in my spacious office answering emails and planning for another busy week ahead. Or I could be at home, surrounded by all my comforts, reclining on my large sofa and watching my widescreen TV whilst sipping a lovely glass of red wine. I could even be at the gym, getting my heart rate up, burning off a few calories, doing the work to maintain my slim physique. But I'm not in any of those places doing any of those things. Instead, I'm sitting in a dark movie theatre with a baseball cap over my head to help disguise my appearance, whilst staring straight ahead at what I came here to watch.

But it's not the movie on the screen that has my attention.

It's the woman in the seat three rows ahead of me. And the man sitting beside her with a tub of popcorn.

As I watch Jade enjoying the movie with her date, as well as enjoying a few mouthfuls of popcorn when she occasionally reaches into the bucket on the man's lap, I think about how tonight is the perfect time to strike. I've seen this pair go on at least three dates together now, which means they are getting past all the early awkwardness and starting to like each other. That's important because I want that to be the case, at least from Jade's point of view. My wish is for her to be growing close to this man, starting to develop feelings for him, allowing him into her heart a little and giving her hope for the future. That's what budding romances do, they give hope.

But I'm going to do my best to take that hope away from Jade this evening.

The movie has been underway for over an hour now, and having discreetly checked the running time of it on my phone whilst sitting here, I know there should be only half an hour left. When it ends, I'm eager to know if Jade and her date will go their separate ways or if they plan to go for a drink later. Jade walked here tonight, a fact I know because I followed her from her home, and I presume she'll walk back again. But will her date offer to walk her home? Will she invite him inside? Could this date just be getting started?

I hope not. I hope Jade is the kind of woman who will take things slowly, and I hope her date is the kind of man who will appreciate that and take his time too. It's not the end of the world if they do spend the night together. In fact, it might hurt Jade even more when I do what I plan to do, but I'm getting impatient now so I'd rather end this tonight. I'm a busy woman, and I've already invested enough time in Jade, so the sooner this is over, the better. I've decided that this is the last thing I will do to her, a parting shot to punish her for involving the police and giving me a headache at work. She could've destroyed everything I've worked for, years of my life, my sacrifices and my dreams. While nothing came of all that nonsense a few weeks ago, I want to hurt Jade one more time for even daring to try and take me on.

I have hurt her professionally, not only ending her chances of working at my place but at any big cosmetics company in

London, thanks to the email I sent out to all my contacts in the industry, warning them to be wary of any application they received from a Jade White because she had caused problems for me. Now it's time to hurt her personally, in her love life, because that will cut deeper. Work is one thing, but there's another level to get at her and I am looking to exploit that.

A few people in this dark auditorium laugh at something on screen, including Jade and her date, but I totally missed it because my eyes are still on the couple ahead. It's been easy to follow these two as they have been dating, mainly as neither of them seems to possess the funds required to go anywhere expensive. A park. A food court in a busy shopping mall. And here, a cinema. All cost-effective places to have a date and very simple places for me to follow them around unseen. This would have been much trickier if they had been going to fancy restaurants, but that's not been the case and I shouldn't be too surprised. Jade doesn't have much money, being unemployed, and judging by where she lives, her budget for dating is small. But I guess this man's is too, or maybe he just prefers to keep it simple. He is rather handsome, something I noted when I first saw him with Jade, and maybe he presumes that his good looks can make up for the rather unimaginative places they have been together so far. Whatever it is, the two of them seem happy and seem to be getting happier.

But not for long.

The film finally finishes, the entire movie passing by without Jade and her date stealing as much as a quick kiss in this dark room, which I thought was an obligatory thing to do on a date like this. Then again, maybe things have changed. It's a long time since I was a teenager kissing some boy from my school in the back row at the movies, and adults probably don't do that kind of thing as easily. Or maybe Jade and her date are really, really nervous.

I wait for them to leave their seats before I get up from mine and then I follow them out, keeping my eyes on the two of them as they wander towards the exit along with all the other people who just watched the same film as them. There is a low hum of chatter accompanying us all as we leave, people talking about the film, which parts they liked or disliked, and Jade and her date seem to be discussing it too. Or maybe they're discussing what to do next.

I really need them to separate, so I'm hoping they go different ways when they get out of this cinema, and as I hang back and watch them through the glass of the front doors, I see them still together. He is looking at her and she is looking at him, nervously nibbling her lower lip before her eyes drift down to his lips too.

She wants him to make a move.

She wants a kiss.

I guess he wants the same thing.

And then it happens.

I watch from a safe distance as Jade and her date lock lips, a gentle kiss, nothing too passionate or risky, just a simple smooch that shows the affection they have for one another. This is how it starts, the first kiss leads to everything else. Another kiss. Hand holding. Hugging. Sleeping together. Making plans. A holiday. Living with one another. Buying a home together. Starting a family. Growing old. The possibilities are limitless, and who knows where it could end?

Well, I do.

It ends tonight.

As their lips part, I wonder if either of them is confident enough to quickly go in for a second kiss. But that doesn't happen, though not because the first kiss was so bad. It's simply because they are smiling, clearly happy at the progress that has been made tonight, but neither one of them wanting to push their luck and risk ruining another date going as well as this one has.

They chat for a moment before they hug and then they separate, Jade walking one way, him walking the other. But it's him I follow, as he's the one I need to talk to. Jade doesn't need to know that I've been watching them tonight. But he does, and when he finds out why, he'll eventually thank me for it.

I follow him down the street, glancing over my shoulder as I go to make sure that Jade has definitely left in the other direction and won't see that I am trailing her date. She has, she's out of sight, gone and totally oblivious to the fact that she will never see this man again. That warm fuzzy feeling she carries in her stomach as she goes home and thinks about that first kiss is soon going to be replaced by a dull, aching void when she wonders why she has never heard from him again.

'Excuse me?'

I call out to the man walking ahead of me, and when he turns around, he looks surprised that a stranger would be trying to attract his attention.

'Hi. Sorry, I didn't mean to startle you. I was just coming out of the cinema, and I saw someone I recognised. It was the woman you were with. Your friend, maybe. Or girlfriend?'

'Erm? Yeah,' the man says, clearly unsure as to how much information to give me about the date he has just been on.

'Her name is Jade, right?' I say, and he hesitates for a moment before nodding.

'Look, I appreciate that this is weird,' I go on, trying to appear as helpful as possible. 'And maybe I should have just left it, but I feel like I have to tell you, just in case.'

'Tell me what?'

'Jade is dangerous.'

'I'm sorry?'

The man looks confused, but I need to convince him, so I keep going.

'I don't know how long you've known her, and she might seem totally nice and normal now, but trust me, she is not.'

'What do you mean?'

'She's a stalker,' I say before looking around nervously to give the impression that I'm afraid Jade might be creeping up on me now.

'A stalker? What are you talking about?'

I know Jade's past, at least the part where she was arrested for stalking an ex-boyfriend in Manchester, some guy called Adam. I discovered that when the police were trying to establish what had happened between Jade and me, though it was not the police who told me. It was the investigator I hired to look into Jade to see if there was anything useful that could help me shake her off. It turned out that there was, and now I'm about to use that same thing to tell a white lie and steer this man away from her forever.

'I had a friend who she dated once,' I say, beginning the lie. 'He thought she was great, but she totally ruined his life. She got obsessed with him. Followed him around at work, his house, wouldn't let him go anywhere without her in the end. He tried to end it, but she didn't make it so easy for him, so he had no choice but to get a restraining order.'

'A restraining order?'

This poor man looks shocked now, but that's better than confused. Now to drive this home, so he'll thank me for what I've just done.

'I thought that when I saw you two together, she might be doing it again to somebody else. So that's why I'm warning you to stay away from her. But you don't have to listen to me. I just felt like I had to say something, or I'd regret it if anything bad ever happened to you in the future.'

I'm really selling it, and I should because I'm good at this kind of thing. I convince people at work all the time, so surely I can persuade this hapless guy to take my word. I guess he is starting to believe me, as he stops looking unsure and says something promising.

'Thank you, I guess,' he says, scratching his head. 'I had no idea she could be like that.'

'Of course you didn't. Neither did my friend. Jade is very good at hiding it. Until it's too late.'

The man looks helpless now, so I try to make him feel better.

'I'm really sorry. This must be a difficult thing to hear, especially if you liked her.'

'Yeah,' the man says, looking very lost before he speaks again. 'I need a drink.'

'That's probably a good idea,' I say, laughing to break a little bit of the tension. 'There's a pub just up there.'

I point up the road, and the man nods.

'Do you want one?' he asks then.

'Me?'

'Yeah. I suppose I should thank you for saving me from making a big mistake with Jade.'

I wasn't expecting to go for a drink with this guy, but this is good because if he warms to me, he'll be even more likely to stop thinking about her.

'Okay, sure. But you don't have to buy me a drink. I was just trying to help. Seriously, it's no big deal.'

We start walking towards the pub, and I notice the man is still looking a little dazed, which makes me feel guilty for making him feel bad. As for Jade, I couldn't care less, but this poor guy is innocent.

'I'm Avril, by the way,' I say to him, extending my hand and smiling. 'And again, I'm sorry for having to do this.'

It could be a risk to give my name when he could mention it to Jade, but I have a feeling that I've done a good enough job of spooking him that he won't be contacting that woman ever again.

He shakes it and smiles back at me, appearing more cheerful. Maybe he's starting to see the positive side of having had a lucky escape. Then there's also the fact that he's about to walk into a pub with me, so it's not as if his night has been a total waste of time.

'Don't apologise again. There's no need,' the man says as he shakes my hand and, just before he lets go, he gives me his name. 'Bobby.'

NINETEEN

JADE

Eight weeks. That's how long I've been living with Avril's baby. Eight weeks of having this terrible secret. Eight weeks of raising someone else's son while they raise mine. Eight weeks of being afraid that every knock at the door is the police and every passerby on the street knows what I've done. Eight weeks of anguish. Where has that time gone? It feels like it's flown by, but that's only because it's all been a blur of confusing thoughts, anxious moments and sleep-disturbed nights when I was never sure if I'd just had a nightmare or was actually awake the whole time and simply experiencing my real life.

But it's not all been bad. The baby I took, the baby who was called Luca by his birth parents, is a dream as far as children his age go. He's so placid, sleeps through the night and sleeps a lot in the day too. Most of the time, it's as if he isn't even here. That has made things easier for me. It's allowed me to get some sleep myself, to quiet my restless mind, to keep the paranoia at bay before it overwhelms me and to give me a brief respite from the guilt I feel about what I've done. If I do sleep badly, it's all down to me, not the baby. He is not to blame for all the stress and guilt that wakes me up in cold sweats. He's certainly not to blame for the times I dream of my real son, the baby I gave away, though those dreams quickly turn into nightmares when I see him screaming at me and telling me how he wishes he had never been born.

I don't know how my real baby is getting on, but the baby I have with me has changed a lot in his first eight weeks of life. He's growing, putting on weight, 'thriving' as Linda put it when she last came to visit us, which she does every other day. It's not so bad now I've learned how to handle her questions and keep my guilty conscience at bay in her presence. She's learned not to keep bringing up the subject of the father, probably because she knows she won't get to see me or the baby anymore if she doesn't drop it.

The baby. He might have been named Luca, but that was not the name I gave him. Linda kept reminding me I needed to name him sooner rather than later. I had to come up with something original myself and I've done it.

This baby is now called Calum.

There's no special meaning behind it, which is why I chose it. I'm not allowing myself to get any closer to this child, so the name is just that. A name. A box-ticking exercise. Something that had to be done as it allowed me to cover my deception further. So it's done. That's it. No need to dwell on it anymore, and there is to be no dwelling today because I'm getting out of this flat and I'm taking Calum with me.

We're on our way to a baby sensory class, one that Linda told me about after she had seen it advertised online.

'It sounds great. It's free and Calum will love it, if he stays awake for more than five minutes.' She chuckled. 'And it'll be good for you too. Getting out and meeting other mums. Give it a try. I can come with you if you like.'

I'd politely declined Linda's offer to come with me and had

also been close to declining going to the class at all. It didn't sound like fun; in fact, it sounded like my idea of hell. Being surrounded by loads of other kids when I didn't even plan on having one of my own. That's not to mention being surrounded by all the gushing new parents battling to show off how cute their child is whilst secretly judging all the others. Yeah, I was pretty sure that a sensory class was the last place I would ever end up.

So why am I on my way there now?

I only changed my mind this morning when I looked outside and saw that the sun was shining. If it had been raining then I definitely would have stayed in all day, but the blue sky made me think that it would actually be nice to get outside and do a little socialising today. I figured I could try the class and if it was as bad as I expected it to be, I didn't have to go again. It's free for first-timers, so there's no cost, and if I go, I get the added benefit of being able to give Linda a positive answer when she inevitably comes around here and asks me if I attended. I can say yes, I went, I gave it a try and it wasn't as good as advertised. End of story.

As I push the pram along the sun-soaked streets and get some much-needed rays on my vitamin D-depleted skin, the optimism the good weather brings extends to my thoughts about finances. I've been receiving child benefit payments since I registered the baby's birth, alongside the Universal Credit money I qualify for due to being out of work, and those payments combined are allowing me to keep going without having to work. It's weird, but after so many years of struggling to get by, of gaining and losing dead-end jobs and feeling fed up of being poor, I'm in a better financial position than I've been in a long time. It's not much, but it's enough to get by. As a single mother, the payments I'm entitled to are higher than they would be if I had a partner bringing in a second stream of income, and while a lot of it goes on the baby, there's just enough to keep me going too. It's been a relief but I know that children need more things as they grow, though I'm trying not to think about that yet.

I see the children's centre up ahead, right next to a tube station I have used many times before. I've walked past this building dozens of times in the past and never given it a second glance. Why would I when I was childless? It might as well have not existed back then. But now, it's become a place I'm going to step into, like all the other parents who need to find a way to get out of the house and pass an hour before returning to their regular routine at home. This nondescript building is a beacon of hope to parents who need a safe change of scene for them and their little ones. As I spot a few mothers pushing their prams through the entrance doors, it looks like this class is going to be popular.

Before I can go inside myself, I'm struck by another bout of paranoia, one that tells me that if I go in here, I'll quickly be outed as a faker. The other parents will figure out that this is not really my baby, he's someone else's, and then I'll be in trouble. Is that what's about to happen?

I consider going home, but I'm here now, and either I go inside or I just wander around aimlessly with the pram before eventually ending up back at my flat. That seems like a boring and fairly bleak way to spend the next part of the day, so I forge ahead and enter the children's centre, determined to see what this will be like. I'm not expecting to enjoy it, but I am expecting it to be quite easy. Either Calum will sleep through the class, or he'll watch the other kids. Either way, I shouldn't have to do much.

I sign in at reception, jotting down our first names, Jade and Calum, which seems strange to look at. I also write down his birthday because this sign-in form asks for that too. I put it underneath the list of other names already on here for this popular class, before entering a large hall where I see several toys are already set out. There are shakers and rattles and tambourines and shiny objects, all things that babies will love to grab, experiment with or just gawk at. The parents are sitting around this pile of toys in a large circle and each of their babies is in front of them, some very alert, others dozing. It's generally how I thought it would be as I take a seat on the floor in between a couple of other mums who are far too busy holding their children to worry about me and the baby I've just arrived with.

'Let's put some music on and then we'll have a little play,' a woman wearing a pink T-shirt with the children's centre logo says, and as a serene song comes out of the speakers, I notice Calum's eyes open and he looks up at me.

I look away quickly, as if afraid that any moment where we might bond will make things even harder because I'm still considering giving him up and trying to carry on my life alone. But he does look cute, and he's clearly comfortable in my arms. I notice another mum looking at me; she smiles as if to acknowledge what a good job I am doing. It's also like she is seeing me as I would hope to be seen: as a good person, a kind, caring, nurturing one.

But that's not the real me.

I'm a woman who swapped two babies out of nothing more than a crazy need for revenge.

I want to go now. I can't be here, surrounded by all these good parents and their cute babies. All this innocence in one room. My guilty conscience cannot handle it.

I am just about to get up and make my excuses when I hear a baby crying outside the room. I look in the direction of the noise and see another mother entering the hall with a baby in her arms. When I do, it's as if my body has suddenly been set in stone and I cannot move a single fibre of it.

That's because I recognise the two new entrants.

It's Avril and the baby I gave birth to.

TWENTY

AVRIL

I hope this isn't going to be a total disaster, but I have a strong feeling that it will be. That's why I tried to shoot the idea down when a friend pitched it to me. They told me about this free sensory class and suggested I should go. Well, me and the baby, obviously. It would look weird if I came alone. My friend said it helped them to get out of the house when their baby was young, so it might help me too. But I don't want to be here. If I have to be, I wish Bobby were by my side. I asked him to come, and he said it could be fun, but not fun enough for him to skip work for the day and come here with us. My husband is out driving his taxi while I'm here with the baby having all this 'fun'.

Of course, he's crying. The child in my arms. Luca, although I haven't actually said his name out loud for a while now. That's because I've spent the first eight weeks of his life feeling like there is something wrong with him. Not in a physical way in terms of his health, but something wrong as in he can't possibly be mine. He looks nothing like me, and from what I can tell, most of the time, he doesn't even like being with me. After the disaster that was my attempts to breastfeed him when we first arrived home, I gave up on that and have tried to bond with him in other ways. Like holding him, playing with him, kissing him, all the usual stuff. But none of it seems to make this baby like me any more and, if I'm honest, none of it is making me like him any more either.

But it's not depression. I'm not allowing Bobby to label it as that. No, it's something else, something I still can't quite put my finger on. I just feel so detached from this baby, and while I wake up every day and wish for this to be the day when our bond suddenly forms, I'm yet to be pleasantly surprised. Instead, every day is a total grind, which is why Bobby suggested I break the gruelling routine and come here, to this sensory class. The fact that it is free is hardly the selling point because we could afford to pay to go somewhere, but the fact it is in a place that is easily accessible on the Tube means it was a simple and short journey to get here. I'm still not comfortable driving, so just three stops on the Underground and here I am, trying to pretend like this isn't going to be a shambles.

'Hi! Welcome! Please, take a seat,' a woman in a pink T-shirt tells me, her smile seemingly almost as wide as the circle of parents and babies I'm expected to join.

It's overwhelming to see so many faces here, other tired parents, each of them with a child, all seemingly blurring into one as I find a space and sit down. Miraculously, Luca has stopped crying and is looking around at this new environment. The longer he is quiet, the more it makes me think this trip might have been worth it. Anything to get a break from the sound of his sobs.

I feel bad for him, especially since he was diagnosed with colic, which has not helped matters at all, but while the colic has gradually got better, the general crying has remained. A few friends I have spoken to have said he could just be 'a crier', as if labelling it makes it easy to put up with. But it doesn't, and the fact all their kids were seemingly silent little angels at this age doesn't make it easy either.

I'm not quite sure what to do here, so I look at the mum next to me and see that she has picked up a shaker from the centre of this circle and is shaking it in her daughter's face. Her daughter is watching it intently, seemingly transfixed by the sound it is making. It must be nice to be that age when the most basic of objects can hold your attention. Better than being an adult and constantly being bored despite having access to absolutely everything we could ever want.

I decide to try and make myself fit in a little more here by picking up a toy, and I opt for a tambourine. Gently shaking it in front of Luca's face, I'm hoping I get the same reaction from him as the little girl beside us, in that he enjoys it or is at least watching.

But no such luck because he just starts crying.

I try and shush him as quickly as I can, not just for his sake or mine, but for the sake of all the other people in this room. I'm sure none of them came here to listen to a baby crying. They can probably get enough of that at home. As always, it takes longer than I feel it should to quieten Luca and, as such, I can feel the eyes of several of the mothers here boring into me as the melodic music is drowned out by Luca's lungs.

I look up to see just how many people are staring at us, which is a terrible idea because it's hardly likely to make me feel any better. It turns out that I'm right because I see a few faces looking back, and I feel ashamed that I'm not as capable of keeping my baby quiet as they are. Before I look back down at Luca, I notice a face that seems familiar. Trying to place it, I draw a blank, but I definitely feel like I recognise the woman on the other side of the circle from me from somewhere. But where? She's looking at me too, making me feel like she recognises me as well, but she doesn't say anything to indicate that she does. Instead, she just looks down, though only a second later, she looks at me again.

I look at the baby in her arms now, as if that will help me, but it's just another little boy and his eyes are closed. How is he asleep while Luca is crying? It's so frustrating that I didn't get an easy child like so many others did. I return to trying to shush Luca and temporarily forget about the fact that I'm sure I know that woman from somewhere.

'When was he born?'

I look up when I hear the question, only to see that one of the mothers around the circle has asked it of another woman here.

'Twentieth of June,' she replies before asking the same thing in return.

'Fourth of June,' is the answer there before the woman turns to me. 'What was your birth date?'

I'm not sure why this is such an interesting topic for people, but I guess it must be how all these strangers break the ice and start communicating, and I guess it makes sense considering babies are the only thing we have in common.

'Tenth of June,' I say, my mind instantly flashing back to that warm day on the hospital ward two months ago when I did not quite have the magical birth I was hoping to have.

'All similar ages,' the woman says with a smile, stating the obvious, but I don't care; I'm just glad that Luca stopped crying when I spoke. I watch as the woman turns to the person beside her and asks the same question, and I'm interested in the answer because the person about to respond is the woman I feel I recognise.

'Me?' the woman replies, hardly answering with confidence. 'Oh, erm.'

She doesn't answer, looking at me instead.

'Erm,' she says again, looking away from me before finally answering. 'The twelfth of June.'

She seemed nervous to speak, which could simply be because she is shy in front of this large group of strangers. Or it could be something else. It was as if she wasn't entirely confident of the answer, which is weird, because a person can forget lots of things, but the birth date of your child is surely something that is etched in your memory forever.

Her baby was born two days after my baby was born, I think, as I process her answer. But there's little time for processing anything else because Luca starts crying again and, this time, it's much louder than before. He's really ruining the calm vibe that this sensory class is surely aiming for. As I struggle to quieten him, I decide to cut my losses and get out of here so I don't ruin this hour for everyone else.

I make my apologies to the woman running the class before heading for the door and quickly finding my parked pram amongst all the others by the entrance. I put Luca inside and, thankfully, he quietens a little, so I have a minute to hear my own thoughts without him drowning them out.

I'm bugged by that woman in the class, the one that seems familiar, but I can't quite place her. Then I see the sign-in sheet on the reception desk, and I walk over to it and steal a glance.

My eyes scan the list of parent and baby names and I'm looking to see if there is a familiar name on here that might help me figure out where I might know that woman from. But nothing is jumping out at me until I realise something. On this sign-in list, alongside names, is a box where everybody has to write the birth date of their child. But there is no twelfth of June on here, which is weird because that's the date that woman in there just gave. However, there are two tenth of Junes. One of them belongs to me. Is the other one hers?

That's when it hits me.

I know where I recognise that woman from.

She was in the bed beside me in the hospital when I gave birth.

It's her, I remember now. And the way she was looking at me during that class, I guess she remembers me too.

I suppose it's no big deal and I could just go home, but I need to know something.

I need to know why she just lied about her baby's date of birth in front of me.

TWENTY-ONE
JADE

I should have known it was a bad idea to come to this class.

But it was confirmed the moment I saw Avril walk in.

I'd been so close to leaving before she even appeared, preparing to get out and quit while I was ahead because of the bad feeling I was getting. But then I saw her, and the baby in her arms, and it was too late. I couldn't just leave then as that would only have drawn more attention to me and given her a possible reason to be suspicious. So I stayed where I was, sitting in the circle of parents and babies, trying to pretend like I was playing with toys and having a good time. But really, all I was doing was stealing glances at Avril and praying that she didn't remember me from the hospital.

I saw her look in my direction several times, but I'm not sure how much I can read into that. She might simply have been observing everyone and I just happened to be there. But there was a nerve-wracking exchange when one of the other mums, an annoyingly chatty and nosey person, asked everyone in the circle what their baby's birthdays were.

I knew that I couldn't tell the truth and say the actual date in front of Avril because we have the same one. That's why I lied and gave a date two days after when I really gave birth. But did she buy it? I guess so, as she didn't say anything to me or anyone else. She just left early, her baby crying and clearly frustrating her. Or rather, *my baby*.

It was surreal to see him again, the boy I gave birth to. Being in the hospital was such a confusing time, I didn't feel like I loved or wanted my baby, so I swapped him, in the process gaining some measure of revenge on Avril for the past. I never expected to see him again, see how he had grown, study the progress he was making. See parts of myself in him, in his eyes, his mannerisms, *his smile*. That was a very difficult encounter I didn't think I'd ever have to go through. Nor did I think I'd see Avril again, be so close to the woman I took from, the woman whose son I held in my arms while she didn't even know it.

I'm guessing the secret is safe. Avril left early; I've stayed until the end so she must be long gone. Although I'll never take a risk like this again. This is the first and last time I go to a baby class. Of course, none of the other parents here know that and, as I'm heading for the exit, another mum approaches me.

'It's so good to get out of the house, isn't it? I've been going mad at home being on my own with this little one all day.'

I look at the daughter she is holding, the angelic face, and the fact she most likely has a parent who is just as innocent and pure. *I wish I was like that.*

'Your baby is so placid. He seems like a dream,' the woman goes on, commenting on the baby I'm holding, who, as usual, barely made a sound over the last hour. He really is an easy baby, although the difficulty increases somewhat by him not actually being mine.

'Oh, thank you,' I say, still walking as I don't want to linger and get caught in any awkward conversations here.

'Are you coming next week?' the woman asks me, possibly desperate for a new friend.

'Yeah, I think so,' I lie without looking back, and then I'm out of that hall, away from the parents and babies and toys, and I strap Calum into the pram before pushing him out the door. It's a relief to be back outside in the sunshine and each step I take gets me away from all those people, as well as the memory of sitting opposite Avril.

'Excuse me.'

I freeze at the sound of the voice behind me because I recognise it straight away. *It's her.*

I don't want to turn around. All I want to do is run. But that will make it too obvious.

With great reluctance, I look back, and when I do, I see Avril with her own expensive pram right behind me.

'Were you talking to me?' I ask, trying to sound innocent, as if there must be some mistake.

'Yes. I was just in the class then and I remembered you. We were in hospital at the same time. We were in the beds next to each other when we had our babies.'

Oh no. Where is she going with this?

'Erm,' I say, stalling, pretending to be figuring it out, as if I needed the reminder.

'You remember, right?' Avril goes on, and what am I supposed to say to that?

'I need to get him home for a feed,' I say, hoping the baby in the pram is my ticket out of here before any more can be said.

Except before I can go, Avril does something unexpected.

She bursts into tears.

It's a very bizarre sight to witness this woman I have hated for years appear so vulnerable in front of me, and I'm really not sure how to react. There's no way it would feel natural for me to try and comfort her, but I'm also wary of appearing incredibly rude and ignoring her distress because that might seem odd and make her suspicious. So I settle for somewhere in between, which consists of me standing still and open-mouthed.

'I'm sorry,' Avril says, wiping her eyes and trying to compose herself. 'It's just so hard. Being a new mum. I'm not usually like this.'

I know better than to agree with her there as she continues to wipe her eyes.

'Sorry,' she says again, a word I never heard her utter once in the time she was making my life a misery. 'I just need someone to talk to. Do you want to get a coffee?'

I really don't, so I try my excuse again. 'I need to get him home for a feed.'

'Please,' Avril begs, totally desperate. It feels impossible to walk away now.

'Okay, a quick one,' I agree, and Avril points out where we can get a drink.

As we head for the nearest coffee shop, the pair of us pushing prams with the other one's child in it, I wonder why fate has conspired against me in such a way. This must be my punishment for what I've done. Me, being in this nightmarish situation, forced to somehow try and navigate it without ending up in prison, or worse, dead, after Avril attacks me when she discovers what I've done.

'Take a seat. I'll get the drinks,' Avril says, pointing to a table near the window as we enter the café. 'What would you like?'

'Just a normal coffee,' I say, not wanting anything fancy that will take the barista more time to make. The sooner this is over, the better.

'Be right back,' Avril says, and wheels the pram away while I push mine to the table and take a seat.

I look inside my pram and see Calum, or Luca, is asleep. But someone is awake, and I hear the crying coming from the queue at the counter before seeing Avril trying to shush the baby in her pram.

It must be exhausting trying to pacify that amount of crying, and it explains why Avril was so emotional just then. She is being pushed to her limits, when in reality, she should have this easy baby that I have. She still seems to be surviving, somehow, whereas I know for a fact that I'd have given up a long time ago with all that crying and probably put my baby in someone else's care by now.

I glance out of the window and see all the people walking by, people who are free, unlike me, trapped in this coffee shop with the last person on Earth I want to be with. Avril recognised me from the hospital but surely, the longer we spend together, the more chance there is of her recognising me from before. I'm losing my baby weight, returning to something slowly resembling my former figure, and even though my hair is very different and I have the extra piercings, I'm worried she'll eventually see past them. If that happens, there is no telling what comes next.

'Sorry, can I leave the pram here? There's not much room up at the counter with all the people in the queue,' Avril says, snapping me out of my daydream. I turn to see she has pushed her pram over to the table. 'I'll be right back. I'm just waiting for the drinks.'

She rushes back to the counter, leaving me with two prams now, and more importantly, with my actual child. I look down at the little face in Avril's pram and see that the baby boy inside looks rather red and frustrated.

Then he starts crying again, and without even thinking what I'm doing, I pick him up and hold him. He stops crying instantly and while it's a relief to not have to listen to that anymore, it's not a relief when Avril returns to the table with our drinks.

'Oh my god, you got him to stop crying!' she exclaims, seemingly amazed. 'He cries all the time. You have to teach me what you just did there!'

'It was just luck,' I try, but Avril isn't buying it.

'No way, you're a natural!'

Yeah, I think, as I look down at the baby in my arms.

I'm a natural, all right.

This child's natural mother.

TWENTY-TWO
AVRIL

I take a sip of my hot drink and savour both the taste of it and the silence that exists now that Luca has stopped crying. He's back in his pram, but it was being held by this woman from the sensory class that got him to calm down in the first place, and I'm extremely grateful to her for that.

'How's your coffee?' I ask her, aware that she has barely touched it.

'Yeah, it's nice,' she replies unconvincingly, before glancing out of the window, struggling to make eye contact with me and not for the first time.

I know her name is Jade because I saw it written on the sign-in form. I knew a Jade once, but she was nothing like this woman, thankfully. I also noticed another name on the sign-in sheet beside her. It was her son's name, Calum, and he has the same birth date as Luca, but I don't want her to know I've been stalking, so I have to try and keep the conversation natural.

'I'm Avril, by the way,' I say with a smile.

'Erm, Jade,' she replies quietly.

'So how are you finding being a new mum?' I ask. 'Are you

loving it, or am I not the only one who feels like it's absolute hell most of the time?'

'It's okay,' Jade replies vaguely, which causes me to laugh.

'Wow, there are a lot of words that could be used to describe having a newborn, but I'm not sure I've ever heard okay used as one of them.'

'I mean, it's hard,' Jade tries again, being a little more specific.

'You got that right. Is he sleeping through for you yet? This one isn't. We're up every night for at least a few hours and he cries most of the day too. He had colic, which was awful, but things haven't got much better since. I had to give up breast-feeding too as it stopped working. And I've been arguing a lot with my husband. Silly things, really, but we're both tired, so it makes everything seem worse.'

I catch myself then, aware that I'm unloading all my problems onto this poor woman who barely knows me, but that's the reason why I am finding her much easier to talk to about this. I hate being vulnerable with people who know me well because that's not the person they know at all. I'm strong, independent, fierce Avril. Not this weepy, woe-is-me Avril, so I get embarrassed when other people see this. Unless it's someone who doesn't know the real me.

'Erm, yeah, he sleeps through sometimes,' Jade tells me, brushing over all the other problems I complained about and just answering my sleep question. Her affirmative answer that she is getting some sleep makes me envious of her, which I know it shouldn't, but tell that to my exhaustion.

'That's good. Sleep's the most important thing,' I say solemnly. 'If that goes, everything goes.'

I shake my head as I think about how the accumulation of fatigue has caused tension not just with my baby but with my partner too. But does Jade have anyone to share this experience with?

'Excuse me for asking, but is the father around?' I venture, wondering if I might have overstepped the mark, though I've never been one to be shy and not ask the pertinent question.

Jade looks uncomfortable again, which might give me my answer, so I talk to fill the awkward silence.

'Sorry, it's just that I don't remember seeing anybody with you when you were in hospital,' I go on, before realising that sounds just as bad. 'Not that I was spying on you, of course! It was just kind of easy to notice because we were in the beds next to each other, that's all.'

Jade really does not look like she is enjoying this interaction and is hardly talkative either. Is it just that she wants to go home and get on with the rest of her day, or has two months of looking after a baby rendered my conversation skills useless?

'I'm not with the father,' Jade admits quietly before glancing at the two babies in their prams beside our table, though there's no need because both of them are quiet and peaceful.

'Oh, I'm sorry,' I say, feeling bad for bringing it up, even though I was keen to know the answer.

Jade says nothing as she keeps looking at the babies, which makes me feel sad for her, as well as intrigued.

'So you're doing all this by yourself? Wow, I'm in awe of you,' I have to say. 'I can't imagine not having anybody to help.'

'My neighbour visits sometimes,' Jade adds, as if that is enough.

'That's good. But what about anybody else? Family?'

Jade shakes her head before looking at her untouched coffee.

'I feel like this conversation is going to fizzle out quickly if I don't work harder to get Jade engaged with it, so I try and find a way to make it more interesting.

'Well, whatever you are doing, you're obviously doing a great job because your baby is so calm,' I tell her. 'And I don't know what is going on, but my baby is calm too. I've never seen him so quiet.'

It's true. Luca is very placid, just staring up from his pram at Jade.

'I guess you're a natural and I'm not,' I admit glumly, voicing my biggest fear that motherhood was a mistake for me.

'I wouldn't say that,' Jade tells me.

'What would you say then? Because I spend every day wondering if I've made a mistake. I mean, how can I be so bad at this? And how can things ever go back to normal if I'm not getting any sleep?'

'It'll get easier,' Jade tries, voicing that useless platitude people offer when someone is going through hell, as if a promise of it being better months or years down the line helps with the immediate issue.

'Maybe,' I reply before sipping my hot drink and thanking my lucky stars that somebody created caffeine so I can get through these long days. Does anybody need coffee more than a new mum?

'I'm sorry for taking up your time,' I say, figuring this probably wasn't a great idea to force Jade to come for this drink and letting her know she can leave if she likes.

'That's okay. I better get going,' she replies, quickly latching on to her opportunity to escape. She stands up and reaches for her pram. But just before she can go, I say one more thing.

'Sorry if this seems like I was snooping, but I couldn't help but notice something back at the class,' I say as Jade pauses. 'You didn't give the right birth date for your baby when you were asked.'

Jade looks at me in horror.

'I didn't?'

'No, you said the twelfth, but it was the tenth. I know because I was right there in the hospital with you. Our babies have the same birthday.'

Jade stares at me, not saying a word, which makes this even weirder than it was when I discovered the error.

'You must have misheard me,' she tries, but I shake my head.

'No, I don't think so. You definitely said the twelfth.'

Jade turns to her pram then and goes to push it away, so I stand up so she can't leave like this.

'Sorry, maybe it was just me getting mixed up,' I suggest. 'I was on so many meds in hospital after the birth. Ignore me. You obviously know your baby's birthday better than me.'

I wonder if that attempt at an apology will relax Jade, but she still seems keen on leaving, so I guess this is the last I will see of her and my last chance to share my problems with somebody who doesn't know me as well as everyone else in my life. *Unless...*

'Can we swap numbers?' I ask. 'It's just that it would be great to meet up again sometimes and I feel like it's helpful to have another new mum to talk to. And I promise not to always burden you with my problems. Do feel free to ask me if you need anything too. I'm happy to help where I can. Us mums need to stick together, right?'

I smile at Jade, wondering if she will like the idea of doing this again, whatever this is.

'Erm,' she says, pausing, looking as awkward as ever, but not leaving yet. 'Okay.'

She takes out her phone, so I quickly grab mine and then she gives me her number.

'Thanks, that's great,' I say as I save her number in my phone. 'See you at the next class, maybe?'

'Erm, yeah, maybe,' Jade replies before finally leaving, exiting the coffee shop as quickly as she can, but at least I got her number so I can always arrange to see her again in future.

No sooner has Jade left than Luca starts crying again.

TWENTY-THREE

JADE

I lock the door to my flat as soon as I have walked through it, afraid that Avril has followed me home and wants to get another look at the baby that I'm with or ask me more questions about motherhood. I'm being paranoid because I didn't see her following me back here. I made sure to check enough times, looking back over my shoulder the entire walk home. I was fearful of seeing her pushing her pram, not letting me out of sight, suspicious of me and how I was able to get her baby to calm down so quickly when I held him.

My baby.

I feel sick at the thought of having held the boy I gave birth to and having to deal with all the confusing, conflicting emotions it brought. I never thought I'd see him again, but that was brutal. The guilt was overwhelming, as was the shame. I couldn't let Avril know how much I was hating myself as I sat there and, fortunately for me, I'm not sure she noticed because she was seemingly too busy hating herself.

It was beyond weird to be in Avril's presence when she was like that. She was a far cry from the woman I knew before, and it shocked me to see her seem so weak and needy. That was on top of the shock of seeing her again in the first place, something I never thought would happen in a million years. The hatred I held for her still burned, but seeing her so vulnerable was very strange, particularly when I have only ever known her to be strong. Or at least as strong as a bully is, anyway. But I couldn't worry too much about her, or allow thoughts of regret to creep in, not when I was in a very difficult position myself, tasked with keeping my secret safe in the face of all her questions.

She knows I lied about the birth date.

Is that a big deal? I hope not. I tried brushing over it casually, and even Avril admitted she may have made a mistake due to all the meds she had been on, so maybe it's not such a problem. But Avril did raise the question with me, which makes me think it must have been playing on her mind. If that was, what else might have been? She also commented on how natural I was when holding Luca. What if she starts to piece this all together?

She doesn't seem to have seen through my altered appearance yet, nor did she seem to recognise my voice. But it has been many years since she heard me speak, plus I've lost more and more of my northern accent the longer I have lived in the south of the country, so that helps. But I cannot ever get too complacent, which is why I have to make sure I never see her again. While that seems like a strange thing to wish for after I swapped numbers with her, I know the truth of that exchange. I gave her a fake number. I changed the last three digits, so she does not have my real contact details. If she tries to message or call me then she will get somebody else, and sure, she'll figure she was given a fake one, but so what? She won't be able to contact me and ask me any more questions, and that's the main thing.

I certainly won't be returning to that damn baby class again. It was foolish of me to take a chance like that, even if the odds of running into Avril there must have been astronomical. Of all the baby classes in all of London, we walked into the same one.

I've managed to navigate the stressful experience and make it back here without the police getting involved, and I just need to make sure I keep it that way. I also comfort myself with the fact that I live in a different flat to the one which Avril barged into back when she threatened me for making the complaint about her, so even if she remembers that place and tries to locate me there, she won't have any luck. I hate that woman for what she did to me in the past, but that doesn't mean I'm not smart enough to be wary of the threat she could pose to me now.

But I should be safe from her.

That chance meeting was very much a one-off.

As I check on Calum, or the real Luca, and see that he is still sleeping, I think about the hell Avril seems to have been through. All the sleepless nights, the colic, the fear that she had made a dreadful mistake. That would have been my reality if I hadn't swapped our babies, but I've had it easier than her, even if I share one thing in common with her – the fear of having made a dreadful mistake. At least I've been sleeping and, because of this, seem to be functioning a little bit better than she is. But only just, and I am still doing this on my own, whilst she has the help of her partner, although there seems to be tension between them too.

But why should I care about her relationship?

Why should I care about her and the man she stole from me?

TWENTY-FOUR

JADE

I don't understand what happened. Why did Bobby stop replying to my messages?

Our last date went so well. We kissed outside the cinema and as first kisses go, it was good. Not perfect, like the one we had watched unfold on screen during the movie, but it was nice. It was very sweet, a little sexy and, most of all, it had potential. I figured it was the first kiss of many. There would be more to come. Another kiss or two on the next date before things progressed even further, and soon, we were to be sharing kisses whilst lying in bed together on a lazy Sunday morning. But something's gone wrong since then.

Bobby seems to have got cold feet and it's been a month without hearing from him now.

Was my kiss really that bad?

Or has something else happened?

It's impossible to know because he isn't telling me. If he won't text me back, how can I know what bothered him? I've even tried calling him a couple of times, but there has been no answer from his end, just more radio silence. This has left me analysing everything about our last date and how it ended and what could possibly have gone wrong in the meantime.

It's so weird. I thought this was the start of something special. But now it seems it's over, and the worst part of it all is that I have no idea what I did wrong. No, actually, that's not the worst part. The worst part of all this is that I thought giving up on my lofty career ambitions and trying to focus on finding happiness with a man could actually bring me some joy. It seems I was wrong. I'm just as miserable having pursued romance as I was when I was pursuing a career in cosmetics.

So what is left for me now?

I vow that I won't try and chase Bobby anymore from this point on. Whatever happened, he is obviously done with me, so I have to assume that either he wasn't very interested in the first place or he was dating other people alongside me and found a better fit elsewhere.

Oh well, it's his loss.

I won't waste a single second more on him and what might have been.

It's time for me to get going to my latest shift in my latest dreary job, this one in a supermarket, so I leave my flat to catch the bus. Once on the bus, I do what I usually do on this fifteen-minute journey, which is to waste away my time by browsing the entertainment news on my phone. It might not be a particularly good idea because I occasionally see stories from the cosmetics world, my phone's algorithms having learned that's the thing I like to see, which then makes me feel sad that it is a world I have given up on ever getting into. If I do see anything, I'll just remind myself like I always do that it's better to give up on a dream if there is a risk it could turn into a nightmare. And if the price to pay for me ever being successful in that realm was to end up like Avril, good riddance to it.

I did apply for other jobs in cosmetics but all applications were rejected, and I began to wonder if Avril had spoken to her contacts in the industry and warned them off me. The fear that she had really turned my name to mud and already set everyone in that world against me always caused me to hesitate before clicking 'Apply' after that paranoia had taken hold. Then I would delete my applications before finishing them, simply because I didn't want to give Avril the pleasure if she knew I was still out there trying to break in, and she was the sole reason I was being kept out.

Better for her to think that I had moved on with my life and gone on to bigger and better things.

If only that was the case.

I read a couple of news stories from the world of film and television, just some gossipy things that help take my mind off my long day ahead and the fact that Bobby is firmly in my rear-view mirror now. Then I scroll down, looking for one or two more articles that might catch my eye before I'm due to get off this bus and report for duty.

And I see something that certainly catches my eye.

It's an article with a headline and accompanying photo that almost cause me to drop my phone, such is my level of surprise at stumbling across it.

BUSINESS INSIGHT – A DAY IN THE LIFE OF COSMETICS POWERHOUSE AVRIL ANDERSON

It looks like this online publication has done a featured article on the woman I hate and, despite knowing better, I can't resist clicking the link to read more about it. Once the article fully opens on my screen, my eyes quickly move down the page, curiosity getting the better of me.

I see a photo of Avril, this one of her with her arms folded as she stands in front of her office desk, the same room where she so easily dispatched me and my hopes of working for her. Then I read the words beneath it, the journalist having put together this piece that seems to be an hourly itinerary of what the 'busy and wonderful Avril Anderson' actually does.

6 a.m. – I like to start my day with yoga. It centres me, and as I'm in my mid-thirties now, I need to prioritise health and fitness as well as my career.

7:30 a.m. – I'm at my desk at this time every weekday, although I've already checked my emails on the way into the office to see if there is anything major that needs dealing with that day. There usually is.

9 a.m. – Meetings. Whether it's with a model, a designer or company directors, I can be found in one of the many meeting rooms in our offices, strategising and looking to grow our brand further around the world.

I keep scrolling down, my eyes scanning over all the writing and the occasional photos, feeling nauseous as I go because, as expected, this article is painting Avril as some superhero who maximises every minute of her day. But as I reach the end of reading about her working day, I'm wondering what nonsense she is going to pretend she does in the evenings. She's a workaholic, obsessed with her job, so I bet she works late every night, but will she admit to that here or will she try to make out like she is a balanced, rounded person with a personal life as well as a professional one?

Then I get my answer.

When I do, not even this bus suddenly crashing could shock me as much as what I see.

8 p.m. – I arrive home, very much looking forward to a healthy meal and a glass of red wine after a long day. Or perhaps I'll have a date night with my boyfriend, Bobby. We only met recently, but ours has been a whirlwind romance, and we are currently planning our first holiday together. We're thinking Greece. It's my favourite destination and I cannot wait to escape the dreary London weather and be soaking up the sun overseas with him.

This cannot be real. Avril and Bobby? An item.

I stare at the photo beneath the text and I'm holding my phone so tightly that it's starting to shake. I see Avril and she is smiling as she sits on a sofa beside her man. It's him. The man who stood me up after our seemingly perfect date. How did this happen? When? Why?

Unfortunately for me, the answers to those questions are obvious. She must have followed me and seen me with him, and at some point after we separated after our first kiss, she must have approached him. I don't know what she said to him, but maybe she made up some lie about me or perhaps she just did a better and quicker job of seducing him than I did. Did she fast-track her relationship with him knowing that I might see an article like this one day and realise what she did? Whatever the case, she is with him and that explains why he has stopped communicating with me.

Somehow, some way, she stole him from me.

I thought I was done with Avril.

But she obviously wasn't done with me.

TWENTY-FIVE

AVRIL

Present Day

I'm not sure of the exact moment when the magic of love and romance wears off and gets replaced with a crushing sense of mundane reality. It could be when a couple move in together and see each other all the time, rather than only when they're at their best. It might be when conversations are more about bills and chores than they are about which restaurant to go to or which bottle of wine to open. But if you ask me, I'd say it's when there's a baby thrown in the mix and each of them is exhausted, flustered and in desperate need of a break from the other. That last example is the point that Bobby and I have reached, where the heady days of our whirlwind romance feel like a distant memory when compared to the current situation we find ourselves in. Bobby arrived home in need of a rest after a long day's work, I've muddled through another day of motherhood, but before we can crawl into bed and get some sleep, we have a crying child to calm down.

I'd never regret starting my relationship with Bobby. Sure, initial contact between us was made simply because I wanted to ruin Jade's new romance, but once I got to know Bobby, I realised he was the perfect man for me. After I had persuaded him away from his cinema date with Jade and told him that she was a super-stalker who was best ignored, we had gone for a drink in a bar. That drink had turned into several, and by the end of the night, Bobby had planted his lips on two women. I might have been the second one, but that was all Jade was beating me at as far as this man was concerned. I made sure to get his number and arrange to see him again quickly. Once we were back together again, I knew he had forgotten all about her and was fully focused on me.

The online article I made myself available for, the one that asked me to tell the journalist about a typical day in my life, was one that I did in the hope that it would be read by Jade. I had no way of knowing for sure if she would see it, but I knew there was a good chance that she would if she had an interest in the cosmetics world. That's why I made sure to not only mention my new man, Bobby, in the article but also to request that a photo of the two of us be featured as well. A double whammy indeed, should Jade ever come across it and, if she did, she would figure out what I had done. I'd screwed over her love life as well as her career aspirations and that meant finality. It was definitely over between us. I had won, she had lost, and all was right with the world. Such was the simple way I viewed life back then. Even now, I tell myself I went as far as I did because of the complaint she made against me at work, a complaint that could have derailed my career. But it had to be more than that. I went way too far with her and, deep down, I'm not sure why. I just couldn't stop myself, not at that time of my life.

I like to think that I'm a better person now. I love Bobby as much for who he is and how he makes me feel, not just because he fitted into my plans for getting one over on Jade. Since then, things have been great between us, but there is no doubt we have hit a roadblock since our baby arrived, and as another draining night approaches, I fear another argument may be on the horizon. That's why I try to avoid it by talking to him about my piece of news from the day, the news that has been playing on my mind for hours, and it'll be good to share it and break it down with somebody else.

As Luca cries and Bobby tries shushing him, I give it a go.

'Guess who I bumped into today,' I say, my voice having to be louder than the crying. 'The woman who was in the next bed to us in hospital. Do you remember her?'

Bobby either looks like he doesn't remember or he doesn't care, so I go on quickly.

'She was at the sensory class I went to. Small world, huh? We went for coffee afterwards and had a chat. She was nice. A bit quiet. But we swapped numbers.'

I don't mention to Bobby the fact that since that coffee we shared, I have messaged Jade to say I enjoyed it and would like to do it again sometime, only for her to not reply to me yet. But she'll be busy dealing with her baby on her own, so I'm sure she'll get back to me when she gets a free minute.

'Do you think he needs more milk?' Bobby asks me, ignoring what I've just said and only trying to figure out what it is that our son needs to quieten down and go to sleep.

'No, he had a full bottle half an hour ago. He can't still be hungry,' I say before taking Luca from him and trying to settle him myself. It's not working, but I don't let that stop me from finishing what I had started saying. 'Anyway, the woman from the hospital. Jade is her name. A couple of weird things happened while I was with her.'

Bobby doesn't say anything as he starts tidying up some of the mess that has accumulated around the house since he was out at work.

'Hey, I said two weird things happened. Don't you want to know what they were?' I ask, annoyed Bobby doesn't appear to care about my day.

'What were they?' he replies wearily, with all the enthusiasm of a man who just wants both his wife and baby to be quiet so he can get some sleep.

'She lied about her baby's birth date,' I tell him. 'She said she got mixed up, but nobody gets that mixed up, do they? She said the twelfth, but it was the tenth. She had her baby on the same day as us.'

Bobby shrugs and carries on tidying while Luca calms for a second then starts up crying again, prompting us to switch roles.

'And the other weird thing was with him,' I say, gesturing to the baby in my husband's arms. 'He cries all the time, we know that, but he went quiet when she held him. It was surreal. It was as if she was some kind of miracle baby whisperer or something.'

'There's no such thing as miracles,' Bobby laments as he has another go at quietening Luca.

'You should have seen it. She was a natural with him. It was freaky.'

'Then get her to come over here and help us now because we obviously don't have her skills,' Bobby replies sarcastically. 'Seriously, how is this story helping us right now? Can we focus on the task at hand?'

'I was telling you about my day,' I try, but Bobby is not in the mood for it, and carries Luca into another room, eager to get away from me, but at least it provides me with a break. I won't feel bad for him taking over because I've had Luca by myself since breakfast, and as tiring as driving a taxi around all day must be, it's not a patch on caring for an almost permanently unhappy child. In fact, the only time Luca seemed happy today was when Jade was around, which really is strange and makes me wonder what she was doing that we're not.

I check my phone again, eager to see if she has replied to my earlier message, but she has not. Then I check the time and decide it's not too late to try and call her. She's probably up because which new mum isn't at this time?

I hit the call button next to her number and put my phone to my ear whilst wandering around and picking up a few dirty bibs and Babygros. It's multi-tasking at its finest, but as the call keeps ringing, I'm fearing I won't get to have a chat while I do this tidying up. But then it's suddenly answered.

'Hello?'

I frown at the sound of the man's voice at the other end of the line.

'Sorry, I was trying to reach Jade,' I explain, wondering who this person could be. She doesn't have a boyfriend, so maybe it's just a friend. She mentioned a neighbour often calls around to help her. I presumed that neighbour was female, but maybe not.

'Sorry, who?' the man asks me.

'Jade,' I repeat, thinking he must have not heard me clearly the first time.

'I think you've got the wrong number,' comes the unexpected reply.

'The wrong number? No, I don't think so. This is Jade's number. She gave it to me earlier, when we were in the coffee shop after the baby class.'

'I have no idea what you're talking about. This is my phone, and I'm definitely not called Jade,' the man replies, seemingly making a joke, though he is not laughing.

'I don't understand,' I say, very confused at this turn of events. 'You're saying this isn't Jade's number?'

'No, it's mine, and if you don't mind, I've got to go now, so I'm hanging up. You've got the wrong number.'

With that, the man does as he says and ends the call, and I'm left staring at my phone as if it has just betrayed me. But it hasn't because I know I saved the number correctly when Jade gave it to me, so there has been no mistake from my end. That means there can only be one other explanation.

Jade gave me the wrong number earlier.

But why would she do that?

I think again about why she would lie about her baby's birthday, and suddenly a pattern is forming here. There's something going on with that woman. She lied in my presence and now she has tried to get rid of me by giving me a fake number, ensuring I cannot contact her again.

This is just one more weird thing to go with the two weird occurrences earlier today.

They do say things happen in threes, and while I don't know about that, I do know one thing.

I need to find Jade again and figure out why she's lying.

TWENTY-SIX

JADE

I'm halfway through another long and lonely day in my flat, with only another woman's baby for company, when I find myself thinking about Avril and wondering if she has tried to get in touch with me yet. Does she already know that I gave her a fake number, or is she still none the wiser? She might not have bothered to message me yet, and if that's the case, she'll have no clue, which is good. If she has sent a text, she could just assume I'm too busy to reply, which will at least buy me a few more days before she realises. But if she has tried to call, the deception has probably been revealed because somebody else would have answered and surely told her that the phone number she had for me was wrong or it might even be an unknown number.

It's difficult to predict what Avril might do once she finds out that I gave her a false number, as if I was some Lothario in the dating world who, after getting what he wanted during a one-night stand, gave fake digits to his lover so they never had to meet again. Except the stakes are much higher than that here. I didn't give her a different number out of personal choice, but because that was the only sensible thing to do.

I cannot have that woman near me again.

I glance outside and see that it is dry, so I figure a short pram walk will do me good, and while it's never as quick getting out when I have another person to get ready, I'm eventually ready to go. But no sooner have I opened the door than I wish I could close it again and stay inside forever because there is somebody on my doorstep who I want to see even less than Avril.

'Gavin? What are you doing here?' I ask as I stare in horror at the man who has come to visit me, but as his eyes lower from mine and land on the baby in the pram, the answer to that question is an obvious one.

'When were you going to tell me?' he says as he stares at the baby that he assumes is his.

'I thought you were in prison!' I cry, trying to fathom how he could have got out so soon.

'I got released early. Overcrowding issues.'

Oh no. Prison's overcrowding issue has now become my overcrowding issue.

'I got out this morning and just saw a friend. He told me he'd seen you pushing a baby around in a pram and when I thought about it, I figured the dates would match from when we slept together.'

'He's not yours,' I blurt out, as if I expect him to take my word for that and leave us alone, but it's worth a try because it is the truth.

'Are you sure? The dates fit,' Gavin claims as he takes a step nearer to the pram, but I pull back.

'Yes, I'm sure!'

'He looks like me.'

'No, he doesn't!' I reply, thinking about how he couldn't possibly be further from the truth.

I hear a door open and Linda appears,

'Is everything okay?' she asks, quickly inserting herself into this chaos on my doorstep.

'Yes, everybody just needs to leave us alone,' I say before I try to shut the door on the both of them, but Gavin blocks it with his arm and forces himself inside. I retreat with the pram, and then I realise this situation isn't going to get better.

'I want to hold him,' Gavin says, reaching for the pram again whilst Linda hangs back, looking helpless.

'Just leave us alone!' I try, but Gavin has the pram and now he's picking up the baby he thinks he has fathered.

'Everybody needs to calm down and let's talk about this,' Linda tries, but we both ignore her, our attention on the baby, who is now crying, either at all the noise or the fact that this stranger has just picked him up.

'Give him back to me. He's not yours!' I repeat, but Gavin does no such thing, holding the baby with care, the kind of care he rarely showed me when we were together.

'I can't believe you wouldn't tell me,' he says. 'What is his name?'

I look at Linda, wondering if she will answer for me. But she just looks back at me, waiting for me to do it. So in the end, neither of us speaks. But while she is probably just waiting for me to let this man know the name of his child, I am withholding it because it's so complicated that it would blow both of their minds if they knew the truth.

'Seriously, you need to leave, right now,' I tell Gavin, trying to take the baby back from him, but he turns away and what am I supposed to do then? I can hardly wrestle a child from him.

'Stop pretending like he's not mine!' he cries. 'The dates match from when we slept together, and you told me you weren't sleeping with anyone else. You obviously got pregnant and kept it quiet, but I know now. I want to be a part of his life. I don't care about anything between us and it's obvious that you don't either, but I'm here for him and I have every right to have access to him. You know that.'

Gavin makes a compelling case, but if only I could tell him the truth, he would quickly hand back the baby and walk out the door, such would be his desperation to get away from me. If only I could let him know that I stole this baby from another woman, he would walk out that door faster than the last time he went through it. He'd disappear back to whatever life he has on the outside after being in prison, and I expect I'd never hear from him again. But I cannot tell him, because I cannot tell anyone, so I'm stuck with him here thinking he has access rights to this baby.

'He looks like me,' Gavin says again, which is total nonsense. How can he when he was conceived by two other people totally unrelated to us? 'He has my eyes.'

'No, he doesn't,' I tell him firmly. 'Because he's not yours.'

Gavin stops pretending to be enamoured with the baby and looks up at me.

'You were seeing somebody else?' he asks, the flash of jealousy that crosses his face a hint at the potential danger this man might pose.

I definitely don't want to say that because not only is it not true, but it's the most likely answer to cause Gavin to turn violent and I cannot risk that when there's more people than just myself to think about here.

'Please, everybody just calm down. How about I make us all a drink?' Linda feebly offers, as if that could possibly de-escalate this tricky situation.

'I'll call the police!' I threaten, which is a massive bluff. They're the last people I need here poking around in my life, but I'm hoping it will spook Gavin and he will leave.

'Call them! I want a DNA test. I want to see if this baby is mine and, if he is, I'm not going anywhere, and they won't blame me!' Gavin snaps back, prepared to stand his ground.

'I'm not doing a DNA test because there's no need!' I try, but Gavin doesn't like that either.

'You won't do a test because someone else is the father? Then maybe you should call the police because when we met, you told me you weren't the kind of woman who sleeps around, so I have every right to get angry!' Gavin shouts at me, his face bright red now, almost as red as the baby's he is holding. 'I know you were telling me the truth when we slept together. You said I was the first guy you'd been with in ages. So I'm the father, aren't I? Just admit it!'

This is a total nightmare, and I can't see any way out. The worst thing I can do is tell him the truth, so what does that mean? I'm stuck having to live a lie with Gavin in it now? Pretend like he is the dad and give him time with this baby? Better that than having him know that his real son, the one he did conceive with me, is currently being raised by another couple who have absolutely no idea about the swap either. I really don't want to do a DNA test, not when I don't know if I'll end up having to submit anything myself. I can't risk the results showing I'm not his real mother, plus I really don't want there to be a record on the system anywhere that this baby had a DNA test. Avril might be investigating one day and it's the kind of thing that might be flagged by a PI.

I look helplessly at Linda, hoping she has some sudden solution to how to make it better. But she looks as panicked as I am, and as Gavin asks me how to get the baby to stop crying, I have no answer for him. That's because the baby hardly ever cried when it was just us two, so I don't have much experience of it.

Our real baby is a crier, though.

The problem is our real baby is with someone else.

TWENTY-SEVEN

AVRIL

As I walk into the daily baby class with Luca, the same as the one I attended yesterday, I see several mums in the familiar circle in the centre of the room and all the toys in front of their babies. But unlike yesterday, I do not see Jade or her baby, and that is frustrating, although potentially, not totally damaging.

I was hoping to find her here so I could speak with her, ask her why she gave me a fake number, and then try to figure out exactly what is going on with that woman who seems to act so mysteriously around me. But of course she wouldn't come back here. Why would she if she doesn't want to see me again? She wouldn't take that risk, and as I join the circle and pick up a rattle to entertain Luca with, I think about how she must feel like she will be able to successfully avoid me forever now.

But she might be wrong.

Even though it's annoying to not see her here, it's okay because I've got another idea. A potential way I can track down Jade and see her again. It might not work, and it is very desperate but it's my only option and last chance considering she has tried to lose me with a fake phone number.

Every attendee of this baby class had to complete an online form before they came. It was obviously just a health and safety thing, a way to get us to accept the terms and conditions and cover their insurance policy if anything happened while we were on the premises. But one thing I remember from that online form is that it asked for our address, and I remember entering mine.

If I entered mine, it surely means that Jade entered hers too.

I'm hoping I can get the chance to learn what Jade's address is so I can go straight from here to there and see her. In order to have a chance of obtaining that address, I need to get a look at the online system, and I need an opportunity to do that.

'I'm sorry. I really need to use the toilet. Would you be okay to look after my baby? Just for a couple of minutes?'

I smile at the woman who runs this baby class and the only woman in here who isn't currently holding a child of her own.

'Yes, of course,' she replies, hardly able to say no in front of all these other parents, not when she's projected this image of being a baby lover who has set this class up not only for profit but for a passion for children and their development.

I hand Luca to her and then hurry to the door, glancing back as I go to see that everybody has stayed in the circle and nobody is following me out, which is perfect because I really need to be alone once I get on the other side of this door.

As I leave the hall behind and enter the reception area, I see all the prams parked in one corner of the room, but most importantly, I don't see anybody sitting behind the large desk opposite them. That's because the woman who runs the class also operates the reception area, her own small business that she runs all by herself. The front doors to the building are locked while the class is underway, meaning nobody can come in halfway through, which is why this area can be left unoccupied. That gives me the opportunity to snoop around the desk and see if I can find the sign-in forms every attendee has to complete.

I check the computer first, but it is password protected, which is to be expected, but is no less annoying. I cannot waste time trying to crack a password I have no hope of ever guessing, so I move my attention away from the computer and start opening the drawers of the desk. The basic sign-in sheet sits on top of the desk, but that only has the baby details on and I need the parent details more, so I'm hoping to find what I'm looking for quickly.

I look up at the door to the hall briefly before returning my attention to the drawers, and as I find a large folder, I take it out and inspect the contents. There are pages and pages of paperwork in here, but I get my hopes up when I see that these are all printouts of the online form.

This is exactly what I'm looking for!

My heart starts racing as I sift through the forms, looking for one with the name Jade at the top. I'm aware there might have been more than one Jade who has been here, it is a very common name, after all, but at least if I can narrow it down then I have a chance.

I hear a noise, something that makes me freeze, and look up, expecting that I've been caught and will have to somehow explain my actions before I'm thrown out of here or the police are called. That's why it's a huge relief when I see that it was a noise from inside the hall, rather than the noise of somebody coming out of it. For now, I'm still alone out here. It's a reminder that I need to be quicker, as my excuse of going to the toilet will only allow me so much time and that time is quickly running out.

So many papers, so many previous visitors here. The woman who runs this class must make a fortune, although I remember that the first class was free, and a lot of these parents might never have returned. I wonder if that's what this pile is. A historical record for safekeeping if there's ever an audit. A collection of parents who never came back. Parents like Jade.

But whereas most never return presumably because they either didn't enjoy the class or don't deem it worth paying money for, Jade has not returned for another reason.

She's not come back because she's trying to lose me.

As I find the page with her first name written on it, *I realise I have just found her.*

There is no surname, but I check the bottom of the form and see the address she entered. Now I have it, I quickly fold the form up and stuff it into the pocket of my jeans. Then I close the folder and put it back in the drawer before rushing away from the desk, just in time to see the door to the hall open and the class leader appear, holding a crying Luca in her arms.

'I was just coming to check everything was okay,' she says to me, looking a little flustered at having to deal with my child while also managing a room full of other people.

'No, it's not actually,' I say, lying to this poor woman again. 'I'm not feeling well. I think we're going to have to leave early. Is that okay?'

'Of course,' she replies, handing Luca to me and then taking a bunch of keys from her back pocket. 'I'll unlock the door for you now. I keep it locked in case people who shouldn't be here try getting in. And I'm sorry to hear that you aren't well.'

'Thank you,' I say as I put Luca in his pram and then push him to the door that is quickly opened, giving me access out onto the street, where I am eager to go because that is the way I get to the address in my pocket.

'I hope you're feeling better soon,' the woman tells me as I exit, and I thank her again before walking away, hoping that she is right.

I might be feeling better soon when I get to this address and see Jade again to find out why she has been so weird with me. That woman is a puzzle I am eager to solve, and the strange feeling I have in my gut when I'm around her is only imploring me to investigate further.

But if I do feel better when I see Jade and figure out what is going on with her, the opposite might be true too.

Jade won't be feeling better when she sees me.

TWENTY-EIGHT

JADE

The last hour has been excruciating. That's how long it's been since Gavin turned up and demanded to see the baby that he believes is his. I have refused to talk with him anymore because of how angry he was acting, and I think Gavin finally understood, because he eventually calmed down. But this isn't over, as he is still nearby. He's at Linda's place now, having gone there after she invited him for a cup of tea and a chance to cool down. She only did that because Gavin was refusing to leave the area, telling me that he was afraid that as soon as he did, I would pack my things and flee from him and he would never see 'his baby' again. To be fair, he would be right. If he had properly left, I would have fled so I'd never have to deal with him again. If only I had left before he had even turned up. That would have been better. Or maybe adoption was the best thing I could have done for this baby and anything else is just prolonging the pain for all of us.

Gavin is currently next door and he'll see and hear me if I try and leave, so I guess I'm stuck here. At least it's just me and the baby in the flat now and, with a bit of luck, it'll just be us two for the rest of the day.

I don't want any more visitors for a while.

I need time to think and make a plan.

Then I hear a knock at the door.

'Oh, go away,' I shout at the door, assuming it's Gavin who has come back to try and stake another claim to the baby.

Another knock.

'Leave me alone!' I cry out, waking the baby as I do, which is annoying, but I can't control my frustration.

And then there's a third knock.

The red mist descends, and I storm towards the door, preparing to fling it open and launch into a barrage of insults at the person on the other side of it who has stupidly chosen to ignore my pleas for peace.

'What part of leave me alone don't you understand?' I shout as I open the door, only to be stunned when I see that it's not Gavin who is the object of my anger.

It's Avril.

What the hell is she doing here?

'Are you okay?' she asks me, which is probably the most logical question considering how much shouting I've been doing since she started knocking.

'How did you know where I live?' is the question I fire back at her.

'I got your address from the baby class.'

'What?' I cry, assuming that data would have been secure.

'I know, I probably shouldn't have, but I wanted to see you again and this was the only way after you gave me the wrong phone number.'

I look at Avril, and her pram. My mind races to figure out why she has tracked me down, and I feel like I'm losing control. The only way this could get worse now would be if Gavin came out from next door and started asking questions about who this other woman was. That would be awful, especially when the baby in Avril's pram is the one he really fathered, which is why I need to try and avoid such a scenario. What if he noticed a resemblance to the other little boy?

'Come in,' I say, ushering Avril inside, which might make me seem incredibly friendly, but it is simply because I need her off my doorstep before the people next door see her.

'Who did you think was knocking?' Avril asks me as she pushes her pram inside and I get another glimpse of my real son as she passes me. 'You sounded very upset.'

'It's a long story,' I say as I close the door and lock it just in case Gavin has another go at coming in. But while applying the lock keeps him out, it also keeps Avril in and that might prove to be even more uncomfortable for me.

'Is everything okay?' Avril asks me as she glances at her real baby in his crib, making my heart skip a beat as I wait for her to suddenly claim that he is hers. 'I tried getting in touch with you, but like I said, the number you gave me wasn't right.'

'Oh, really? I thought I gave you the correct one?' I say lamely, my brain so scrambled from the events that have already occurred today that I can't come up with a better answer than that.

'No, it was definitely wrong,' Avril says, her eyes still on the baby I stole from her. 'So what's the deal? Did you not want to see me again?'

'What? No, of course I did,' I lie. 'It was just a mistake. I've changed my number a few times recently, so I must have just given you an old one by accident.'

Avril finally looks back at me, and while she still seems sceptical, she doesn't press me on the number issue anymore. Although she does have other questions.

'What's going on with you?' she asks.

'Me? Nothing!'

'You were acting weird in the baby class, giving the wrong date for your baby's birthday. You were being weird in the coffee shop too, and then it turns out you gave me the wrong number. And you're being weird now. So what's going on?'

I need an excuse and fast.

'Oh, sorry. I didn't realise I was being weird. And you say I gave the wrong date? Must be baby brain. I swear there are days I forget my own name since becoming a mum.'

I hope that has worked, but Avril doesn't seem to be buying it, saying nothing but eyeing me sceptically.

Oh my god, she sees right through me. She knows I've done something terrible. She's going to find out that we have each other's babies and I'll be in prison by the end of the afternoon.

I feel like doing the only thing I can then, the one thing that will come easily.

I'm just about to start crying.

But Avril beats me to it.

'I'm sorry,' she says as she starts sobbing, and suddenly my tears are kept at bay while hers are let loose. Except no sooner has she started crying than the baby she came here with starts crying too.

'I can't cope. I can't do this,' Avril admits, sitting down on my sofa and seemingly ignoring her baby's cries to try and deal with her own. I'm conscious of how loud the baby's crying is and if Gavin hears it next door, he might come around to check on us, so I rush towards Avril's pram and scoop up the baby inside.

My baby.

No sooner do I have hold of him than he quietens again, just like he did in the coffee shop. I feel a horrible pang of guilt now, as if I've just realised my baby is not as troublesome as I first thought he was and maybe I could have dealt with him better if only I hadn't been so overwhelmed in the hospital. He's certainly calmed now in my arms and, just like the first time it happened, Avril notices it.

'There it is again,' she says. 'How do you do that?'

'It's nothing,' I pretend, but, of course, it's actually *everything*.

'No, it isn't. He calms down as soon as you hold him, like he's settled in your arms. But why would he do that? Why wouldn't he settle for me?'

'I don't know, he's just a baby.'

Avril wipes her eyes and with her tears having stopped as quickly as the baby in my arm settled, she turns her attention to the other child in the room.

'There's something about him,' she says as she leans over the real Luca.

'What do you mean?' I ask, my question fraught with anxiety.

'He looks like my husband.'

I force a nervous laugh out.

'What?'

'He looks like my partner. He has his features. I thought I saw a glimpse of it in the coffee shop, but I definitely see it now. How can that be?'

Oh no. This is getting worse. It feels like I'm waiting for the inevitable now. The moment when she tells me she knows I swapped our babies.

'Maybe I'm just going mad,' Avril says, surprising me. 'I've not slept properly for weeks, and I went cold turkey on the painkillers I was supposed to be taking. That probably wasn't wise. My head's all over the place. I guess I'm seeing things.'

I wasn't expecting her to talk her way out of this awkward situation for me, but she has done a good job of it. That's why I stay quiet and allow her to keep talking.

'I'm just really lonely and fed up. And tired. So, so tired. Do you think I could have a lie down here in your bedroom? Just an hour or so. It's just I don't have anyone to help me with Luca today, so I can't sleep at home. And you're so good with him, I know he'll be fine. Would that be okay?'

Avril wants to have a nap here? It seems very random, but it's certainly a lot better than what I feared might happen when she arrived, so I guess I can't be picky.

'Erm, sure,' I say, figuring she can't suspect me of anything after all if she feels comfortable enough to try and fall asleep in my home. 'It's that door over there.'

'Thanks. Just an hour, max,' Avril says. 'I know I'll feel so much better after it. Come and get me if you need me.'

I watch her go into my bedroom, and as she closes the door, I think about how this is very bizarre. But also good.

My secret is still safe.

Although I can't relax.

Not when Avril is still here and I'm now looking after both my baby and hers.

TWENTY-NINE
AVRIL

I close the door to Jade's bedroom and take a deep breath. One thing I certainly won't be taking is a nap. That's because I lied to Jade about why I wanted to come in here.

I'm not here to sleep.

I'm here to snoop.

Convinced that something very weird is going on with Jade, from her attempts to lose me and how my baby quietens down as soon as she holds him, I am looking around for clues. Something, anything, that might give me a better idea of who this woman is, why she seems so suspicious and why I can't shake the feeling that something is terribly wrong with my baby.

The first place I try is the dressing table by the unmade bed. The top of the dressing table is full of cheap make-up products, but it's the drawers underneath them that I am most interested in. I pull open the first one and am met with the sight of various items like phone charger cables, headache tablets and other banal items that don't tell me anything about the person who owns them. I rummage around but there's nothing much of interest, so I move on to the other drawers, though they are all filled with underwear and some T-shirts.

None of this is helping.

I give up on the dressing table and head for the wardrobe, opening the doors carefully, anxious about one of the doors being creaky and alerting Jade to the fact that I am prying. Thankfully, they don't make a sound, though there's nothing of interest in here, anyway. Just cheap and basic dresses and sweaters hanging on racks, a far cry from the types of expensive and aspirational fashion items I used to work with in my career.

I'm starting to fear that coming in here under the excuse of having a nap has been a waste of time and I'm not going to find anything that helps give me a better picture of who Jade is and what she might be trying to hide from me. She's clearly not going to tell me much herself, so my only way of getting some real answers will be if I can uncover something without her knowing. But how can I do that if I can't find anything more personal than her underwear and lipstick choices?

I look around the rest of the room, but aside from a few piles of worn clothes on the floor, there is nothing else but the messy bed in the centre. I hardly expect to find anything amongst the crumpled duvet and tangled sheets, but what about underneath the bed itself?

I quietly drop to my hands and knees, thinking this would be an awful time for Jade to come in and check on me only to catch me in this position. The door remains closed, so I peer under the bed, and when I do, I see a few more miscellaneous items scattered around what looks like a shoebox.

I reach under and pull the box out, and as I take the lid off, I see that this is where Jade keeps her most valuable possessions. But I'm not here to take jewellery or watches or anything like that, because she doesn't appear to have the money to afford those kinds of lavish things. Instead, I see her passport, and I freeze when something catches my eye.

'Oh my god,' I say as I realise, to my absolute horror, that the woman in this passport photo is a woman from my past. She looks a lot different from the way she does now, which is why I have not recognised her, but now I have got this snapshot of the past, I know exactly who she is.

I drop the box, which makes a little noise, but I don't care about that. I just want to get away from the passport. As I stand up and back away to the door, recoiling in disgust, I feel like I'm going to be sick.

'This can't be happening,' I utter under my breath.

I only stop backing away when I bump into the door behind me, and it makes enough noise that I'm sure Jade must have heard it.

I can't believe it's her. The woman I was once enemies with. The woman I did my best to ruin. The woman whose boyfriend I stole and made my husband. I thought she seemed vaguely familiar when I first saw her in the hospital, but she looks so different. Different hairstyle. Different hair colour. Different shape. With the seven years that have gone by, she looks like an entirely new person. It's a long time and she's certainly done a lot to look different to how she did back then. But I know it's her now and, despite all *her* changes in appearance, I still look pretty much the same as I did back then, so she must know it's me. She must have known it was me back at the hospital when we were in neighbouring beds. She must have recognised me instantly. Bobby too, because neither of us has made such drastic alterations to our appearances as she has.

So why didn't she say something then? Why didn't she say anything, a single word, to either one of us? Why did she stay so quiet behind that curtain that was nearly always closed around her bed?

My head feels like it's spinning as I think about all of this, but I try to tell myself not to panic. Maybe nothing bad has happened here. Sure, she probably recognised and remembered me, which would explain why she has been so keen to get away from me ever since, but that's it, right? That's all that's happened?

I wish I could believe that, but thinking back on how the pair of us hated each other, I find it hard to believe that she could just let things go so easily after randomly seeing both me and Bobby again. She would have had every right to start an argument or even just say something disparaging like we are welcome to each other, anything to at least give the sense that she had moved on and felt she was better than us in the long term. But she didn't do any of that. She didn't say so much as a word to us. She just left the hospital with her baby and that was it and, since then, even though we have been together a couple of times, she still hasn't said anything about the past.

Why?

There's only one way to find out.

I take hold of the bedroom door handle and at the same time, take a deep breath. I'm preparing to step out of this room and walk into the next one where I will confront Jade about what is going on here. But just before I go, I realise how the stakes have increased between us since last time. It's different to before, when it was just the two of us. There are two babies involved now, both of whom are in this flat with us. Is it a good idea for me to make a scene now, on her home turf, when both myself and the two babies are in a vulnerable position? I need to be smart about this. Do what the old Avril would do. She would make a plan. Be meticulous. And most of all, *make sure to win.*

I open the door and lay eyes on Jade holding Luca, and all of my resolve falls away because I get an awful, gut-wrenching sense of what this woman might have done to take her ultimate revenge on me. It would explain why my baby went from being so placid to seemingly hating me. And why the baby I have calms down whenever she is around.

The thought is unbearable, but as I stare at her with the baby I came here with, I wonder if that is her real child and the other child, the one that was already here when I arrived, is... *mine?*

'Are you okay? I thought you were having a nap?' Jade says as she notices me lingering in her bedroom doorway.

I try to speak, to move, to do anything, but I can't because the thought that she might have done something as despicable as swap our children has me rooted to the spot and unable to get any words out.

'Avril? Are you okay?'

I really need to answer. To say something. But what can I do?

I realise that despite our past and the feeling that I had won, I really don't know who I am dealing with here and what this woman is truly capable of. So, with that in mind, I decide that I will leave and then speak to Bobby about involving the police. Better that than potentially not being able to leave this flat at all if Jade turns on me or, worse, *our innocent babies.*

'I can't sleep. Sorry, I think I'm best just leaving and going home,' I say, walking to the pram I came here with, though, of course, there is no baby in it because Jade is holding him.

'Oh, okay, no problem,' Jade says, barely disguising how pleased she seems to be that I am leaving after all. She gently places the baby back down in my pram. But as I look at him, the child I thought was Luca, I see a flash of her in him and I know now that this is her child.

She really is playing this sick game. Which means I'm about to leave her with my real son.

Can I do it?

I turn and look at the tiny infant I believe is the real Luca, the real life that I grew inside myself for nine months, and it breaks my heart that we seem to have been separated for this first part of his life. But the most important thing is that I give us both a chance of being reunited properly one day, when it's safe, so I remind myself to stay calm and just get out of here.

The police can deal with the rest.

'I'll be going now,' I say, pushing the pram to the door, and Jade doesn't try and get me to stay any longer. As always, she's happy to let me go, and of course she is, because she is hiding a terrible secret.

But not for much longer.

THIRTY

JADE

While it should be a relief to have Avril out of my flat, something feels wrong. Like it was too easy. What happened? One minute, she was keen on having a nap in my bedroom, the next, she couldn't wait to get out. It's as if something made her change her mind suddenly. But what could it be?

I'm drawn to the bedroom, figuring it must have been something she saw in there, and as I walk in, my heart is racing as I fear she might have seen something she should not have. As I look around, I see my bed, dressing table and wardrobe, but all seems okay with them. But there is something under the bed. It's the box I keep my personal documents in. Avril wouldn't have seen that, would she? That would have required her to crawl under the bed on her hands and knees – and why would she do that?

Unless she suspected something was wrong.

I quickly drop to my hands and knees and look under the bed and, when I do, I see the box with my valuable documents in lying on its side, the lid half off and something poking out from within.

It's my passport.

I wish I could tell myself that I'm just being paranoid, but I'm not because this box was definitely upright when I left it, with the lid closed and the passport safely stored inside. Now it looks like the box has been disturbed, and if it wasn't done by me, it could only have been her.

Avril has looked at my passport.

Which means she knows what I used to look like.

If she has realised who I really am, she might figure out why I've been acting so weird around her. Even worse, she might figure out why our babies have been the way they have with each of us.

She left in a hurry. She seemed desperate to get away from me, despite being initially eager to find me. That tells me one awful thing.

She knows who I am now and, potentially, she has worked out what I did.

The game is up.

I go from hoping for the best to accepting the worst and instantly start piling things into a rucksack, the large piece of luggage I keep under my bed beside my passport now being filled with as many of my things as I can cram in, because I realise I need to leave here – fast. If Avril knows who I am, and if she suspects I swapped our babies, she will be back. And she won't be alone. She will bring the police with her, and she might have already called them as she left. I need to be gone. I need to escape Avril and Gavin.

I need to escape everybody.

I don't know if I'm going to be able to make it out of here, but I have to try, so I keep packing my rucksack with essentials. I then haul it out of my bedroom before remembering I'm not the only one I have to pack for.

I look at Calum lying in his crib, his eyes open, staring at me, the innocence of youth watching the guilty adult but being far too unaware and immature to judge me. What do I do with him? I can't just leave him here on his own. I'll have to take him with me. Maybe I'll see somewhere on the way that is a safe place to leave him. There might be an old couple who will do the right thing by him. I could have left him next door with Linda, but not now Gavin is back on the scene. Or maybe I'll keep him with me and take him wherever I go next, so I'm not starting a new life totally by myself.

I can't believe I'm having to do this.

I scoop up a few of Calum's things and throw them in a small rucksack that I sling over the opposite shoulder to the one currently holding my bigger rucksack, and then I carefully scoop up Calum and put him in the pram before pushing him to the door. I'm praying he doesn't cry and alert Gavin and Linda nearby, but of course he doesn't because this baby is not a crier, which allows us to leave my flat in silence.

I don't even bother closing the door to my flat, not only because I don't have a spare hand to do it with but because I can't spare the two seconds it would take to even try. I just have to be gone from here as quickly as possible. I rush in the direction of the train station, which is a ten-minute walk from here, or a five-minute run; I am hopeful this can work.

And then I get confirmation that it won't.

That's because I hear somebody calling out my name.

THIRTY-ONE

AVRIL

'Stop!' I cry, grateful that I lingered outside Jade's flat in case she left because I've caught her doing exactly that. Although I'm still afraid that she might be able to escape.

I see Jade turn around and spot me, the surprise visible on her face even from the distance between us, which is about ten yards or so. I've just watched her leave her flat with a big ruck-sack, a smaller one, a pram and my baby, but I'm not letting her get any further. No way. Not until the police have got here and we have done a DNA test on our two children.

I've already called them, dialling 999 as soon as I left her flat and finding a hiding place just around the corner. I phoned them and told them exactly what was going on, that I feared a woman had stolen my baby and she was dangerous, meaning they had to come to this address as quickly as possible to arrest her. Obviously, a frantic call like that warrants immediate atten-tion, and I was told by the operator that officers were being dispatched, so they should be with me as soon as possible. But they're not here yet and, until they are, I'm the only thing stop-ping Jade from getting away with this.

She only stops for a second. No sooner has she seen me than

she unburdens herself of the heavy-looking rucksack and takes off running. She is still with the smaller bag which I am guessing is full of baby things, and also the pram, the one with my baby in it, having abandoned her belongings but running away with the one thing that I believe belongs to me.

'No! Stop!' I cry as I run after her, pushing the pram with her baby in. If it's not crazy enough that each of us has the other's child, it's even crazier that we're now running along a busy street past dozens of bewildered pedestrians.

'Somebody stop her. She has my baby!' I cry out, but nobody listens or at least acts on what I say, probably because it is so wild and unfathomable. They stand and stare, watching us go, unsure or unwilling to get involved, and those with headphones in wouldn't hear my anguished cries for help however loudly I shouted.

Jade runs around a corner and I temporarily lose sight of her, which is an awful experience. But I quickly have eyes back on her again as I round the same corner and see her up ahead. Judging by the direction we are running, I'm guessing she is heading for the train station. That would make sense considering she had a big rucksack with her. Although that rucksack is currently lying behind us in the gutter, so wherever she plans to go now, she won't have much to start with. Her passport might be in the small rucksack she still has, and that would mean she could go abroad.

She could flee the country with my baby.

Luca, or at least the child I used to call Luca, starts crying in the pram; the speed at which I'm pushing him is clearly upsetting. For once, I can't get frustrated at his crying: I'd probably cry too if I was him. It can't be comfortable to be pushed down the street at these speeds, having the wheels of the pram bumping over kerbs, such is the haste in which I'm going. There's no denying he is slowing me down, but I can't just leave him, even if he isn't my baby. I keep pushing the pram right up until the moment the wheels seem to lock and, suddenly, it's tipping over.

'No!' I cry as the pram topples to the side and I have to dive to ensure the baby inside doesn't fall out onto the concrete. I'm able to keep him inside it, though I hit the ground hard myself. As I lie beside the fallen pram, a stranger rushes over to offer his assistance. He's not the only one who appears, and this other person is not so helpful.

'What did you expect to happen, running down the street like that? What a dangerous thing to do with a pram. You should be ashamed of yourself!'

I can't believe I'm being scolded by a random member of the public, but they wouldn't be so judgemental about my behaviour if they knew why I was in such a rush.

'That woman has my baby!' I cry out, tears in my eyes, not just because I hurt my knee when I fell but because I have lost sight of Jade again. She's gone around another corner, and even though I feel I know where she is headed, there is the chance I'm wrong and she could slip off in a different direction, meaning I could lose her forever.

'What?' the man trying to help me up asks, shocked at my reason for running.

'She has my baby and she's getting away! Please, help me!' I beg as I get to my feet, the crying baby in my arms and the pram lying on the pavement, one wheel totally broken, just like my heart as I contemplate the horror that my life has become.

I try to run again but the pain in my injured knee is too intense. It buckles easily, causing me to cry out, though it's nothing compared to the pain I feel at the thought of Jade escaping with my baby. Thankfully, the helpful man believes me and says he will catch Jade for me, so he takes off running after her. Watching him go around the corner, I shout out to him that she must be going to the station. With a bit of luck, he will catch up to her there, well before she can get on a platform and board a train away from here.

I feel utterly helpless as I wait and hope he's successful; it's an awful position to be in. Things get worse when, a few minutes later, the man reappears from around the corner with a sorry expression on his face.

He doesn't even need to say anything because I know what it means.

He's lost her.

Which means I might have just lost my baby.

Forever.

THIRTY-TWO

JADE

I look back out of the bus window as it leaves the stop where I just boarded and, to my relief, I cannot see Avril anywhere on the street. That gives me hope that she doesn't know I'm on this bus and I might have got away from her.

I was planning on going to the train station but as I was running there, I saw this bus and, realising it was about to leave, I jumped on board. It was a spontaneous decision, but I figure a better one, as Avril must have presumed I was going to the station. If she goes there, she won't find me. I don't actually know where this bus is headed, only that it's going to a different part of the city and that's fine by me. I can figure things out from there.

I just had to get away from her and I have.

But I don't know what happens next.

As the adrenaline decreases, my emotion increases and I start sobbing, attracting the attention of a few of the other passengers on this bus, who look in my direction and must be trying to figure out what is wrong with me. I need to stop crying and try to be as unmemorable as possible, because if the police start searching for me, it won't help if half the people on this bus remember seeing me and can say which direction I went in. It's so hard to stop the tears, and as I fail to do so, a woman takes a seat beside me.

'Are you okay, dear?'

I look at her, this saint of a woman who seems to be concerned for my wellbeing, and think about how I do not deserve the kindness of a stranger. She shouldn't be trying to help me. She shouldn't be worrying about me. She should be phoning the police and getting as far away from me as possible. But she doesn't know my secret. No one on this bus does, which is why it's still driving to its next stop as if it's just another normal journey with normal passengers on board.

'Yeah,' I reply feebly before the woman turns her attention to the baby in the pram beside me.

'Have you been keeping your mummy awake all night?' she asks him jokingly before looking back to me. 'I'm guessing it's sleep deprivation. I didn't sleep well for years when I had my kids. It does get easier, I promise. Now I'm lucky if they come to see me and I'd give anything to go back to when they were little and needed me for everything.'

I should just leave it. I should just stay quiet, smile, and maybe thank this woman for her kind words before letting her know that, yes, it is just sleep deprivation that is causing me to cry, and I appreciate that, like with all new parents, things get easier after the hard stage. That would be the sensible response and, if I did that, this woman would probably just wish me well and then go back to her own seat. But I can't. I literally cannot do it. I cannot take this kindness when I know I don't deserve it, which is why, against my better judgement, I reply with an honest answer.

'It's not sleep deprivation,' I say as I wipe my tears with my hand. 'This baby is fine. He sleeps well every night. That's not the problem. The problem is that he isn't mine.'

The woman frowns, as if she must have misheard me.

'Excuse me, dear?'

'I said he's not mine. This is someone else's son. I stole him from her at the hospital, and I ran onto this bus because she was chasing me and now she's going to go to the police and they'll be looking for me. There's nothing I can do except keep running until they catch me. And then I'll go to prison, and I'll be the most hated woman in the country when this is on the news. When I get out – if I get out – I'll have even less than I had before, which makes me think the best thing for everyone is if I just end it all before then.'

The woman is horrified but I'm not done yet.

'You take him. You have this baby. He'll be safer with you than me. Just tell the police everything I told you and that he needs to be returned to a woman called Avril Anderson. You got that?'

This poor woman must be wishing she hadn't sat down next to me because her quiet bus ride has suddenly taken a very strange turn, and she doesn't look ready to accept the responsibility I am trying to give her.

'I don't understand what you're telling me,' she says as I stand up and press the button that alerts the driver that I wish to get off at the next stop.

As the bus slows down, I consider what I am about to do. To get off the bus and leave this baby with this woman while I try and go on alone, surely improving my chances of success if I'm not slowed down by a pram and child.

'Wait. Let's just talk about this,' the woman tries again, but I've already said way too much and I'm not exactly sure why I confessed everything to her. Now, as the bus comes to a stop, I'm not sure I can even do what I just suggested.

I can't leave the baby with her. I'm sure she would do the right thing, but I cannot be all by myself. For someone who never wanted a child, I suddenly can't face life without the company of one. That's why I change my mind and push the pram towards the doors as they open, causing the woman to call after me as I go.

'Wait!' she tries, but I don't look back.

Once I'm off the bus, I hurry away down the street until I'm out of view of it. I expect that woman is talking to the bus driver now, telling him what I just told her and possibly wanting the police to be called before the bus moves on. But I'm only focused on what's next and when I see the sign for a tube station up ahead, I decide to take a train as far as I can and then figure things out from there.

I see the camera above the ticket machine as I buy a single fare that will get me through the barriers and onto the platform, and I see another camera when I'm there waiting to board. I presume there'll be a camera on the train itself too, another way for an investigating officer to trace my movements, especially when corroborated alongside the witness statement from the woman on the bus. But as the train arrives at the station, I only know one thing.

I've already gone way past the point of no return.

Whatever happens next, I won't go down without a fight.

THIRTY-THREE

AVRIL

As I sat on the cold concrete of the pavement, the pain in my twisted knee competing with the pain in my heart at what I believed was the sight of Jade running away with my baby, it felt like the whole world was crashing down on me. That's why when a member of the public asked me if there was anyone they could call to come and be with me, there was only one answer.

I needed my husband.

I handed over my phone, gave the contact name to the stranger helping me and then allowed them to make the phone call while I sat and wallowed on the hard floor, the crying from the pram next to me as loud as the traffic from the road beside me and all the chatter from the other strangers who had gathered to try and find out what was going on.

As I wait for Bobby to arrive, after no doubt being shocked to receive such a phone call telling him that his wife is in distress in public and needs help, I think about contacting the police again. I already called them when I was outside Jade's flat, and presumably, they have arrived there expecting to see me, though they won't find much because both the occupier of the flat and I are several streets away. I wonder what they will do next. Will they be in touch with me to ask what happened? Or do I need to call them again and tell them what has changed? I don't feel up to making such a phone call and have decided that I will get Bobby to do it when he gets here. He'll be more composed than I am. He's stronger than me. I fear I'll come across as crazy and delusional and it will affect how seriously the police take my claims.

Where is he? He should be here by now. He's a taxi driver, for heaven's sake. He's always in his car, on the road, whizzing around the city. Surely, he could have driven himself here already.

Then I see him, or rather, I see his vehicle. It turns onto the road and comes towards me, stuck behind another car until that one turns left and now Bobby is free to speed up before parking beside me. He leaps out from behind the wheel, looking stunned to see me in such a vulnerable position in the middle of this very busy place, and he quickly tries to help me back to my feet.

'What happened? Can you stand up?' he says, trying to take my arm. I allow him to have a go at lifting me up, though with my injured knee and weak disposition, I doubt I have the strength to stand.

'What have you done?' he asks me as he sees me wince in pain.

'I've hurt my knee,' I cry, trying not to weep but struggling as Bobby continues to attempt to lift me up and, surprisingly, I'm able to get back to my feet, though I need my husband's support to keep me propped up.

'Is Luca okay?' he asks me as he looks in the pram, but I don't bother checking myself.

'That's not Luca,' I say coldly.

'What?'

'That's not our son. *She* has him. We have hers.'

'What the hell are you talking about? Who has him?'

'Jade.'

'Jade who?'

'Who do you think? Jade, the woman you had been on a date with before you met me! She was the one who was in the bed next to ours in hospital and she swapped our babies!'

Bobby stares at me like I'm some insane person who has accosted him on the street, rather than his loving wife who he should trust more than anyone else in the world.

'You're not making any sense,' he tells me as a car horn blares behind him, coming from a frustrated driver who is annoyed the taxi has parked haphazardly at the roadside and is now making it harder for other vehicles to pass.

'She looks very different now to how she used to, but it's definitely her! It's Jade! I was in her bedroom and saw her old passport photo!'

'You were in her bedroom? What are you talking about?'

The horn blares again, only adding to the sense of chaos and confusion on this hectic street. While some members of the public who had stopped have wandered away now, presumably figuring whatever drama was going on is finished, there is still plenty to distract us, making our serious conversation even more difficult.

'You need to believe me!' I cry, grabbing Bobby's shirt collar and pleading with him. 'She has our baby. The real Luca! She ran away with him when I chased her! Why would she do that if she wasn't guilty?'

I feel like that's a perfectly legitimate point, but Bobby has a counterargument that shows me who he believes more at this moment in time.

'You chased someone and accused them of having your child?' he says, incredulous. 'They were probably running away to safety, not because they were guilty of anything!'

I don't believe it. He isn't trusting me on this?

'What part of this don't you understand? Jade, the woman you ditched for me, and who has a reason to have a vendetta against us, has our child! It explains everything. Why our baby was so calm on the first day he was born. How he took to breastfeeding so well. I felt so happy with him, like we had bonded instantly. Then it all changed on day two. He wouldn't stop crying and didn't breastfeed anymore and that's when I felt totally disconnected from him. So it must have happened sometime between those two days. She must have swapped the babies during the night while we were asleep!'

As I'm getting louder and more expressive, Bobby seems to be shutting down, growing quieter and more subdued, and the contrast couldn't be starker between us. All the while, more traffic is building behind his hastily parked car and more horns are blaring. But that isn't the worst thing. That would be how it feels like the distance between us is growing, not reducing.

'I honestly don't know what to say,' Bobby admits, running a hand through his hair, which looks a little unkempt but only because he was up early and didn't have time to groom himself between helping me and the baby and getting out the door to go to work.

'I know, it's hard to believe,' I agree with him. 'We have to act fast. We need to go to the police together and tell them everything and they can catch her. And the hospital can investigate how this was possible. But the most important thing is that we are reunited with our son. We have to get Luca back, before it's too late.'

'No, I don't know what to say because this is so ludicrous,' Bobby replies, shattering my illusion that he might have been starting to believe me. 'Would you just stop and listen to yourself? Baby swapping? Chasing people? The police? Have you lost your mind?'

'What?' I cry, aghast that he thinks this is somehow all in my head.

'I told you to get help. I said you were struggling. You didn't listen and now look what's happened. We don't need the police, we need a doctor, someone to help you because I don't know what to do anymore. And we need to get Luca home because this is no environment for a baby.'

He opens the boot of his car and takes out the spare baby seat he keeps in there that he uses when he's not working, and he quickly starts setting it up on the backseat. He obviously wants to get us in the car and get us home before we can cause any more problems on this street. As he fiddles with the seat, a driver passes by with his window down and shouts an obscenity at my husband for his careless parking, which does little to improve his mood and most likely will make him hate me even more. But I have to shout out to him too.

'You need to believe me!' I try again. 'I already called the police and they'll be at Jade's flat now. We should go there and see them. I can tell them what just happened and they can try and catch her and—'

'You already called the police?' Bobby says, stopping what he's doing and looking mortified.

'Yes! I had to!' I maintain, but he doesn't seem to believe that and as the seat is ready, he takes the baby and starts putting him in the car.

'That's not our son!' I cry out, trying to get him to slow down. 'He is Jade's baby, and she has Luca! Will you stop and just listen to me!'

I'm pulling at Bobby now, trying to get him to turn around and look at me and generally making his task harder, which is why he eventually snaps and spins around, though I wish he hadn't when I see the anger on his face.

'It's been hard since we had Luca, I'm not denying that, but you're the one who is making it harder,' he tells me. 'Now either you get in this car with us and we go home together, or I leave you here by the roadside. But I am getting our son out of here because it's not fair on him, and it's not fair on me to have to listen to your wild theories in public!'

Bobby shuts the back passenger door and gets in behind the wheel, and in that instant, I fear I am losing him just like I have already lost Luca. That's why I rush to get in the car before he can drive away, not wanting to be left by the roadside surrounded by gawking pedestrians and angry motorists.

No sooner have I shut my door than Bobby starts driving, pulling out into the busy traffic and attracting even more car horns, but we're moving away now and leaving that chaos behind.

The problem is the chaos won't disappear that easily.

All the while, I have no idea where it is that Jade is going.

THIRTY-FOUR

JADE

I disembark from the train one stop short of the end of the line, still living as a free woman, but for how much longer remains to be seen. It might be a while yet if I can find somewhere to lie low around here, and as I make my way through the small station in this town, I am pleased when I don't see a camera tracking my every move. I'm well out of the busy city now, swapping those hectic, CCTV-covered streets for this quieter place that is popular with commuters who want to earn the big city wages but live somewhere with a slightly cheaper postcode.

I push the pram out of the station and look around the first street I arrive on, trying to get my bearings, looking for somewhere I can stay for tonight. Anywhere cheap will do. A basic bed and breakfast, or even a homeless shelter for people down on their luck if they have such a thing here. Somewhere affordable I can hide out until my next child benefit payment comes in, which is due tomorrow. Then, when I've got that extra bit of cash in my bank account, I can make a firmer plan about what to do next. For now, I just need to get off the streets and out of sight, so I keep walking, pushing the pram while looking around hopefully for somewhere to stay.

I've gone about ten minutes from the station when I see the sign for a motel, and the closer I get, the more I feel it might fit my criteria. It certainly looks basic, which equals affordable, and it's big enough for there to be a few people here but not so big as for there to be too many who might recognise me should my face make the news later today. Then again, I don't want to be the only person staying, as that could make me stick out even more. I just want to try and blend in, though it remains to be seen if that's possible considering I have a baby with me.

I go inside and instantly find the reception, offering a smile to the young man behind the desk.

'Can I have a room for tonight, please?' I ask him hopefully, holding my breath as his eyes survey me and then the pram. I really hope they don't have some kind of 'no-children' policy, because if so, I'm out of luck.

'Just the one night?'

'It might be more. I'm not sure yet,' I say as I take out my purse and rummage through the last bit of cash I have. The next child benefit payment can't come soon enough, and I'm grateful it gets paid digitally so it can get to me wherever I am.

'Thirty-five pounds,' the man says, and I hand him the price for the room. Though I'm pleased it's cheap, I don't expect it will get me very much. Probably just a bed and a communal bathroom, but it's better than wandering the streets all night.

'Last door on the right,' the man says as he hands me a rusty-looking key, and I take it before hurrying away to find my room, more than eager to get inside.

In the corridor I take a deep breath without anyone else's eyes on me. Well, anyone apart from the baby staring up at me from the pram. He's been on quite the journey today, but hopefully it's over now.

As I find the last door on the right and slide the key in the lock, I know I'm not going to spend the first ten minutes in this room doing what most people do after check-in. I won't be unpacking my belongings, as I don't have many. Not after I had to leave my large rucksack behind during the chase with Avril. All I have now is the small rucksack on my shoulder that is full of items for Calum – bottles, milk and nappies. At least he has what he needs. As for me, I'm going to have to learn to live off even less than I was living off before.

I push open the flimsy door and see what I expected, which is a very basic room with a bed and wardrobe, and there's only just enough room for me to push the pram in and close the door behind me. I figure Calum can just sleep in the bed with me, if there's any sleep to be had – the mattress hardly looks the most comfortable, but it'll do for tonight.

It's a surprise to notice a small TV on the wall, and I can't resist turning it on to see if I've made the news yet. I desperately don't want to see my face on the bulletins, but it's a possibility, and I'm better off knowing if it's happening. I can't find anything yet. No mention of me or any baby-swapping incidents. But just because everyone with access to the news channels doesn't know yet, it doesn't mean Avril doesn't know. She's figured out what I've done and if I was in her position, I'd be telling anybody who would listen, so it can't be long until this is big news. There's also the fact that it's scandalous: a hospital where members of the public go to have their children being at the centre of such a shocking thing as Avril is going to accuse me of. There'll be investigations, public outcries, calls for people to lose their jobs, people desperate to know how such a thing could happen and, heaven forbid, if there's a chance it could happen to some other family in the future. The publicity for the hospital won't only be bad, it will be damning, but I'm sure they'll find a way to apologise, pay a fine and survive it. But as for me, there'll be absolutely no coming back from it once the accusations are out there, especially when it will only take a simple DNA test to prove that I have Avril's baby, and she has mine.

. . .

I spend some time crying into the thin and flat pillow I've been provided with, and then I feed Calum after he started to make sounds which I have come to know mean he is hungry. Then I change his nappy before realising that I can't put off using the communal bathroom forever, so I will have to venture out of my room if I want to relieve myself before going to bed.

I unlock and open the door and peer out into the corridor, but there's no one around, so I carry Calum with me to the bathroom. When I enter, it's even more of a relief to see that no one else is in here. I see three toilet cubicles as well as a rather grim-looking shower curtain hanging down in the corner, so I enter the nearest cubicle quickly and try to do what I need to do whilst holding a baby at the same time.

It's awkward and uncomfortable but I manage it, simply because I have no choice but to. While I have previously and strongly considered leaving Calum with somebody I deem to be trustworthy, I am certainly not leaving him unattended here in my bedroom, when I have no idea of the character of the people who might be staying in a room nearby.

I flush the toilet and leave the cubicle and I'm eagerly rushing back to my bedroom, thinking that I've done well to not be seen by anybody since I left, but then, just at the last second, I hear a door open and a man pops his head out from the bedroom two doors down from mine. He has long hair, a beard and the kind of eyes that offer more darkness than light. I instantly sense that this is not the kind of person I want to be chatting to. But he seems eager to talk to me.

'Hello there. You're new. When did you get here?'

I consider answering but realise I don't have to, especially if I'm feeling uncomfortable in his presence, so I step into my room.

'What's your baby's name?' he asks me, but I ignore that too and go to close the door, hearing him say one more thing as I do.

'I'll see you soon, beautiful.'

The short and simple sentence sends a shiver down my spine, and as I close and lock the door, I'm hoping it's just a casual thing he has said and not something that he actually thinks might be true. But I get my answer a few seconds later when I hear movement on the other side of the door.

I freeze as I hear a foot drag across the carpet, and I fear that man is now right outside my room and about to try and come in. Sure enough, I hear a knock a second later.

I stay quiet.

But he doesn't.

'Open up. I just want to talk. Let's get to know one another. I'm great with kids if that's what you're worried about.'

I realise he isn't going to leave me alone unless I make it obvious that I don't want company, so I break my silence and call out to him.

'Sorry, I'm really tired. I'm going to sleep,' I say, hoping he'll respect that and leave.

'I'm sure there's room in that bed for the both of us,' comes the chilling reply, and then to my horror, I see the door handle moving.

He's trying to get inside.

'Go away!' I call out, glad there is a lock keeping him out, but this door isn't the thickest and I fear he could force his way inside if he really wanted to. And I guess he does because the handle wriggles faster before he knocks again.

Realising I can't put all my trust in the cheap lock, I put Calum down on the bed before pushing the pram up against the door and holding it against it as hard as I can. I'm hoping the extra weight from this side will prevent the door from opening should the lock break. But the man is not discouraged, trying the handle several more times as well as calling out to me with the nonsensical idea that we could keep each other company tonight.

Finally, after what feels like an age, Calum and I are left

alone when the man stops trying to open the door and walks away, though he doesn't leave without a menacing warning.

'Maybe I'll see you during the night,' he says.

As I listen to him leave and hear his bedroom door close down the corridor, one thing is for certain now: I am not going to get a wink of sleep in this place. I'm going to have to sit up all night and watch the door whilst watching over Calum too.

But as bad as that is, I doubt I'll be the only one having a restless night.

THIRTY-FIVE
AVRIL

My husband has made it clear that he thinks my theory about the baby swap is the newest and most dramatic symptom of my postnatal depression yet. I'm pretty sure that, at this point, he thinks that he and the baby we are caring for would be better off without me getting in the way. I might even go so far as to say he hates me. But if he doesn't already, there's a strong chance now because he's really not going to like what I've just done.

I received a phone call from a police officer who was following up after the events earlier today. They wanted to know where I was when they arrived, probably thinking I had made a prank call and caused a fuss over nothing on account of not being at Jade's apartment. I could have just apologised, said there had been a mistake and left it there. That's what Bobby would have expected me to do considering he was mortified that I called the police in the first place. Instead, I did what feels right, and what I've been wanting to do this whole time, except Bobby has always kept me from doing so. I told the police that Jade still has my baby and has done a runner, and they have to locate her immediately. I was able to do all this after going upstairs under the pretence of taking a nap. Bobby was hardly going to get me to stay downstairs with him and the baby, not after all the arguing we had been doing since we got home. But no sooner had I left him than I answered the call and told the police to come here and, by my calculations, they should be here any minute now.

Bobby is really not going to like it when they turn up.

As I hear a car parking outside, I go to an upstairs window and look out. When I do, I see two police officers walking down our driveway. There's no going back now, so I rush downstairs to let them in. Rather me than my husband, who is currently preoccupied with a crying baby.

Jade's crying baby.

I open the door and see two very stern faces looking back at me.

'Mrs Anderson?' the older, more grizzled officer asks, and I nod my head. 'I'm PC Barlow and this is PC Kane. You made the call earlier about your baby?' he asks next, wanting confirmation before we go any further.

I can give him that and more.

'Yes, that's right. I believe he was swapped not long after his birth, and I know who has him. Her name is—'

'What's going on?'

Bobby's voice behind me interrupts my flow, and as I turn around, I see him standing in the kitchen doorway, a baby in his arms and an incredulous look on his face.

'Come in,' I say to the officers whilst ignoring my husband. 'I need to give you as much information as I can about Jade so you can find her. It's already been too long but I don't think she has much money so she can't have gone far and—'

'Avril, what is going on?' Bobby repeats, his voice much louder than the first time.

'They called me back. They wanted to find out what happened earlier, so I told them,' I explain. 'I told them how I chased Jade, and she ran away, which proves she is guilty!'

The more I say, the more disgusted Bobby seems to get, and as I look back at the officers, it appears they are not sure what to make of the dynamic between us.

'I take it you're the father of the baby in question,' PC Barlow assumes.

'Yes, he's the father and that baby he is holding is not ours. We thought it was our son, but I knew something was wrong, though I had no idea what it was until I bumped into her. She was in the hospital bed next to us on the maternity ward, and when I saw her after that, she was acting strange. She was trying to avoid me, but I was able to track her down to her flat and when I went inside, I found out who she really was and—'

'I need help,' Bobby interrupts. 'I can't do this anymore. My wife has not been herself since we had our baby, but this is going too far. To accuse somebody of swapping our baby. It makes no sense. Why would a woman give up her own baby to take ours?'

'Because we know her, and she has a vendetta against us!' I say, which is something I've said to him several times since he first came to me on the street earlier, but he hasn't taken it on board yet.

'You say you know Jade. What's your relationship?' PC Kane enquires.

'He was on a date with her on the night we met, but he obviously ended up with me. I guess when she saw us together at the hospital, she wanted revenge. She's crazy. She's a stalker.'

'We don't even know it's her for sure,' Bobby says, exasperated. 'The woman I saw at the hospital looks nothing like the woman I went on a date with years ago.'

'She's changed her appearance!' I cry. 'But it is her! I saw her passport!'

The more frustrated I get, the more I fear I am looking and sounding like a paranoid, crazy person, which is the point Bobby is trying to make.

'You say she wanted revenge on you?' PC Kane says, looking at me. 'And she did this by swapping her child for yours.'

'Yes, that's exactly what I'm saying!' I am pleased that somebody seems to be listening to me.

The two officers share a glance, and I recognise the look on their faces as the one Bobby has been showing me all day. They don't believe me. They think it sounds too far-fetched. They think a mother would never give up her own child in the name of revenge. But that's what has happened here. How do I make everyone believe me?

'Let's do a DNA test, right now!' I suggest. 'That will prove this baby did not come from me! You'll see that I'm right then. Please, I'm begging you, just give me a chance to prove what I know. Jade has my baby. I can feel it. I know it's him. It's my baby boy. She has him and...'

My voice trails off as I collapse to the floor, sobbing and shaking and feeling like all the strength has just suddenly drained out of my body. It's too much, it's overwhelming, the thought that I might have lost my son and will never see him again. Who knows what Jade is capable of? If she can do something as drastic as this then she can do anything. Like harm my baby. Or leave him somewhere where he isn't safe. Somewhere he can't be cared for. Then what if it's too late to save him?

'Help me, please,' I weep, tears pouring down my face as I sit in a crumpled heap on the hallway floor. 'Please do something to get my baby back.'

I feel hands on me then and realise I am being helped back to my feet by both the officers, who guide me into the lounge where I take a seat on the sofa, still sobbing but at least a little more comfortable now.

One officer stays with me, though I'm not sure who because my vision is blurry and I don't lift my head to take a proper look at him, partly out of shame but also because I'm simply too upset. But I hear the other officer talking in the hallway. He's speaking privately with Bobby, though I can just about make out what is being said, despite their low voices.

'Sir, this is highly unusual, and while we will look into the accusation your wife is making, I need to ask for your opinion on this,' the officer says, and I have a feeling it's PC Barlow. 'I'm getting the impression that you don't believe what your wife is telling us. Is that correct?'

I listen out for Bobby's answer, as if the future of this investigation hinges on it, as well as the future of our marriage. I know he's said so far he doesn't think it can possibly be true, but right now, this is the moment of truth. What will he say to this police officer?

'She needs some help,' he tells PC Barlow with sorrow in his voice.

'I see,' the officer replies, understanding exactly what he means by that response – and so do I.

Jade is the villain here.

Yet my husband has just told the police that I am.

THIRTY-SIX

JADE

It's hardly a surprise that I got no sleep last night. That's just what happens when you're in an unfamiliar place and have had to stay up and guard the door in case a crazy man tries getting inside your bedroom. Thankfully, the man who tried unsuccessfully to get in earlier did not return, possibly because I reported him to the guy on reception, but maybe just because he realised I wasn't going to be a pushover and would fight back even if he did get inside. But that didn't mean I could rest. I had to stay awake and keep watch, make sure I was safe, and Calum too.

I've been finding myself calling him that a lot more, as well as worrying about him more frequently too. Not only has that surprised me, but I know it's wrong. I shouldn't be getting attached to him. He's not mine and he never can be. But all this time we are spending together is forming a bond between us. I am his guardian and safekeeper when it's just the two of us, there's no denying that. He depends on me, and the longer this goes on, the more I feel like I'm starting to depend on him too.

As I've been awake all night, there's been no need to set an alarm to wake up. I get up as soon as I see the first evidence of daylight beyond the thin curtain over the window. Calum is still sleeping so I work quickly around him, gathering up our things because I plan to get out of here as soon as possible and never come back. My next child benefit payment should have hit my account today, so I plan to withdraw that money and then find somewhere more suitable for us to stay. The thought has occurred to me that if the police are looking for me, there may be someone monitoring my bank account, but I just have to hope that's not the case yet. Even if Avril has reported me and made her allegation, there will have to be an investigation, which takes time, and that's assuming the police believe her. But will they? Or will what she tells them sound very unbelievable?

I check the news while Calum sleeps, the volume turned down low, but I only need to see the pictures anyway. I will recognise my photo if it shows up on any of the early morning bulletins, but it does not, which gives me the confidence boost I need to leave this room and go back out into the world again.

They say to never wake a sleeping baby, but I take that risk by stirring Calum from his slumber, and while he grizzles a little bit, he soon relaxes when I give him a quick bottle of milk. Then, with Calum already back in a contented and sleepy state, I push his pram out of the dingy bedroom, unfortunately having to go past that nefarious man's bedroom on my way to reception, but thankfully, he does not emerge. He's probably asleep, as I assume most people in this motel are, but there is somebody behind reception as I pass it. It's a young woman this time and she's flicking through a fashion and cosmetics magazine while sipping an energy drink. I consider telling her that this really is not a safe place for someone like her to work, but I decide against it, as she's most likely just like me: a person who needs money so accepts whatever job they can get to survive. I also consider telling her something else, which is that the magazine she is reading, the one with the model on the front in the bright red lipstick, is all an illusion and that the cosmetics world is not as glamorous as it is made out to be. Maybe she has ambitions of trying to get a job in that world one day and I could save her the potential heartache or worse. Or even if she's someone with only an interest, I could enlighten her as to the darker side of that world, away from all the colourful make-up and bright camera flashes. But in the end, I leave it, passing her by with my pram. Although as I go, she looks up at me for a fleeting moment and she seems sad at my appearance, as if she knows this is no place for me to be either.

The cool morning air goes some way to easing my crushing fatigue, and the further away I get from the motel, the better I feel. The sun is out, so maybe this won't be such a bad day after all. As I find a cash machine, I quickly take out my bank card and insert it so that I can get my cash and get out of here.

I nervously look over both shoulders after entering my pin number, as if I believe a team of police officers are suddenly going to swarm on me now they have electronically pinpointed my location. But that doesn't happen, although that doesn't mean I'm happy. That's because, despite trying to withdraw the money I need, I am met with the dreaded words that nobody ever wants to see when they are desperate for cash.

Insufficient funds

'What?' I say out loud, as if asking a question of an inanimate object is going to get me anywhere. Of course, the cash machine cannot answer, so I have little choice but to try again, re-entering my pin and assuming there simply must have been a fault the first time. There was no fault, at least not with the bank. I'm told the same thing as the first time. There is not enough money in my account for me to complete the withdrawal.

'No,' I say, fearing that something has gone wrong with my latest child benefit payment. Could the police have put a stop on it? No, surely not. They couldn't have moved that quickly, could they? Maybe there's an issue with the benefit system. An IT glitch or something. Maybe the money will come through soon. I can't just hang around and wait for it to do that, though, so I decide to be proactive and call the benefit office to find out exactly what is going on.

I'm on hold for what feels like forever, but it's always the way with these kinds of things, and as I wait, I wonder if I'll even get to speak to a human or will it be some artificial voice prompting me with infuriating questions that don't help me at all?

It's a relief both when my call eventually connects and when I hear there is a real person on the other end of the line.

'Hello. Yes, I'm ringing because I haven't received my child benefit payment today,' I say quickly before I'm forced to slow down a little and answer several questions, including my name, my child's name, dates of birth and more things that don't get me my money any faster. Once all that is done, I hope to be told that there must have been a mistake, and they'll send the money now.

But when is my life ever as easy as that?

'It seems there is a problem,' the person at the other end of the line tells me.

'Yes, I know there is, that's why I'm calling,' I reply, growing frustrated.

'We're missing some details for you on our system which we need to complete the next payment.'

'What details? I gave you everything I needed when I applied!'

'Yeah, sorry, we've been having a few issues with our IT system and it lost some data over the weekend,' I'm told, which is not my fault but seems to be my problem.

'So what does that mean? When am I going to get the money I need for my child?' I ask, cutting to the chase.

'I'm afraid we can't process the payment until we have the

information we need. Could you come in to your nearest centre and we can sort it then? It shouldn't take more than ten minutes.'

'Come in? No, I can't,' I cry, fearing the thought of having to take the train all the way back to where I just ran away from. 'Can't we just do it over the phone now?'

'I'm afraid not. We need you to re-sign a few documents. Like I said, it shouldn't take long, and we'll be able to process the payment then.'

'I can't come in. Please, there must be another way. Can you send me what I need to do online? I have my phone. I could do it that way and—'

'I'm sorry. Like I said, we're having IT issues and we apologise, but I can't send anything to you digitally. When would be the most convenient time for you to come in?'

'There is no convenient time!' I cry, feeling like my only way of having any money has just evaporated before my eyes.

This feels like rotten bad luck, the kind only reserved for the people who deserve it most, but while that thought makes me feel sad, my next thought makes me feel afraid. What if this isn't some IT glitch, but rather a trick by the police to get me to come to them? They could have put a stop on my payment and then come up with this ruse of me needing to go to the office to get it sorted. That way, rather than having to try and find me, I would walk right into their handcuffs.

Is that what this is? If so, I can't go to the office, can I?

But if I don't, I have no money, and this is my only chance to get it.

I leave the woman hanging at the other end of the phone line as I look down at Calum in his pram and ask him a question he is far too young to answer.

'What do I do?'

THIRTY-SEVEN

AVRIL

I must have passed out from exhaustion at some point last night, or maybe, after crying for so long, the gods took mercy on me and made me have some rest, knowing there were only so many tears I could possibly shed in such a short amount of time. Whatever it was that caused me to drift off, when I wake up I see that I've only been out for an hour. But I hear nothing but silence, which makes me worry even more.

Where is everyone?

I get out of bed and rush downstairs, but every room is empty, barring the furniture, though most of it is covered by various baby items like clothes, muslins, towels and packets of nappies and creams. But as for the baby? Nowhere to be seen. Neither is my husband.

'Bobby! Where are you?' I call out as I wander around my spacious home, but they're definitely not here and I get confirmation of that when I notice Bobby's car is not on the driveway.

Panicking because I fear he has left me, I try calling him, but while he doesn't answer, I do receive a text message a few minutes later, suggesting he ignored my calls because he didn't want to hear my voice.

*I've taken Luca to my mother's. She's watching him while I go
to work.*

He's still calling him Luca. He still isn't listening to me.
Then another message comes through.

I can't do this anymore.

That's the confirmation, not that I needed it, that Bobby is
not on my side and has had enough of me and what our relationship has become. I could get angry at him now, or upset again
like I did last night when I heard him tell the policeman that he
didn't believe me, but I don't, as that would be a huge waste of
time. What I need to do is take action. My husband's scepticism
is the reason the police aren't rushing to help me like they
normally would when such a serious crime is reported, and he's
obviously expressed enough doubt to make them think this is all
some symptom of my struggle since becoming a mum. I need
them to help me; I certainly don't need them suggesting I get
professional help for my mental health because that would be a
total waste of time. That's why I went for a lie-down. All it does
is confirm that I will have to help myself and prove that everybody is wrong, and I am right.

*I will do a DNA test on the baby we brought home from the
hospital.*

All I need to do is figure out the fastest way to obtain such a
test, but I presume I could get it online like anything else. That
must be the quickest way, plus it would come without the added
complications of having to explain why I'm doing it, if I was to
go via a doctor or someone else in a hospital. Why would I want
to do that if they will think I'm mad? And why would I ever put
my trust in those kinds of people and places again if they helped
contribute to this disaster in the first place?

I use my phone to search around online for a DNA test and

then I place my order, opting for the quickest delivery option possible, which is actually later today. According to this website, if I send back the test before 10 a.m. tomorrow, I can have the results later that day, which means, potentially, I will have definitive proof in twenty-four hours. With the DNA test ordered, I am still wishing there was something I could make happen faster because every second that I think of Jade being with my baby is terrifying. But at least it feels like I've done something, although I know opening the test results will be extremely daunting.

Either I am told that my baby has indeed been swapped, which is truly frightening. Or I am told that I have the right baby at home with me, in which case, I guess I have been the worst mother in the world and it's no wonder Bobby wants to leave me.

But I am right. I feel it in my gut. Jade has Luca, which means, right now, Bobby's mother is looking after a baby who is not her real grandchild.

I consider calling her and explaining what is going on, but I assume Bobby has already told her about my theory and, as his mother, I presume she is on his side rather than mine. Therefore, it might be a waste of time to try and get some sympathy from her, so I leave it, though I will make a call to somebody.

I try the police again, seeking an update on what they are doing. It takes a while for me to get through to the person I need, but eventually, I get a police officer who can help, or at least pretend to.

'We are still seeking Ms White, but so far, we haven't been able to locate her,' I'm told.

'What are you doing to find her?' I ask, hoping there is a long list of tactics they can use.

'She hasn't returned to her address yet, and her next-door neighbour hasn't seen her. Neither has her baby's father.'

'Excuse me?'

I have no idea what he means by 'her baby's father'.

'There was a gentleman outside the address with the neighbour, and he claims to be the father of the baby Ms White is with. He is as keen to find her as you are.'

So I'm not the only one with a vested interest in finding this baby. By the sounds of it, the man who believes he is the father is very much trying to be a part of his child's life too. But it's not his baby. Which means I have his baby, or at least I did until Bobby took him to his mother's.

'You need to find her. This situation can't be resolved without her,' I say, overwhelmed by how much of a mess this is and how many different lives it is impacting. The only saving grace is that the two babies involved are far too young to remember any of it, but that's only if this gets fixed quickly. The older they get, the more this will impact on the people they grow up to be.

I miss what the police officer at the other end of the line says because I choke up, the thought of my son growing up hitting me hard, or rather, the thought that he might never grow up because Jade might do something awful to him.

'I just want my baby back,' I cry down the phone, the blood-curdling, anguished cry of a desperate mother that is loud enough for the people several streets away to hear.

As I sink to the floor, the phone drops from my limp hand. I lean back against the wall and weep. I feel the odds of finding Jade are diminishing rapidly.

There's no way she'd ever come back.

She might be crazy and deluded, but she's smart enough to not take that risk.

She must be getting further away from here by the second.

THIRTY-EIGHT

JADE

I can't believe I'm going back into the city.

Back to where I ran away from.

Back to where Avril and the police and everybody else will be looking for me.

I have no choice. I need my child benefit money, likely the last bit of money I will get before the police freeze the account. Maybe they've already done that and I'm walking into a trap, but I have less than ten pounds to my name now, so I have to take this chance. I've simply run out of money to run any further. Hopefully, I can get the money I'm owed and be gone again and that will buy me a week or so to figure out another income stream. But as a single mum, I know I won't be able to work with such a small baby alongside me, not in the few and poorly paid industries that would ever hire me. That is why, as this train reaches the station and I prepare to get off, I'm having to accept the fact that, at some point, I'm going to have to leave Calum behind. But not yet. One, because it will look good if I turn up to collect my child benefit payment with an actual child in tow, but two, because I am not quite ready to let go of him.

I push the pram off the train, smiling weakly at the kindly

man who offers to help me and holds back some of the passengers who are trying to board so that I have space to disembark. That's one huge thing I've noticed since having a baby. *People notice me now.* Before, I was just a solitary, sad figure, but now, with a baby, it's as if everybody sees me and not only that but they smile at me.

She's a mother. She must be so caring. She must know what she's doing.

She must be a good person.

I'm not ready to go back to being totally invisible just yet. I guess I've gradually got used to motherhood, and even started to enjoy it. From thinking it was the last thing in the world I would be good at, what if my lack of confidence in myself has destroyed my real destiny? What if I had given it time with my baby, fighting through that initial stage in hospital when I felt overwhelmed, both by his crying and a need for revenge on Avril? I could have bonded with my baby, and he could have given me the purpose that I have been lacking for so long. But it's too late for that now. Even if I have started to enjoy the way people look at me when I have a baby with me, it's not much use if I'm on the run and trying to avoid attention.

I obviously don't want to be recognised now, so I keep my head down as I push the pram along the busy streets before I reach the address the woman on the phone gave me earlier. It's a fairly bland building, and as I walk inside, I see several employees in bland attire walking around, which fits with the general aesthetic of the place. Fortunately, I don't see any police officers, and as I join a large queue, I'm thinking I was told the truth about the IT glitch. That's because it's obvious that all the people in this line are here for the same reason as I am. I get confirmation of that when I hear the person at the front arguing with the poor employee behind the desk.

'Where's my money? I need my money!'

Yep, they're definitely here for the same reason as I am.

Relaxing a little, but only ever so slightly, I impatiently wait my turn to be seen. When I reach the front, I explain why I'm here, and the weary employee who has been dealing with this issue all morning then begins to deal with it for me.

I have to complete some paperwork, but it's nothing that I didn't do the first time when I applied for the benefit payment. However, my circumstances have changed because I'm no longer at the address they have listed for me. I don't tell them that, though, opting for speed and success rather than creating the confusion that would come if I told them I was currently moving around with my baby with no fixed abode.

'Your money should be in your account by midday,' I'm told, which is only an hour away, so that will have to do. I leave the exhausted employee to deal with the next person in the line.

Stepping outside, I'm conscious that I should probably stay in the area rather than leave straight away, just in case my money doesn't go into my account at midday, and I need to go back. So I decide to while away that time by going in and out of a few shops, taking the chance as I do to check the newspapers that are on sale in a few of them. I'm making sure that my face isn't on any of the front pages, or indeed any of the pages inside. But it's not. There is no news yet about a baby swap and Avril's desperate search for me.

The longer I'm here, the more emboldened I am feeling, but I know that I shouldn't push my luck.

When the clock strikes midday, I go to a cash machine to check my balance. To my eternal relief, the benefit payment has landed in my account, so I now have the funds necessary to keep going.

I withdraw all of the money just in case the police do freeze the account at some point, and then I march to the train station, pushing my pram with a little spring in my step because I am feeling optimistic for the first time since I ran away from here.

It's amazing what a little money and freedom can do.

I see the station entrance up ahead but have to slow down when a car drives in front of me. I steer the pram around the vehicle blocking my route and am just about to go inside when I hear somebody shouting.

'Hey! Excuse me?'

I turn around instinctively, not expecting that the person calling out is speaking to me, just a natural reaction to hearing a noise behind me. But as I do, I realise my mistake. The person is talking to me and when I see their face, I know exactly who it is.

It's Bobby.

'Hey, thanks for stopping. Sorry, I didn't mean to startle you,' he says as he reaches me, and I realise he was the one driving the car that just parked in front of me.

As shocked as I am to see him, I'm just as shocked at how polite he is being with me. Why isn't he shouting at me and accusing me of stealing a baby and, most of all, why isn't he trying to take the baby away from me now? Basically, why is he not acting like his wife?

'I recognise you from the hospital. Do you remember? We were in the bed next to you,' Bobby says, still sounding very friendly.

'Erm,' I mumble, trying to get a read on him. Surely Avril told him about me and what she thinks I've done? And surely she mentioned who I really am, which means he would know I'm the woman he once went on a couple of dates with.

'Look, I just wanted to apologise,' he says, surprising me further. 'My wife, Avril, has told me what happened between you. How she chased you and how she thinks you swapped our babies in the hospital.'

So she has told him.

'Obviously, it's a ludicrous accusation and I'm sorry for any distress it might have caused to you and your baby,' Bobby goes on, looking into the pram. *Looking at his son.*

'Avril has been struggling a lot since the birth and I fear this is just another symptom of that struggle,' he says, seemingly still on my side. 'I'm trying to get her help. I just wanted to make sure you were okay. I saw you walking down the street as I drove past, so I wanted to catch up with you and just check everything's all right.'

I honestly have no idea what to say to all of this, but if Bobby seems fine with me, maybe I should pretend like I'm fine too.

'I'm okay,' I reply, figuring that's all he needs to hear.

'You are? Oh good. I've been worried. Especially since Avril got the police involved. I didn't know if they'd been hassling you too, but hopefully not.'

The police? *So they do know about me.*

'I need to get going,' I say, turning back to the station, but Bobby reaches out and takes hold of the pram handle, stopping me from going anywhere.

'Look, I know who you are,' he says as I stare at his hand. 'Avril told me. We went on a few dates together. You've changed a lot since then, and I admit I didn't recognise you at the hospital, but you must recognise me? I haven't changed at all, well, barring a little extra weight over the years.'

He chuckles then as he pats his stomach with his spare hand, while his other one remains firmly on the pram.

'You do recognise me, don't you?' he asks, and I nod. 'I just wanted to say that the reason I didn't contact you again after our date was because Avril told me a few things about you. Things that may or may not be true, but I believed her at the time. Anyway, after what's happened recently, I'm starting to think that it might be Avril who is the one with issues. That's not your problem, so I just wanted to make sure you are okay and there are no hard feelings.'

I can't believe this. *Bobby is taking my side over his wife's?*

'I'm okay, thank you,' I say, figuring I should quit while I'm ahead. 'And there are no hard feelings.'

'Great,' Bobby replies with a smile and then, to my relief, he lets go of the pram. 'All the best to you and your son.'

I move away, pushing the pram into the station and leaving him behind as quickly as I can. My heart is still thumping even after I've made it onto the platform, and it doesn't slow down as the train arrives and I get on board. Only as the train is moving away do I start to relax a little.

That was far too close for comfort, but I got away with it. I also have some useful information. Bobby doesn't believe his wife's baby swap theory and that means the police might not believe her either.

If so, maybe I can get away with this after all, and what I have done has clearly worked. It sounds like Avril's life has been in ruins recently, which was my initial intention based on how she ruined mine. But I had underestimated the impact my revenge would have on me too. How much it would take out of me. And how much I would end up regretting giving away my son.

Was it worth ruining Avril if I've ruined myself in the process? I thought it was about which one of us would win.

But what if we both lose?

THIRTY-NINE

AVRIL

It's going dark and I'm still home alone. I understand Bobby has left the baby with his mother, but I would have thought he would have come back to talk to me at some point. But he hasn't phoned or sent me a text message, and he certainly hasn't shown up here to speak to me face to face. I'm just sitting here in our quiet house wondering what to do, but confident about one thing.

My husband is actively avoiding me.

He must be because he's never stayed out this late at work before. Even though taxi drivers can work unusual and unsociable hours, Bobby never did. He worked in the daytime while I was out so he could be home with me in the evenings. If anything, I was the one staying out late while he waited for me to walk through the door. But things have changed, although I doubt it's because he's out there still driving around trying to earn extra money.

It's because he does not want to be anywhere near me.

I stop looking at the door and look down at the thing I've been holding ever since it arrived this afternoon. The package in my hand was given to me by a smiling delivery driver three hours ago, and I've been clutching it ever since because, as far as I'm concerned, this item holds the key to getting my baby back. It's the DNA test I ordered online this morning and, since it got here, I have read and re-read the instructions of how to use it, though it still remains in its packaging. That's because I don't currently have a baby to test it on. I considered driving over to Bobby's mum's place, but I feared I wouldn't get time alone with the baby to get what I needed without her seeing me and stopping me. I figured I'd wait until Bobby got home and then explain how the DNA test would sort this out once and for all, and then I expected we would both drive over and collect the baby together before taking the test as a couple. But I wasn't banking on Bobby being home this late. As the kitchen clock keeps ticking on, there is still no sign of him.

To my surprise, I see the flash of headlights through the curtains and hear an engine getting closer, and as I go to check the window, I see my husband parking his car on the driveway.

So he has come home.

Now I suddenly wish he hadn't.

My stomach is churning as I fear we are about to argue all over again, but as Bobby walks through the door, it seems I'm bracing myself for the wrong thing.

He doesn't look angry.

He looks like he's up to something.

'You never work late,' I say quietly as I try to gauge what is going on, but I could never have predicted it in my wildest dreams.

'I wasn't working,' he replies as he closes the door. 'I was following someone.'

'What?'

'I bumped into Jade outside a tube station at lunchtime and then I followed her,' he says as if it's the most casual thing in the world to be telling me. 'That's why I'm so late. I ended up going pretty far. But I know where she is now.'

'You saw Jade?'

'Yep.'

'Why didn't you call me? Have you told the police? Do they have her now? Where's our son? Is he okay?'

I rush towards my husband and take hold of his arms, desperate for information. While it's good news that he saw her, I'm wondering why he doesn't seem particularly elated.

'I talked to her. I wanted to get an idea of her state of mind. I didn't call you or the police because she was about to board a train, and if I lost sight of her, I figured she'd be hard to find again. So I got on the train too.'

'Where is she?'

'She's staying at a motel about an hour's drive from here. I just came back on the train and picked up my car.'

I cannot believe Bobby has been following Jade all this time and not just avoiding me like I thought he was. This must surely mean one thing...

'So you believe me now? That she has our baby? That she swapped him!' I cry, desperate for him finally to be on the same side as me.

'Let's just say that she definitely seemed nervous when I was talking to her,' Bobby tells me. 'She was eager to get away. She also looked spooked when I mentioned the police.'

'Of course she did. It's because she's guilty!' I cry.

'I know you're convinced of that, but I'm still not sure. That's why I think we should be cautious.'

'Cautious?'

'Yes. I've asked Mum to have Luca for tonight.'

'Jade has Luca,' I remind him, but he just ignores that.

'Mum has the baby tonight,' he repeats. 'I thought we could go to this motel in the morning and try and speak to Jade again. The three of us. Talk this through. Sort it out once and for all.'

'We're not waiting until the morning,' I tell him, grabbing my coat from the hook and looking for my shoes. 'We're going tonight. I'm not letting that woman out of my sight, and you shouldn't have done so either. You should have stayed watching her and I would have come to you. She could have gone out again. She could have moved on, then how would we find her?'

I locate my shoes and now I'm ready to get going, but Bobby is not moving as quickly as I am.

'What are you waiting for? We need to get going!' I tell him.

'We need to stay calm and be sensible,' he replies. 'If you're wrong about this, you'll be the one in trouble with the police, not her.'

'But she has our baby! I thought you believed me now! You followed her because you must believe me!'

'I followed her because I'm not sure what to believe anymore,' Bobby admits. 'I just know that we need to resolve this one way or the other, and I'd prefer to do it without getting the police involved unless we absolutely have to.'

'Okay, we'll play it safe and sensible if that's what you want,' I concede. 'And I swear if I'm wrong then you can leave me and do whatever you want, but I'm not wrong, I'm telling you, I know it for sure. She has our son, Bobby. She has our baby boy and it's time we got him back. So please can we stop wasting time and go to that motel before Jade has the chance to get away again.'

'Okay,' Bobby says, letting out a sigh as he prepares to leave the house no sooner than he has got home. 'Let's go.'

Three simple words from my husband but they are music to my ears. For the first time since this ordeal began, they mean that he is finally listening to me and believing me.

It feels like a pivotal moment, but there's no time to waste, which is why I don't consider calling the police as we head to his car. It took me this long to convince my husband; I don't want to waste more time trying to convince them. We're going to resolve this ourselves.

As soon as we set off in the direction where we'll find Jade, I feel it in my bones.

I'm getting closer to my baby by the second.

FORTY

JADE

Having not slept last night, I was sure I'd get some rest this evening, especially since I was able to get the benefit money and find myself a new and safer place to stay than the last motel. But that's not the case because of what happened before I got here.

I bumped into Bobby.

I can't believe it. What were the odds? Seriously, what were the chances of him seeing me and stopping me to talk? I can't even fathom how unlucky I had to be for that to happen, even as someone who has had bad luck follow me around since childhood. But it happened. It was real. I really stood in front of the man whose baby I stole and had to somehow make it through a conversation with him.

It was excruciating. Nerve-wracking. Sickening.

Yet, somehow, bizarrely, it ended in my favour.

Not only did he not seem to believe his wife and her accusation that I took their baby, but he also actually apologised for her actions. He even went as far as to ask me if I was okay.

From cursing my bad luck, I couldn't believe my good fortune.

He really believes me over her, or at least he did when we

were together outside that station. But he might not do so forever, which is why I cannot risk ever seeing him again.

He did recognise me, though, or at least he knew who I was. His wife must have told him. He said I looked very different to the past, which is true, whilst commenting on how he looked almost the same, which is also true. Then he told me something I'd already figured out long ago, which was that after our last date, Avril approached him and told him some malicious lies about me. They were lies that must have been both convincing and ominous enough for him to cut off all contact with me, and eventually, to end up with her instead, proving that taking him from me was part of her revenge during our bitter dispute.

He actually told me that.

He was open and honest with me.

I just couldn't be the same with him.

I was able to walk away with his son, the one he looked at in the pram as we spoke, and board a train that took me away from him. I feel bad because my revenge on Avril is punishing him at the same time, and by the sounds of it, he is a victim of Avril's too. Her lies. Her manipulation. Her power.

But I had to walk away because Bobby told me that Avril had contacted the police. I got the confirmation of my worst fear: I am accused of a terrible crime, and somewhere, a police officer will have me on their To-Do list. It doesn't matter that Bobby is seemingly not believing his wife. Even if the police are of the same opinion, they will have a duty to investigate the claim just to be sure. That means they will be trying to find me so they can ask me a few questions and resolve the matter. Even if they expect me to be innocent, it doesn't matter because as soon as I'm in their presence, if my guilty conscience doesn't give me away, the DNA test they might request will, the one they might simply conduct 'just to be sure'.

I cannot let them find me, at least not with someone else's

baby, so I am going to have to leave him and go on the run myself.

I look at Calum, sleeping beside my bed in his pram, and I feel terribly sorry for giving him this awful start to life. Just because my life was already messed up, I had no right to drag him down with me, yet here he is.

I know it's best if I leave him with someone but if that feels too difficult, I could always just leave this motel and leave him behind. He'll eventually be discovered by somebody when they hear him crying and come in to check and, while it will be shocking, they'll surely do the right thing and call the relevant authorities. The woman on the reception desk here when we checked in was very friendly and lit up when she saw Calum, so if she finds him, she'll look after him until the police arrive. By that point, I can be long gone and use the money I have to get away before picking up a cash-in-hand job and trying to eke out a living doing that. It will be a miserable life, but it has to be a better one than in prison.

This is it, I decide, as I stare at Calum in the pram. This is the last night I will have with him. The aching feeling I have tells me I am attached to this baby, which is weird because he isn't mine, yet we have been through so much together and the sad reality is, he is all I have. Yet just before dawn, I will leave this room and leave him in it. I'll walk away, past whoever is on reception and out of this building and then I'll catch a bus or a train and I'll be out of Calum's life.

It's the best thing for him.

It will also be the best thing for Avril.

It feels weird to consider her best interests, a consideration I've never made before, but this has gone too far. While she stole a man from me, I stole a child from her and that is many times worse. I have to admit that I am more of a bad person than she is and allow her life to go on, while mine crumbles. I could leave a note with the baby, something that says who his real parents are and what I did. That will make it simple for the police and quickly reunite Avril and Bobby with their child.

What about my child, the one they have at the moment? I presume he'll be taken into care and given foster parents eventually. He will grow up with a family who can love him and provide all the financial things for him that I never could. One day, his new family will most likely have to explain to him how he came to be in their care, and then if he wants to, he might decide to look for me.

But what would he find if he did?

A woman in prison?

Will I even still be alive then?

I almost hope not because the thought of my own child meeting me, looking me in the eye and asking why I gave him away is unbearable. I think I'd take prison and even death over that fate. I knew nothing about what it meant to be a mother when I gave birth in hospital, but now I see what it is really about, and more importantly, how I have failed on every level.

As more minutes tick by, I know it's still several hours until dawn. But I also know that when the sun rises, I won't be in this room anymore.

Only a baby will remain.

By the end of tomorrow, Avril will have her son back.

I guess it means she wins, but I don't care about that anymore. I just need to do the right thing.

But will that be enough for her?

Will she be content with getting her baby?

Or will she want me too?

FORTY-ONE

AVRIL

'She's in there.'

I look to where Bobby is pointing and see a mundane motel across the street from where we have just parked. It's dark, but the streetlights provide enough illumination to get a good enough look at it. It's a basic building, three-storey with three windows on each floor and a front door with a camera in front of it. I'm guessing that surveillance device is there not because the building and any of its contents are particularly valuable, but because this is an undesirable area and a small effort has been made to dissuade any criminal types from trying to break in after dark. Other than that, I can't tell much about this place, but I don't need to. All I need to know is that this is where Bobby saw Jade go after he followed her on the train.

My husband says she is here.

Which means my baby is too.

'I'm going in,' I decide, reaching for the car door handle, but Bobby reaches out too, in his case, to prevent me from going.

'No. Are you mad? What do you think you're going to do?' he cries.

'Get our baby back!' I snap back.

'You said you would be sensible about this. I never would have brought you here if I'd known you were going to be reckless.'

'You never would have brought me here if you didn't think there was a chance I was right about this. Nor would you have followed Jade here in the first place. You obviously believe me, finally, so what are we waiting for? Let's do something about this. Let's get the bitch and make her pay.'

I get out of the car, fending off Bobby's outstretched arm as I do, but he is quickly out alongside me, slowing me down as I try to cross the street towards the motel.

'Avril, please. You can't just storm in there. The door might be locked. There's a camera. They'll never let you in. Just stop and wait for a second.'

Bobby pulls me back to him, so I am forced to comply.

'What do you suggest we do?' I cry, frustrated but also aware that I did lie to Bobby. I told him I would keep calm when we got here and not act impulsively.

'We wait until she leaves in the morning,' he suggests. 'Better to do this in daylight. We can let her come to us rather than trying to fight our way in there. We can sit out here in the car and keep watch. We'll see her if she leaves. If she doesn't come out, we'll walk inside in the morning and calmly ask to see her.'

'The morning? But why not just do it now?'

'Think about it. If we storm inside and try to get into her room, she might panic. What if she locked her door and, knowing we're outside, decides to do something drastic? She might hurt the baby and herself rather than face us. If we wait until she comes out onto the street then we remove that risk. She'll have nowhere to hide then.'

I realise that my husband is right. It would be far safer to allow Jade to come out here with the pram rather than risk her barricading herself in her room and hurting Luca before we can break in.

'If Jade is the woman you say she is and capable of the things you think she has done, we cannot back her into a corner. It's too dangerous,' Bobby goes on, only making more sense. 'We need to catch her by surprise, but most importantly, we need to have eyes on the baby when we do. That way, we can stop her from doing anything terrible if she panics.'

He is right. The calmest voice in the argument usually is. We should wait until Jade walks out. But that means waiting and I've never been good at that.

'Shouldn't we at least check that she is in there?' I suggest. 'Just so we know for sure?'

'She's in there,' Bobby replies confidently. 'I watched her go inside with the pram and I sat and waited to see if she came out. But she didn't, which tells me she was successful in booking a room for the night. Once I'd waited long enough, I went back to get my car and then came straight home to you. Now we're back here. It's not been that long so she will still be in there, guaranteed. She has no reason to leave tonight.'

'You're absolutely sure she didn't see you follow her?'

'Yes, otherwise she wouldn't have led me here.'

'But she might have seen you and been trying to confuse you. Throw you off the scent.'

'She didn't see me,' Bobby assures me again. 'She looked behind herself a few times, but the train station was busy and I was hidden in the crowd. I boarded the train further down the carriage than her. She had no idea I was there. For all she knows, I returned to my taxi and went back to work.'

I can see that Bobby really means it and believes it, which assures me that she is here, and I just have to bide my time before this is over.

'Let's get back in the car,' Bobby suggests.

It is chilly out here on this street, so I agree to that too.

We walk back to his taxi, and as we get inside, I'm preparing for a long night in his passenger seat. But I won't try and sleep. I dare not. I will keep my eyes on that front door and make sure I don't miss anybody coming out.

'You should try and get some rest. I'll keep watch,' Bobby says from behind the wheel, as if reading my mind but not liking the fact that I'm going to stay awake all night.

'Nope. No way. I couldn't sleep even if I wanted to. We're here to keep watch so we will keep watch. Simple as that.'

Having already won one argument with me this evening, Bobby knows better than to push his luck and try for back-to-back victories, so he shuts up then.

But there's only silence for a moment. His phone rings, startling the both of us.

'It's my mother,' he says after checking the caller ID before he answers it.

'Everything okay?' he asks before I hear his mother's voice down the line saying that it is, but she is wondering if the same can be said for us.

'We're fine,' he tells her, which is a simple way of skimming over everything that has happened this evening. 'How's Luca? Is he okay?'

It initially feels weird that he is still calling the baby that name when we both believe Jade has the real Luca, but I suppose it's better than him telling his mum that she is currently babysitting someone else's baby.

I hear her say that there has been a lot of crying, but the baby is asleep now.

'Thanks for having him tonight. I'll be there sometime in the morning to pick him up,' Bobby says, which is far vaguer than giving a specific time, but, of course, he can't do that either, as we have no idea what time Jade will emerge from the motel. Nor do we know exactly how things will play out when she does.

As he wraps up the call, I stare at the motel windows, wishing I knew which one Jade might be behind. But she could be on the other side of the building, it's impossible to know. All we do know is that she is inside somewhere. But she can't stay in there forever.

She has to leave at some point.

When she does, I will be waiting for her.

FORTY-TWO
JADE

I've managed to get a few hours' sleep, though it wasn't the kind of rest my energy-depleted body was craving. That's because I suffered with terrible nightmares while I slept, the kind that cause the person having them to toss and turn and wake up sweating, with an elevated heart rate and an awful sense of confusion and fear.

I dreamt all sorts of things, bad things, things that I might deserve and maybe things that are in my future.

I dreamt of police officers arresting me and throwing me into tiny prison cells. I dreamt of myself scratching at the walls of the cells to get out, only to find there was no way through. I also dreamt of a court case, being in the dock before a judge and jury, as well as being marched in and out of court past incessant photographers with cameras and baying members of the public with insults to hurl my way. On top of that, I dreamt of two crying babies, the pair of them side by side, seemingly united in their hatred of me, making it clear, in their young and childish way, that they despised me for what I had done in the earliest part of their lives. If all that wasn't bad enough, I also dreamt of her. *Avril.* She was standing over me and I was powerless to prevent her from taking her revenge.

The scariest part occurred when I woke up and feared it wasn't just nightmares after all but something even more frightening.

What if it was a glimpse of what was to come in the real world?

Unsurprisingly, I stood no chance of falling back to sleep after that. I spent the next few hours staring into the abyss of the kind of gloom that is only possible in the deepest, darkest part of the night. Thoughts raced through my mind as I tried to figure out which I was afraid of most. The police? The media? The public? The two babies growing up and hating me? But in the end, I realised what it was. It was Avril.

The thing I am most afraid of is being face to face with her. Alone. I just know there will be no limit to the pain she would wish to inflict should she ever get the chance to have her revenge on me.

As I hear a soft snore emanate from the pram beside my bed, I wish I could rest like Calum can. Or Luca. I guess he'll go back to having his original name very soon. It's sooner than I would like because as I check the time, I realise dawn is only an hour away now and I'd made the decision last night that I would be out of here by then.

I guess it's time to get going.

I get out of bed as quietly as I can, even more desperate not to disturb a sleeping baby than any parent usually would be. While they are anxious because they don't want to wake the child and have more work to deal with, I'm worried because I cannot bear to have Calum look at me one more time with his beautiful blue eyes. That will only make leaving him harder and this is going to be hard enough as it is.

I get dressed in the dark and gather my meagre belongings together. Once I'm ready, I'm wishing I had more things to do, just to delay this awful part a little longer. But I'm done. I'm all set to go. All I have to do now is walk out of the door and leave Calum behind and it's over, or at least the part that involves him is, anyway.

Continually envying him and his fledgling, innocent life, I think about how today will likely unfold for him. He'll be gathered by someone who works at the motel, either the friendly receptionist who doted on him when we arrived here or a cleaner who comes in here after the early check-out to tidy up. I'm confident that they will do the right thing and have Calum taken care of while the police are called, whereupon he will be cared for even more when they get here and deal with the fact he has been abandoned. He'll be taken somewhere safer than this place, looked after, fed and changed and cuddled until somebody figures out who he really is and reunites him with his birth mother, where he will only be looked after even more. Basically, he will be loved and cared for whatever happens. It's the total opposite for me. Nobody is going to look out for my best interests. I'm all alone and as I stand over the pram and feel a tear running down my cheek, I feel like this moment right here, as bad as it is, is probably the best I'm going to feel all day.

'Goodbye, baby,' I whisper as I reach down and lightly touch one of Calum's hands. 'I'm so sorry for what I did to you, but you're going to be okay, I promise. You're going to go home, to your mummy, and you're going to grow up to have a wonderful life and you won't remember any of this ever happened.'

A tear drips from my face and lands on his Babygro, but he doesn't stir. Soon that tear will dry, although the same can't be said for the tears in my eyes. As I force myself away from the sleeping child and towards the door, I can barely see, such is the emotion seeping out of me.

Leaving the dark bedroom, I step into the hallway and close the door quietly behind me, not only trying to prevent Calum from waking but also any of the other people in the neighbouring rooms. I want to leave here without being seen in case somebody remembers me as arriving with a baby and wonders why he's not with me now. I need to be far away from here before Calum is discovered alone, and I'm hoping I've got a few hours yet before he wakes up crying and somebody out here figures something is wrong. But I also make sure to leave the door unlocked so Calum can be reached, and thanks to these cheap motel doors, they are not the kind that lock automatically when closed.

I creep towards the reception area, praying the front desk is unmanned when I get there, and it is, meaning there is no need for me to explain to anybody why I am going out at this early hour. All I need to do now is press the electronic release button that will unlock the front door and I'll be safely out onto the street.

It's pitch-black out there, which is what I wanted, but it means I can't really see anything as I open the door and step outside. I see the glow from a streetlight a few yards away and know that it will help guide my way down the pavement and onto the next street. As the motel door closes behind me, there's no going back now. I couldn't get inside again if I wanted to because the door has automatically locked, meaning the only way in would be to buzz and wake the owner. But I'm not doing that, which means Calum really is totally by himself now.

'Come on,' I say to myself under my breath as I start walking, as if I need a little pep talk to get my legs moving the way I need them to go.

My plan is to catch a train north, maybe as far north as Scotland, and when I get there, I'll try and find work. Any work, I don't care, just as long as it is cash in hand, and nobody finds out who I am. I can change my appearance again, I've obviously got a talent for that, and maybe, one day, I could figure out a way to leave the country if I cannot get settled again here.

As I go, the street is eerily quiet, barring my footsteps, but I get the strange sense that somebody is watching me. I pause and look around but can't see anybody so keep going, but as I do, I hear what sounds like a car door opening.

I look around again, but still can't see anything. I decide to speed up my walking, just in case. However, as I do, I hear something other than my footsteps.

I hear another set of footsteps.

These ones seem to be getting nearer.

Turning around and looking towards the nearest streetlight, I am hoping whoever it is passes directly under it so I can get a good look at them and discover that they are not to be feared and are just a member of the public out here walking like I am. But whoever it is, they do not pass under the streetlight. They remain in the shadows, yet the sound of them draws ever nearer.

It can't be the police, I tell myself, and it turns out that I am right, not that it's much consolation when I realise that.

My awful discovery comes when I eventually see who it is out here on this street with me.

'No,' I say in terror, my most recent and worst nightmare coming true when I lay eyes on the face of the woman who has her gaze locked onto me. But there's no point denying it. It is true, as clear to me as the yellow glow from the nearest streetlight.

I've been found by the one person I never wanted to see again. I don't know how, but it's happened.

I am now face to face with Avril.

She looks like she wants to kill me.

And I expect that she is about to try.

FORTY-THREE

AVRIL

'Where is my baby?'

Considering how much I hate this woman and what she deserves, I am being very restrained as I reach her. That's only because I cannot see Luca with her, and I need to establish his whereabouts before I can even think about doing anything else to Jade.

She doesn't speak. She doesn't say a word. She just stares at me, as if frozen in fear, which is an appropriate response from her body because she is in mortal danger. But I can't attack her until I know my baby is safe.

'Where is he?' I scream, my frantic voice piercing the still of the night and surely waking up a few people who were sleeping nearby. I grab her, squeezing her arms, hoping to extract the information I so desperately need.

'Let me go,' Jade tries, but her efforts to pull away from me are weak, as if she's already given up. Or maybe she knows that her attempts to escape can never overpower my desire to see my baby.

'You took him from me!' I scream, right in her face. I want

her to flinch, and she does. 'You swapped our babies! I'm right, aren't I? Just admit it!'

'Please,' Jade says feebly, her voice barely audible and in sharp contrast to my piercing cries.

'I know you did it! What kind of sick person does that?'

Jade starts crying, possibly because she knows what she has done is terrible or maybe because she knows this is over now: I've caught her. But it's not over yet, not for me. Not until I find my son.

My stomach feels like it is doing flips as I fight the fear that she has hurt him and left him dead somewhere, meaning that whatever pleasure can be derived from seeing Jade punished for this will be overwhelmed by the grief of my child not growing up.

'Just tell me where he is! What have you done to him? Is he still alive?'

My grip on Jade loosens as I contemplate the unthinkable. Even though I believed that I would have the upper hand here, that could not be further from the truth. She still holds all the cards, or at least the only one that matters to me.

She knows where my baby is.

And I don't.

'Of course he's still alive,' Jade replies, as if I am the villain here for assuming he was not. But what else was I supposed to assume?

'He is?' I ask in relieved surprise, only for more questions to quickly come to mind. 'Where is he? Why's he not with you? Who is he with?'

'You have to let me go, please,' Jade says, my hands still on her. 'I don't want to go to prison. Just let me go.'

I can see exactly how much she fears prison because it's written all over her face, but she should have thought about that before she did what she did.

'Where is my son!' I cry, my only concern. I see Jade briefly look past me and at something behind me.

I turn around to see what she was looking at, and when I do, I see the motel she just came out of.

My son must be in there.

That realisation causes me to loosen my hold on Jade a little more and, taking advantage of that, as well as having my head turned, she seizes her opportunity to potentially escape, breaking away from me and taking off running down the street.

'Hey! Come back!' I cry, but while I take one step towards her as if to give chase, I quickly stop when I realise following her would take me further away from where Luca might be. I forget about Jade and just focus on trying to get my baby back, which is why I run to the front door of the motel and attempt to open it. It's locked, so I press down hard on the electronic buzzer by the handle, and I can hear it blaring on the other side of this door. It's loud, certainly loud enough to wake those inside, and I make sure it has the best chance of that because I keep pressing it rather than letting go and waiting patiently.

'Come on! Open up!' I cry out to somebody, anybody, on the other side of this door. Eventually, I hear it being unlocked before it opens. Somebody has answered my desperate calls, but I barely see who they are because I burst inside without waiting to be invited in, and then I look around.

'Which room was Jade staying in?' I cry as the poor person who presumably works here rubs their bleary eyes and looks overwhelmed at my sudden arrival.

'What?' he replies sleepily.

'The woman with the baby boy? Which room was she staying in?' I cry, expecting that should narrow it down and hoping there aren't any other guests here who came with babies.

'Erm...'

'Which room?' I demand to know, making it clear this is no time for guest confidentiality.

'The room at the end of the corridor. On the right,' I'm told, and that's all I need to take off towards it.

I sprint down the corridor as a few doors open on either side and agitated, sleep-deprived guests poke their heads out from their dark bedrooms to find out what is going on. I ignore them all until I reach the room where Jade apparently stayed, and as I try the handle, I hear something that tells me I am in the right place.

I hear crying.

Trying the handle, I'm relieved when the door flings open and the light from the corridor filters into the room around me. That's how I am able to see the pram positioned beside the bed. The crying is louder now too with the door open, and I lunge towards the pram to get a look at the baby inside it, praying that the cries are just hunger-fuelled rather than from genuine pain. When I lay eyes on the little face inside, I know what has happened.

I have been reunited with my baby.

'Luca,' I say with tears running down my cheeks as I scoop him up into my arms and try to soothe his cries. Amazingly, he quietens almost instantly. But of course he does, because he is mine and we have been brought back together again after being so heartlessly separated the day after his birth.

'Oh, my baby. I'm so sorry,' I say as I hush him and hold him. 'Mummy's here now and I promise I'll never let go of you again.'

As I cradle him, I'm feeling like a terrible parent even though I can hardly be blamed for what Jade did. Although maybe that's not true because I did plenty to her in the past, which resulted in her doing what she did in the hospital. At least I have Luca back and, seemingly, barring the psychological damage to me and Bobby, there is no harm done. I know it's him, every cell in my body tells me that it is. This is my flesh and blood, my boy, and this is what I have been missing for so long, hence all my struggles since leaving hospital.

'Somebody call the police,' I hear a voice say, and I turn around to several people crowding in the doorway.

'Yes, please do!' I reply, which surprises them. They probably thought I was the one in the wrong for barging in here, but I have nothing to hide.

'It's over now,' I say to my baby as somebody else asks me what is going on. Before I can answer them, I realise that what I just said is not true at all.

I just told Luca that it is over, but I'm wrong. It's not.

It's not over until Jade has been caught and punished for this.

And the last I saw of her, she was running away.

FORTY-FOUR
JADE

I can hear the sound of my feet on the concrete pavement as they carry me away from Avril as fast as they can. But I can't hear her calling after me, which means she has prioritised finding her baby over getting revenge. That has allowed me to get away from her after she unexpectedly found me, so even though she caught me, I'm still free. I intend to keep it that way for as long as possible, and it's certainly much easier to move around without having a pram to push too. My heart aches at leaving Calum behind, even if he was never Calum but Luca, and even if he is back with Avril now whilst I am all alone. More than that, my heart is aching for the baby I gave birth to and the one I'll never get to know. I can get as far away as I want to, but I'll never have what Avril has.

I'll never have the love of my child.

The street is quiet because dawn is only just breaking, barring the sound of me running, though it won't stay this way for long. I want to be at the train station before the carriages get full of commuters, but there's still a fair distance to go if I travel by foot. Then I see a taxi drive past and consider taking the faster option.

'Hey!' I call out, waving as it moves away from me, but I see the brake lights come on so the driver must have spotted me in the rear-view mirror.

As the taxi comes to a stop, I open the rear passenger door and get onto the backseat before nervously looking through the back window to make sure Avril isn't chasing me after all. But she definitely isn't, there is still no sign of her, so she must be at the motel and probably holding her baby and telling somebody to call the police. That gives me more time to escape, time I am making the most of by having a taxi driver get me out of here quicker.

'To the train station,' I say as I put on my seatbelt.

The driver puts us in motion, not turning around or attempting to chat with me, but it is very early, and he might have just started his shift or be coming to the end of a very long one. But I'm not in the mood for talking either. What would I say if he asked me how my day had started? That I've just left a baby by itself and then escaped the clutches of that baby's mother before she tried to hurt me? And now I'm off to start a new life, even though I've only got enough money to last me a week at most, and it all depends on whether the police don't catch me first.

Yeah, best that we don't talk.

I stare out of the window as we drive, passing along the quiet streets and the homes that line them. Inside, people will be waking up. Crying babies being seen to by their parents, or older children running in and diving under their mum and dad's duvets. Or some people might still be sleeping, not yet having had kids or perhaps having already raised them and watched them leave home, to return occasionally but not right now. Everything seems quiet out here, but I'm sure there's plenty of life in all these houses. It's the kind of life I will never know.

None of them would swap places with me, the tired, scared

and lonely woman in the taxi. They'd all hate to be in my position, and they should because it's awful.

I shouldn't do it, as it will only attract questions from the person driving, but I start crying, though I quickly try to pretend like I'm okay.

'Sorry,' I say with my head down so he can't see the extent of my tears, even though he is surely looking in the rear-view mirror to do just that.

The taxi keeps on moving and the driver doesn't speak, so I guess there's no harm done, and eventually, I've composed myself enough to lift my head up and look back out of the window. When I do, I have no idea where we are. It looks like we've left the residential streets behind and have moved onto an even quieter road, one with trees on both sides instead of buildings.

Is this the right way to the train station?

'How far away are we now?' I ask the driver, but he doesn't answer, although he does indicate off the road and steers us onto a shady lane.

Totally surrounded by trees, he keeps going until the road behind us is no longer visible.

'Hey, where are we going?' I ask him, fear lacing my voice. I'm now sure this is not the right route.

The taxi comes to a stop and the engine is turned off. Only then does the driver actually turn around so I can see his face clearly. When he does, I gasp and try the nearest door handle, although it's locked. But I keep trying because I really, really need to get out of this car. It isn't just any taxi driven by any driver.

It's driven by one half of the couple I have been trying to evade.

Bobby is at the wheel.

And he is in control now.

FORTY-FIVE
AVRIL

'Do a DNA test on me and the baby! Do it now! Then you'll see that I'm not crazy!'

That's the first thing I said to the police officers who entered the motel room where I stood with Luca. Even though I'd only just been reunited with him, I was happy to hand him over for a short while if it meant I could then keep him forever.

Of course, I'd need to say a lot more than that, from how I came to be in the motel room to where the woman is who was with the baby before I arrived. But I didn't care. There was all the time in the world for statements and investigations and, ultimately, for me and my family to move on. The scariest part of all of this was over, which was the fear that I might never catch up with Jade and my baby again. Even though it might not seem like it from my point of view, I know there will also come a time to make Jade pay for what she did. Though she ran away from me on the street, I knew she was being followed.

Before I got out of Bobby's taxi, he told me that he would linger, just in case Jade ran and I lost her or had to go elsewhere to find the baby. That way, he said, he would have eyes on her while I was distracted, and that is exactly what happened. I chose to run to Luca after finding out where he was, but that didn't mean I was allowing Jade to escape. I knew my husband was on her tail, and I know he won't have let her out of his sight.

I'm hoping he's already caught up with her, although I'm not sure what might have happened since he has. Did Jade fight back? Did he have to abandon his car and chase her on foot? Or does he have her in his vehicle, trapped and ready to phone the police to get her?

I told Bobby to call me as soon as he had news, but he hasn't yet, so for now, I will deal with the police as best I can. I've been asked to leave the motel room and accompany the officers to the station, while Luca is being watched by a support officer until this has been resolved.

My questions come quickly.

'What happens now?'

'You will do the DNA test, right?'

'How long until we get the results?'

'I'm not under arrest, am I?'

I'm assured the DNA test will be done, critical as it is to my story and the accusations against Jade. For now, I have to be patient and let the justice system run its course. I'm also assured that I am not under arrest but need to answer some questions, which I agree to. Whatever it takes to speed this up and make it clear who is in the wrong. It's much easier to be in this position, the one helping the police, rather than in Jade's position, where she will have to try and wriggle out of it.

Patience is my best friend now and I have to exercise that patience as I wait for Bobby to let me know what is happening with Jade. But the longer I fail to hear from him, the more I begin to worry that Jade has somehow escaped. Maybe he has lost her and is too nervous to call me and admit he let her get away. Then another thought rises to the surface, an even scarier one: what if Jade fought back and, in her desperation to get away from him, he has been injured? Is he hurt now? Or dead?

Jade is capable of anything, after all.

Have I got my baby back only to lose my husband?

At the police station, I go over it all with a detective, everything I've already told his colleagues, and the same thing I've been telling them for a while now. That woman swapped our babies, and I've just corrected it. Although from their point of view, it's not that simple. Even from mine, I guess it's not either. Bobby's mother still has Jade's son, so he will need to be taken into care, and I do want to ensure that he is because he is totally innocent and deserves so much better than the start in life he has had so far. I am also still waiting on the test results to prove Luca is the baby I just found and not the one I took home from the hospital, though I'm confident what the outcome will be there.

Regardless, there's a lot to sort out yet, not least of which is what is going on with Bobby and Jade.

'There's still no word from your husband?' a detective asks me after I've been sitting at the station for hours, and I shake my head.

'No. I don't know where he is or if he's okay,' I say quietly, and I'm starting to fear that things have ended badly for him. I never should have agreed to his idea that he would pursue Jade while I went after the baby. We should have stuck together. That way, all three of us would be safe and even if Jade had escaped, at least our family would be intact. But now it's missing a piece, another one, so soon after the first piece went AWOL.

When my phone rings, I cannot answer it quickly enough.

'It's him!' I cry as I see my husband's name flash up on the screen before I take the call. 'Bobby! Where are you? Are you okay?'

'I'm fine,' I hear him say, but his voice is quiet, meek even. Like he doesn't want to be talking to me but knows he has to check in and let me know what is going on, so here he is.

'Are you sure? You don't sound okay,' I try again.

'I'm fine,' Bobby repeats.

'Did you catch her? Do you have her?' I ask.

There's a long pause.

'Bobby? What happened? Where is Jade?'

'She got away. I caught up to her in my taxi, but lost her again.'

I guess that explains why my husband is not enthused to be having this conversation.

'She got away,' I repeat mournfully for the benefit of the detective eavesdropping on this phone call. 'That's okay. The main thing is that you are all right.'

I would have loved nothing more than for him to tell me that he handed Jade over to a couple of police officers and he is making this call while she is in custody, but alas, it was not to be. But it's not the end of the world, not when I was imagining Bobby being hurt just before this phone rang.

'I'm sorry,' my husband mutters.

'There's no need to be sorry!' I tell him clearly. 'We have our son back and now all three of us will be able to go home and get on with our lives. That's all that matters, so stop feeling bad and come and meet me. I'm at the police station. Where are you? Maybe I can get someone to come and pick you up?'

I look to the detective who nods to say that could be arranged, but Bobby tells me he will drive himself here and will see me soon. With that, the call ends. I'm glad that I'll be reunited with my husband soon. I'm also glad that he is unhurt and now it's just the test results we need.

It would have been the cherry on the cake if he could have caught Jade. But never mind. I suppose it would have been too good to be true. A woman like her always seems to worm her way out of everything. She might be evil, but she's resourceful.

Surely she can't hide forever? Surely she'll be caught one day? Until then, I'll just have to focus on my family. But I'd be lying if I said I wasn't praying I'd see her again. I want to stare at her across a courtroom as her crimes are read out, and I want to look into her eyes as she is sentenced. I really, really want to watch as she is led away in handcuffs to begin that sentence. Hopefully, she'll glance at me as she goes and see the smile on my face that tells her who won.

I came out on top, as I always did between us.

Jade was never a match for me.

Surely now, after all of this, she can admit that I am the better woman.

But there is the possibility that I see her again in another way. Not in a courtroom, but in some other setting, a far more dangerous one, at least for me and my family. What if Jade returns for revenge? What if she tries to harm me or Bobby? Or what if she tries to steal my baby again?

Could she come to our house? Would she try? Would she dare?

I tell myself it's unlikely.

But I also have to remind myself that it's not impossible.

I cannot rule out anything when it comes to Jade.

FORTY-SIX

JADE

It's been forty-eight hours since I fled Bobby's taxi after being able to escape. Since then, I've remained hidden and out of the clutches of the police, who are looking for me in huge numbers now that Avril's theory has been proven correct.

According to the newspaper articles that I have seen, the DNA test proved without doubt that Avril is the mother of the baby boy in the motel room, which means she was right to accuse me of swapping our babies after birth. I obviously didn't need a test or newspaper article to tell me that, but the police and the wider public did. Now that they all know the truth, I guess I'm officially the most wanted woman in the UK. Serious crimes always make the headlines, but nothing quite captures the attention and imagination of the public like a stunning story that involves children. Can there be a more shocking tale than a baby swap?

But it doesn't matter that everybody is looking for me.

All that matters is that I'm not found.

At least not until I have done what I want to do.

It's obvious that there is no getting away with this. I cannot hide from all the people who are desperate to find me, even if I had a lot of money, which I do not. That's why I cannot try and get abroad now. I need time to try and get a job and save up, but it's time I don't have. I am going to get caught. I have accepted that. What I have not accepted is going down in defeat.

I cannot let Avril win.

It seems like she has it all while I have nothing.

But she has no idea what's about to happen.

I know the police are looking everywhere for me. The airports. The train stations. The ferry terminals. The bus shelters. Anywhere I could be mobile, changing location, potentially crossing borders and getting further away. Nobody is looking for me here because nobody expects I'd ever need to come here, nor be so stupid as to try. That's why there is no police car outside this house. It's also why the people inside the house are going about their evening as if everything is normal.

No one thinks I'd try and see Avril, least of all her.

But that's exactly what I'm here to do.

I'm standing in the back garden of her home, in shadow before the sun has set, and there are no security lights back here that could be triggered by my movement. It's perfect because she has no idea I'm here, and that's how I want to keep it, right up until the moment I am inside her house and staring at her shocked face.

I creep to the nearest window and peer inside. I see the happy family going through the motions in the kitchen. Bobby is in there and he is holding Luca; the little boy cradled on his chest looking snug, not crying, just awake and watching his mother.

She has the perfect-looking life.

Here I am, watching on, with nothing.

Avril is using a large knife to chop vegetables, preparing the evening meal whilst looking every bit the domestic goddess she has turned herself into. Gone are the power dresses she used to wear in the office; instead, she has on a light and flowy nightgown, comfortable and perfect for snuggling her baby in later. She is make-up-less but still beautiful and operating the knife with a confidence that suggests while home life is chaotic, she has it all under control.

Of course she does. She's Avril. Superwoman. The nation's darling, the woman everyone feels sorry for because she was the victim of a cruel, cold-hearted bitch who stole her baby. I expect she'll be selling her story to the highest bidder once an appropriate amount of time has passed, and I bet there are plenty in the media who will pay for it. That's because everybody loves her while everybody hates me.

It isn't fair but it is the truth.

Therefore, I've got absolutely nothing to lose at this point.

So it's time to get inside this house and break up this happy family one last time.

I creep to the back door and try the handle, but it's locked, so I move on round to the front, keeping my head down below the level of any windows I pass. When I reach the front door, I try this handle, but it's also locked. Probably to be expected. Avril will be cautious. She lost her baby once and she won't want to risk an intruder getting inside and potentially causing her to lose him again. But there's no way she'd ever expect me to come back here.

It's time to surprise her.

I knock on the front door, the confident kind of knock that a person who belongs here would make. I'm hoping that upon hearing it, Avril will assume it is a family member or friend who has come to visit. She'd never expect that it could be me. Why would I knock?

I wait for the door to be opened, my body tensing by the second until I'm ready to lunge forward into this home. I just need to be given the opportunity. I hear a key turn, and I know I'm about to get that.

The door opens and I see Bobby and the baby both staring

back at me. Bobby knows who I am, and maybe Luca remembers me in some small way from the time we spent together, but it's the older male who reacts more tellingly. His eyes go wide and he goes to speak, but I push past him, entering his house as he cradles the baby before I go looking for the person I came here to see.

'Avril!' I call out into the huge home that seems to have doors going off the hallway in every direction. From one of them appears the lady of the house. As Avril sees me, she stops dead in her tracks, as if she's seen a ghost.

'What are you doing here?' she asks me before she looks to Bobby, but he is still standing helplessly by the door, encumbered by a baby that needs to be protected. So Avril will have to fend for herself here.

I rush towards her, not allowing any time for her to make a plan. She retreats into her kitchen. I follow her in and as she tries to keep her distance, I give her another reason to fear me.

I pick up the knife she was just using and hold it out between us.

'Bobby! Call the police!' Avril shouts to her husband who is still somewhere behind me. The sound of her raised voice causes the baby to start crying, which only adds to the sense of disorder that has suddenly come over this impressive house.

I don't turn around to see if Bobby is doing as his wife asks, but I presume he will call the police. I better be quick, meaning I raise the knife higher as Avril cowers behind a marble countertop.

'You ruined my life,' I tell Avril. 'You took everything from me. My hopes. My dreams. My confidence. And then my boyfriend. So I took something from you. How did you like it?'

'Jade, please, just put the knife down,' Avril tries, pleading for peace, but that will be up to me to decide.

I turn to Bobby, who has got his phone in his hand and is

attempting to make a call while still holding the crying Luca, but he hasn't managed it yet.

'No, stay away from them!' Avril cries, her fear rising as she sees the knife turn in the direction of her husband and child. But I'm enjoying her panic and, of course, I knew it would only increase by focusing on her loved ones, so I make sure not to turn around yet. Not until I know Avril is stepping out from behind the countertop and is coming nearer to me.

'I'm going to have to take something from you again,' I say, figuring Avril will get that very strong hint.

As I step towards Bobby and Luca, I hear her rushing towards me. That's my cue to turn back around, although when I do, I'm no longer pointing the edge of the blade out away from myself. Instead, it's pointing towards my stomach. As Avril gets close, she stops, trying to figure out what I'm doing.

'You think you've won,' I say smugly. 'You think there's no possible way my life can ever be better than yours now, not with the prison time I'm facing. But I don't have to go to prison. You do.'

Avril has no idea what I'm talking about as I keep the knife held firmly in front of my stomach.

'Why would I go to prison?' she asks fearfully.

'For murdering me,' I say, and her eyes go wide. 'For killing me when I turned up here to apologise for what I did. For saying I was going to hand myself in only to see you reach for a knife and kill me in cold blood.'

Avril cannot believe what she is hearing. 'I'll say it was self-defence,' she tells me. 'You were threatening my family. You broke into my home.'

'I didn't break in anywhere,' I remind her. 'I knocked on the door and then I walked in. There's no sign of a struggle anywhere. No indication that I tried to harm anyone else. The only thing there will be is a bloodied knife with your finger-prints all over it and my dead body lying on your kitchen floor.'

'You'll never get away with it,' Avril says, rather foolishly, when she has a second to think about it.

'I don't need to get away with it,' I remind her. 'I'll be dead. You'll be the one left behind trying to get away with it.'

Avril looks to Bobby, assuming he will be her witness. 'You're hearing all this?' she asks him. 'You'll back me up. You'll tell the police that she killed herself and tried to frame me. You're a witness.'

'Why would he back you up?' I ask her.

'Of course he will. He's my husband!'

'That might be correct,' I say as I touch the tip of the blade to my torso. 'But he's not the father of your baby.'

Avril's eyes widen in panic, the kind of panic that can only come when your deepest, darkest secret has just been exposed to the light.

'What?' she says, trying to feign ignorance, but it's too late for that.

'You had an affair at work. I saw you in your office window. I was following you and I caught you. If you think I'm a stalker, I might as well be a proper one. Now I'm telling Bobby because he deserves to know that he is holding another man's child and that he is married to a compulsive liar.'

'It's not true!' Avril tries, but of course she would say that.

'Get a paternity test,' I tell Bobby. 'You'll see who is telling the truth. She only tested her DNA with the baby, not yours!'

'Jade, please put the knife down,' Bobby says, and I see genuine fear in his eyes, which almost makes me follow his order.

But I don't quite do it.

I *can't* quite do it.

Turning away from him, I raise the knife up. Avril rushes towards me to try and prevent me from doing it, but I plunge it down hard and let out a cry of pain as the blade penetrates my skin.

I grimace as I hold the knife inside myself before dropping to my knees and releasing it, the blood-soaked blade dropping to the tiles beside several splodges of red. Then I curl up and wait for the warm, welcoming blanket of death to take me, a fate that might seem awful for many, but for me, a person with no prospect of a bright future, I am anticipating its comfort.

I see Avril standing over me before she drops to her knees to try and stem the bleeding, but it's too late. I'm losing my life and all she is doing is getting more evidence on her hands.

I wish I'd never met Avril; I wish I'd never swapped our babies and that I'd gotten more time with my real son, the one I carried for nine months and should never have abandoned. And I really wish there was some other way out for me that didn't involve prison.

But this is my fate.

The last person I see is the person who sent me down this deadly path.

Avril is watching me die.

At the same time, she is watching me win.

FORTY-SEVEN

AVRIL

As the door to my cell is locked for the first time since I was found guilty of Jade's murder, I know it will be at least ten years before I get to reside in a different room to this one. That's how long I've been sentenced, meaning by the time I get out, my son will be almost a teenager, and I'll have spent almost all of Luca's youth behind bars.

Luca now resides with his biological father, who came forward for a DNA test after hearing all about mine and Jade's story in the news. Once the test proved he was the real dad, he was able to obtain custody and now my son lives with his father and his father's new girlfriend – the three of them living the kind of homely life that I thought I'd be living myself.

From desperately wanting a child to realising that I will now barely know my son as a child has been a daunting truth to face. I tried everything to avoid this fate. I paid for the best defence team I could get. The lawyers who stood up in court and tried to get the jury to believe that I was the victim of one final, devastating plot from Jade did their best. They explained the trauma I had been through. The difficult birth. The fact my baby was taken in hospital while I slept. The fact I had to fight so hard to get him back. But while all of that was true, it was not good enough because another thing was also true. Someone was dead, and the police had found me with her blood on my hands.

That's why the jury came back with a verdict of guilty. I was deemed a killer, and despite what a person goes through, killing is almost always inexcusable.

They believed a dead woman over me. They believed my husband over me too.

That's because he was on Jade's side and not mine.

When Jade looked me in the eye with the knife in front of her stomach and told me that Bobby was not the father of my baby, it was a huge shock to learn that she knew my darkest secret. But with the way she so brazenly said it in the presence of my husband, I had to assume that he already knew it too.

I didn't know how it came out, or when this pair could have discussed it, but it seemed that they knew and had made a plan to get revenge on me. It was the ultimate revenge, in Jade's case, because with her now dead, I can never do anything to her again. She looked like she knew that as I stood over her and watched her die. It was as if she was proud of herself for finally outsmarting me and knew that whatever happened next, I had to have at least some respect for her, respect that I lacked when we first met on the day of her interview.

As Jade died on my kitchen floor, I heard Bobby speaking to the police over the phone, telling them what had happened. But he wasn't telling them what I needed him to. He told the police that Jade had come here, defenceless, explaining how she wanted to apologise, demonstrating how she was struggling with her mental health and saying she was full of regret for what she did with our babies. Then he mentioned that Jade had revealed a secret: I had been having an affair with a work colleague and that other man was Luca's father, not him. Then Bobby told the police that in order to shut Jade up, I had grabbed a knife and stabbed her and now Jade was dead.

The police came to the scene and, despite my telling them the truth, Bobby stuck to what he had told them on the phone and even indicated that he was afraid of me being in the presence of the baby, so they had to arrest me, at least while the investigation was pending. I was dragged from my beautiful home, kicking and screaming, leaving behind Luca, as well as the man who had so cruelly betrayed me.

But of course, the way he sees it, I betrayed him first.

And he is right.

There are no more apt places to do some soul-searching than sitting inside a small cell with a locked door, surrounded by criminals on all sides, and with nobody from the outside world able to come and help you. A person is all alone in a location like this, which makes it the perfect place to look back and reflect on all the choices that led to that person being there now. I'm certainly doing a lot of reflecting as I look back on all of my mistakes that have led me to lose everything, most of all, my child.

There are many. From being rude to Jade during her interview, to visiting her home and threatening her further and then, of course, stealing her boyfriend and having him for myself. All things I regret and should not have done. But my biggest mistake by far was my affair with a work colleague. That is the one that lost me the support of my husband. It also gave Jade the opportunity to gain victory even in death.

She told Bobby about my fling just before she killed herself, the fling I had in the office during a dark period in my life when Bobby and I were finding it impossible to conceive the child we so desperately wanted. It should never have happened, it was a truly terrible mistake, but it did, and when I found out I was pregnant, I knew it was not my husband's baby.

Crucially, I thought Bobby was still in the dark about it, and I had hoped to keep it that way forever. But Bobby found out that Luca was not his, that the child I gave birth to was the result of my fling with somebody else and, therefore, he hated me and also felt no paternal bond with Luca. Maybe he really did only find out that night Jade died, although I suspect it happened before. Jade was far too cunning to leave things to the last minute. Maybe she told him the truth about Luca way earlier, and that was why he was not only able to team up with Jade to enact this devasting plot, but how he was able to stay so calm throughout the ordeal while I was losing my mind. All the time I thought Jade had my baby, I was panicked, restless, unable to do anything else but crave the return of my baby. I thought Bobby didn't believe me and was just being a little heartless, but really, he was just acting like anybody in his position would.

Why would he care about me and my baby when he had no love for either one of us? Throughout everything, it might not only have been Jade who was one step ahead of me, but my husband too. Unfortunately, I cannot prove it. Without concrete facts, dates and evidence, it made it so much harder for my lawyers to convince the jury that such a thing as Jade and Bobby teaming up had happened. It sounded fanciful as a defence on my part, like the desperate theory of a woman who had killed somebody and needed a way out of it. The jury knew I had a strong motive to kill Jade, so even after trying to convince them that it was a con and I was the victim, it was impossible to change the facts that Jade was dead, my fingerprints were on the knife, and I had a very strong motive to want to hurt her.

From their point of view, the victim was Jade. She was dead, after all, and when did a dead body ever come out on top? But that was exactly what had happened here, though no one believed me because once Bobby had the DNA test that proved that Luca was not his, the police knew I was capable of lies and secrets, instantly making any statements I made after that untrustworthy and unreliable.

Through my tears and my frustration comes a maniacal laugh, a recognition that I really did get the wrong impression of Jade when I first met her. I was wrong in that interview. I shouldn't have ridiculed and dismissed her. I should have hired her on the spot. She obviously possessed all the traits necessary to succeed in the cut-throat world of cosmetics. She could have been as good as me, if not better. Together, we could have made a formidable team. But as it is, she is dead, I am in prison, and there are two children out there who will grow up without their mothers.

This all started a long time ago, but things went crazy when the babies were swapped.

I wish I could go back to that night in the hospital. I wish I hadn't fallen asleep. Maybe I wouldn't be in here now if I'd stayed awake.

But I closed my eyes.

When I opened them again, my life was already on a course I could not alter.

EPILOGUE

BOBBY

Everybody knows Jade as the desperate and, ultimately, doomed baby swapper. They also know Avril as the murderous wife who was not as perfect as she seemed. But what about me?

Who do people think I am?

I'm just the poor guy who got caught in the middle of those two crazy women.

At this moment in time, I'm in my happy place, which is not a place that many people would consider to be happy, but it works for me. I'm behind the wheel of my taxi, driving around London, and having just dropped off a passenger at their desired destination, I'm on the lookout for my next fare. I love being on the move, the view out of my 'office' window always changing, and I love the fact that I know every shortcut this city has to offer. Some might say Avril and Jade knew a few short-cuts too, but while their ways landed them in a whole heap of trouble, my ways seem to always turn out fine.

It's these moments here, when I'm in between customers, that I enjoy the most because my taxi is quiet, which means I get a chance to think. Instead of having to make chit-chat with the stranger on my backseat, I get to drive around in peace, and it gives me plenty of time to consider anything that might be playing on my mind.

I've certainly had a lot to consider recently.

It's been a couple of months since Avril went to prison for Jade's murder, and therefore, a couple of months since I've been going home to an empty house. It's the house I shared with Avril, and what I got as part of my share of the divorce, seeing as her accommodation is set for the next decade or so. But I have no wife to greet me at the door anymore, nor do I have a baby to cuddle and play with. Some might think that is a terrible loss, to go from a family to absolutely nothing, but the way I see it, things worked out okay for me in the end. I'd even go as far as to say that things worked out exactly how I wanted them to.

It was in this very taxi that I had my conversation with Jade, just after she had inadvertently got in whilst thinking I was a regular driver who could take her where she needed to go. By the time I'd driven her to that quiet country lane and parked up, and after she had tried and failed to get out of my locked vehicle, she realised the mistake she had made. However, I quickly let her know that she had not been the only one.

'You hate Avril,' I had said, stating the obvious as I looked at her on my backseat. 'That makes two of us.'

'What?' the anxious woman had replied, no doubt wondering why I hadn't called the police already.

'I hate her too. Probably for a very different reason to you, but make no mistake, the desire for vengeance on her flows through my veins as strongly as it does inside yours.'

'What are you talking about?' Jade had asked, stunned as to why I was on her side and not my wife's, who she had just escaped from outside that motel.

'I take it that you realised Avril was a bad person well before me,' I said calmly. 'I realised it eventually too. Unfortunately, I was already married to her by then and going through the process of trying to have children with her. I say process because that's what it became for us. Doctors' appointments, expensive treatments, invoices to pay and results to wait for. Hardly romantic, but I didn't care because I just wanted a baby with the person I loved. But it turned out that person didn't care who she had a baby with.'

It had felt good to get my feelings off my chest as I spoke to Jade, one of the few people in the world with whom I felt comfortable venting about Avril, someone who would never tell me to calm down or go easier on her.

'We'd had multiple rounds of unsuccessful IVF treatments and Avril was not conceiving,' I'd gone on. 'I'd noticed a change in her. Her mood was getting darker around me with each failure and she was spending more time at work. She'd always been a workaholic, but this was on another level. Some nights, she wasn't getting home until midnight.'

Jade had listened as I'd continued to pour my heart out to her. She was locked in my taxi, so what else could she do?

'One night, fearing we were drifting dangerously apart, I had gone to her office to talk to her. To tell her that no matter what, even if we couldn't have kids of our own, I still loved her and was happy for it just to be the two of us. But I didn't get a chance to say that. I'd seen her office light on from out on the street and when I looked up at the window, I saw her with another man.'

Jade had said nothing to that, but in her mind, she might have been thinking what a fool I had been for ever loving a woman like Avril.

'I guess it was a colleague of hers. It didn't matter. What did matter was that she would rather be in the office with him than at home with me.'

'What did you do?' Jade had asked, finding her voice again.

'I went home. I figured I'd wait for her to return and then confront her. Tell her what I'd seen and then that would be it.

I'd leave and we would be over.' I'd shaken my head at how easy things might have been if only I'd done that back then.

'But you didn't?' Jade had asked, and I'd continued to shake my head.

'I couldn't find the words. She came home as if nothing had happened, and I just acted the same. Then the days went by, and it seemed to get harder to say anything, especially as I realised I still loved her and didn't want to lose her. I figured maybe her affair would fizzle out, and if she was still coming home to me, then she must love me too. Then she gave me the news.'

'She was pregnant,' Jade figured, and I had sadly nodded.

'I knew it wasn't mine. We'd stopped physically trying a while before that, and there hadn't been another IVF treatment in between, but Avril told me the last one must have worked after all. She thought I'd just be so happy that I'd believe her, and that's what I pretended to do. But I knew. She was carrying another man's child. What I didn't know was what I was going to do about it. Until I saw you creeping through the curtain in the hospital in the middle of the night with your baby in your arms.'

Jade had been stunned then at my admission that I hadn't been asleep after all when she had made the swap.

'You saw me?'

'Yes. I was awake. It was dark in there and I pretended to be asleep, so you weren't to know. But I witnessed what you did. I saw you swap the babies. And I sat there and let it happen because I knew that it was not my son who was being taken. It was his, the man my wife had cheated on me with.'

Jade had seemingly been lost for words at the news that she had actually been caught committing her darkest act at the time it occurred, rather than months afterwards like she believed.

'I should have left Avril well before she gave birth and was still pretending that I was the father, but I planned to do it when we got home with the baby. I figured that would be the best time to tell her that I had caught her and now she was on her own. That way, she'd be left with a crying baby while I walked out the door, responsibility-free and entitled to request a divorce. Before that could happen, I saw you swap the babies, and I realised something else was going on. So I stuck around to find out what it was.'

Jade had told me then about how she had been depressed both during her pregnancy and after giving birth, which contributed to what she did. But there was also the personal history between her and Avril. After telling me about the interview and the threats after it, she brought up our cinema date.

'Did you like me?' Jade had asked. 'Could we have been together, if Avril hadn't intervened?'

'Yes,' I had replied confidently, as rueful as Jade was that Avril had come between us and changed the course of both our lives forever.

'Avril spoilt everything,' Jade had added then, and I'd had to agree.

'But that doesn't mean we can't get our own back before this is over,' I had replied, and for the first time since Jade had realised she was in my taxi, I saw her look less afraid and more intrigued.

'Unfortunately, I can't see a way where you don't end up in prison for what you have done,' I had told Jade then sadly.

'I can't survive in prison,' Jade had told me. 'So I'll do anything. Even if it means putting my life on the line.'

That last sentence from Jade led to her suggesting something shocking, a way that could end things between her and Avril forever and ensure she finished with the perfect revenge. The problem was it wouldn't just end things for Avril. It would end things for Jade too. That's why I tried to talk her out of it. But options were so limited that it eventually became clear it was the only way we could take Avril down. Even then, I still hoped Jade wouldn't go through with it.

'You can go, and I'll hide for a few days,' Jade said after that, speaking slowly and clearly so I understood the instructions, not that I wanted to. 'Let's say forty-eight hours from now. That should be enough time for the police to talk to you and Avril and get the statements they need and for them to leave you alone at home for a while. Then I'm going to visit you at your house. You can give me the address. I'll come at night. Knock on the door. You'll unlock it, let me in because you can just say you initially presumed it was a friend coming to visit, and by the time the door was open, it was too late to stop me rushing in past you. You will make sure there is a knife in the kitchen that I have access to easily. Maybe you'll have asked Jade to be chopping some veg for dinner, so it will be out on the kitchen counter with her fingerprints on it. I will take that knife and stab myself with it. You just need to promise to tell the police that Avril attacked me without provocation. Depending on how it all plays out, she just might end up in prison for my murder.'

To say I had been gobsmacked at her plan would be the understatement of the century, but she had reminded me of what she had just said. How she knew she couldn't survive in prison. She felt going there was a death sentence. So, if she was going to die anyway, why not take down the woman she hated on the way?

There was a chance she could survive the stabbing, but if she did, she would spend her recovery, and considerable time after that, in police custody because she couldn't change what she had done in the past. There was no way around the fact she had swapped two babies and got away with it for so long. That's why, when Jade kept trying to make me come around to the dramatic idea, she told me she would rather die than go to prison and asked me to ensure that medical assistance did not get to her any quicker than it needed to in the aftermath.

Beyond that, all I had to do then for Jade was promise that if Avril ever got out of prison for her crime, I would ensure she still lived a life of misery, by whatever means I could, ensuring justice was still being done for the deceased. Considering what she had been through, and how I felt we could have been something special if Avril hadn't intervened in our lives, I agreed.

The fact that Jade is now dead, and Avril is in a prison cell, confirms that Jade's plot worked to perfection, although there was a moment when we were all in my kitchen when I tried one last time to get Jade to stop what she was about to do. I asked her to put the knife down before she stabbed herself, giving her one more chance to try and see that she didn't have to do it. But she ignored me, although at least she died knowing that I genuinely cared about her, which was probably the first time she felt anyone cared about her in a long time.

It was over after that. Jade was dead and Avril would go to prison for her murder once I had provided my 'witness testimony'. After Jade had given up her life, there was no way I could have backed out then or she would have died in vain. So I did what she wanted me to and ensured Avril's downfall.

Who would have thought that me, the man in the middle of those two deceitful women, would be the one to help oversee a way for this to end?

As for the two innocent little lives who were caught up in all of this, the last time I checked, I was informed that both babies have been doing well. Their two fathers were contacted by the police and informed of the strange situation and all that had occurred. Social services were also contacted to care for the children in the meantime. The biggest positive to come out of it all is that both babies are far too young to retain memories of what happened. While they may be told about the dramatic events at the start of their life one day, that is years away, and they will be in a better position to process it all then. I promised Jade that I would keep tabs on her son and ensure that he was being well taken care of by his father, who did not have the best character reference, although maybe fatherhood would be the making of him. If it wasn't and the young boy ever needed someone else to look after him again in future, I told Jade I would do everything I could to ensure that was me.

But for now, I am just focusing on myself.

I see a prospective passenger up ahead and slow my taxi, ready to take him on board and deliver him to wherever he wishes to go. As he gets inside, he, like everybody else who knows the story of the baby swap, has no idea that Jade once sat in that same seat and told me how she was going to bring down Avril. If only the police knew, and the media, they would have a field day. But nobody knows and I will make sure to keep it that way.

I might never have swapped a baby, or had an affair, or done any of the other things Jade and Avril did.

But like them, I do have to live with a terrible secret.

Let's hope I do a better job of keeping it hidden than those two ever did.

A LETTER FROM DANIEL

Dear reader,

I want to say a huge thank you for choosing to read *The Baby Swap*. If you did enjoy it and would like to keep up to date with all my latest Bookouture releases, please sign up at the following link. Your email address will never be shared and you can unsubscribe at any time.

www.bookouture.com/daniel-hurst

I hope you loved *The Baby Swap*, and if you did, I would be very grateful if you could write an honest review. I'd love to hear what you think!

You can read my free short story, *The Killer Wife*, by signing up to my Bookouture mailing list.

You can also visit my website where you can download a free psychological thriller called *Just One Second* and join my personal weekly newsletter, where you can hear all about my future writing as well as my adventures with my wife, Harriet, and daughter, Penny!

Thank you,

Daniel

KEEP IN TOUCH WITH DANIEL

Get in touch with me directly at my email address
daniel@danielhurstbooks.com. I reply to every message!

www.danielhurstbooks.com

 facebook.com/danielhurstbooks
 instagram.com/danielhurstbooks

PUBLISHING TEAM

Turning a manuscript into a book requires the
efforts of many people. The publishing team at
Bookouture would like to acknowledge everyone
who contributed to this publication.

Audio
Alba Proko
Melissa Tran
Sinead O'Connor

Commercial
Lauren Morrissette
Hannah Richmond
Imogen Allport

Cover design
The Brewster Project

Data and analysis
Mark Alder
Mohamed Bussuri

Editorial
Natasha Harding
Lizzie Brien

Made in United States
Cleveland, OH
01 March 2025

14792298R00156